THE VAMPIRE PRINCE

Moretti Blood Brothers
Book Two

By Juliette N. Banks

COPYRIGHT

Copyright © 2021 by Juliette N. Banks. All rights reserved.

No part of this book may be reproduced in any form or by any means, electronic or mechanical, including photocopying, recording, or by any information storage and retrieval system without the written permission of the author, except for the use of brief quotations in a review.

This book is a work of fiction and imagination. Names, characters, places, and incidents are either products of the author's imagination or are used fictitiously. Any resemblance to actual persons, living or dead, events, or locales is entirely one of coincidence. The author acknowledges the trademarked status and trademark owners of various products and music referenced in this work of fiction, which have been used without permission. The publication and/or use of these trademarks is not authorized, associated with, or sponsored by the trademark owners.

Author: Juliette N. Banks
Editor: Happily Ever Proofreading LLC
Cover design by Cat Cover Design

ABOUT THE AUTHOR

Juliette first published with Random House in 2013. After three decades as a marketer, Juliette felt the time was right to share the stories and characters who were taking up residence in her imagination. 2020 gifted her with the time to write and learn about the independent author landscape and by early 2021, she had released her first paranormal romance series, The Moretti Blood Brothers.

She lives with her Maine coon kitty in Auckland, New Zealand, frequently travels to the United States, and reads the same books as her readers.

Connect with me digitally on any of the below platforms:

Official Juliette N. Banks website:
www.juliettebanks.com

Instagram:
https://www.instagram.com/juliettebanksauthor

Facebook:
https://www.facebook.com/juliettenbanks

Facebook Readers Group:
https://www.facebook.com/groups/authorjuliettebanksreaders

DEDICATION

To my writing assistant, Tilly. Without your furry little face popping up to remind me to eat, pee, sleep, and feed you, I probably would have been found in a state of rigor mortis with my fingers stuck to the keyboard.

ALSO BY JULIETTE N.BANKS

The Moretti Blood Brothers
The Vampire King (novella)
The Vampire Prince
The Vampire Protector

Realm of the Immortals
new series launching late 2021
The Archangels' Battle
The Archangel's Heart

THE VAMPIRE PRINCE

Moretti Blood Brothers
Book Two

By Juliette N. Banks

CHAPTER ONE

Willow leaned on the counter and slowly counted to ten.

She'd been waiting for the sonographer for over thirty minutes. It was seven in the evening, and as the only person in the waiting room, it wasn't clear why she was having to wait so long.

Her patience was dwindling.

Tap, tap, tap.

Her subtle attempt at getting the absent receptionist's attention wasn't working. This was the last place she felt like being; however, she'd injured her ankle over a month ago, and regular treatments weren't working, so her osteopath had sent her for an ultrasound.

She didn't have a problem with ultrasounds; the problem was the time taken out of her day. With multiple deadlines due, Willow was still learning how to balance her own needs over her well-paying but demanding clients in her new media relations business.

When she'd discovered the clinic was open late, she'd booked a six-thirty appointment hoping to be home by seven where she could heat leftovers and dive back into work.

Yet here she stood thirty minutes later, still waiting. She'd browsed Facebook, put hearts on all the Instagram posts, and sent out a tweet.

"Excuse me," she called out as politely as she could. "Hello!"

The receptionist who had greeted her earlier popped her face around the corner. She held her phone in her hand and looked annoyed at the interruption.

Willow inwardly sighed. The girl was probably making a tick tock, or whatever the kids called it these days. Not that she was old, but yeah, it wasn't her thing.

"Can I help you?"

"Sorry to disturb you"—*no, I'm not*—"How much longer will the wait be?"

Chest heaving, the girl didn't even attempt to hide her annoyance. She walked to her computer and began tapping away with some barely contained huffs. They both squinted as headlights from a large SUV pulled up onto the sidewalk. Willow covered her eyes and looked away.

"Let me see," the girl said once whoever was driving had turned the headlights off. "He should be available soon. We had a delay earlier, which created a backlog."

Willow ground her teeth.

"Oh."

She forced a small smile to her lips, then returned to her seat where she imagined how the conversation could have gone.

Why in the hell didn't you tell me, then I could have rescheduled?

Oh, he won't be long. It's only half an hour.

That's my decision to make. You took that decision from me.

Lady, chill out.

Don't tell me to chill, you tick tocking—

"Oh, they're back," the receptionist said, interrupting her hypothetical argument—which she was winning, by the way.

She *was* winning.

Willow looked out at the big men who had exited the

SUV.

"Who are they?"

The men were all dressed in black. Their attire should have made them look like thugs with all that leather and denim, but there was an air of wealth about them. Perhaps it was the big SUV, the quality of their clothes, or the chunky, shiny watches on their wrists.

One thing was for sure—they were all ridiculously good looking, as if they'd stepped off a movie set. Rough but polished.

"I don't know. For the past few weeks, they've shown up religiously every night before heading upstairs to the medical rooms."

Then they did just that. All six of the men walked in a tight group, gathering around one dark-haired man as if they were secret service. Willow wondered if he was a celebrity or politician hoping for anonymity. Or perhaps she watched too much television.

"What kind of treatment do they do upstairs? Cosmetic?" It was a wild guess, but why else would you sneak in for treatment late at night so regularly.

The girl looked away from the testosterone-loaded view and shrugged.

"That's just the thing; no one really knows. Recently they've been working late into the night. It's weird."

Willow stood to watch their progress, taking in their long, confident strides. Outside, the sky had grown dark, but streetlights poured golden light around the area, offering good visibility.

She'd been right—they were all extremely attractive, each of them taller than the average man, with broad shoulders, thick necks, and solid thighs.

"Perhaps they're security?"

"Hmm, who knows?" the girl mumbled as her finger swiped across her phone screen.

"Pretty hot security if they are," she added with a small grin, despite losing her audience.

Suddenly, one man turned his head and looked directly at her. Her heart began pounding in her chest, racing as she stepped back, gasping.

Silver, ethereal-looking eyes seemed to hold her on the spot. His eyes narrowed, yet his gaze didn't feel threatening. As they continued to stare, she felt her body and face heat unexpectedly.

"What?"

What?

The spell broken, Willow's eyes flicked to the receptionist.

"What?" Willow asked back.

"Oh, sorry. I thought you said something."

She looked back at the man whose eyes stayed on her a moment longer before he turned to the man standing next to him and laughed casually, totally carrying on with his life.

Which was fine. Except she was suddenly overcome with a strange and irrational feeling of loss.

"Willow Thompson-Davies?"

She turned abruptly and found the sonographer standing with an iPad in his hand, greeting her.

"Are you okay?"

Willow blinked. "Yes. Oh, yes, I was just...never mind. Hello."

"I'm Mark. Sorry for the wait; it has been one of those crazy days," he said with a grin that had the power to melt panties.

She grabbed her purse and followed him through to the treatment room, wondering if she was being pranked by a relaunch of *Candid Camera.*

She could just see it.

Now we see Willow being greeted by the male

stripper posing as a medical practitioner. She does not know the men outside will join him in a moment and do a Magic Mike routine.

"Now, let's get your pants off."

Willow's mouth fell open. Mark grinned again and nodded to the door on her left. "Pop right in there and change into the scrubs."

Her face flamed as she began mumbling words which were not of the English language.

I really need to get laid.

Clearly her mind was in the gutter, and judging by the handsome man's grin, he was enjoying her discomfort.

Thirty minutes later, she followed him back to the reception. Her eyes immediately glanced outside and found her silver-eyed man and one other leaning against a power pole. She hadn't stopped thinking about him during her appointment. The absence of his eyes had left an icy shiver throughout her body that she'd been unable to shake.

He was beautiful, in a dark and dominant way. His hair was black with waves that fell just below his ears, and he had a strong, masculine jaw. Even from here, she could see he hadn't shaved recently, which gave him that sexy edge women loved. She was one of them.

The jacket he wore only emphasized his muscular upper body, and as he dug his hand into his jean pocket, his T-shirt and pants separated just enough to expose an inch of silky olive skin.

She licked her lips unconsciously. His head turned. She couldn't breathe. He held her stare for a moment, then glanced between her and Mark.

She whipped her head around as Mark spoke. He was leaning flirtatiously against the counter beside her, smirking.

"I will send the results to your osteopath tomorrow afternoon. They'll call you and talk through them."

"So, you can't tell me anything?" she asked again, trying her luck.

He shook his head. "My expertise is in taking the images. I leave the diagnosis up to your specialist."

"Not even a hint?" She smiled and lowered her eyelashes. It had been years since she'd flirted, so she must have looked like she had something stuck in her eye.

He laughed, confirming her suspicion, and shoved a piece of paper in her hand. "Not even a hint. Now be gone with you."

"Fine." She laughed, and with one last glance at the receptionist, she hoisted her handbag onto her shoulder and stepped out the door.

Like all street-smart women, Willow pretended not to look at the darkly clad men, but she couldn't help herself. The second man was also large and muscular, but an inch or two shorter. He had a very predatory way in which he held himself, which gave off a dangerous vibe the silver-eyed man didn't have. Or at least not as much. She was certain they were military or security of some kind.

The closer she got to them, unable to reach her vehicle any other way, the louder her heart thumped in her chest.

Around her, businesses were turning off their lights, closing for the evening, but the area was lit by nearby streetlights, so she felt safe enough.

The men may be supersized—and my God, they were, from their heads to their hands, legs, and arms—but that didn't make them dangerous. Heck, she was a sucker for bulging biceps. Usually. Today, her inner voice told her to be wary.

A few steps away now, and she felt a zing rush through her. A ringtone broke the silent tension as "Who Let the Dogs Out" filled the night air.

Willow glanced at the man with the silver eyes, and her heart skipped a beat as the corner of his lips twitched. His friend answered his phone and took a few steps away. Silver Eyes stepped away from the pole and watched her. It wasn't a threatening move, yet it made her tense.

"I won't hurt you," he said.

"No. You won't," she replied, deliberately looking directly into his eyes in warning.

His smile grew, softening his strong jawline and sending warm shivers through her body. Warmth that had no place being there.

"Good girl."

God, he was gorgeous. He was just the right amount of bad boy with a spoonful of class. Now that she was closer, she could see just how well his jeans fit, and that his leather jacket was clearly designer. Before she could help herself, a blush hit her cheeks, and she gave him a shy smile.

Damn traitorous body.

Her blush spread its way down her face, across her chest, and descended to her core.

What is wrong with me?

She felt an unreasonable need for him to reach out and touch her. To touch him back.

If I could just run my fingers over those biceps and through his hair.

Willow scrunched her eyes closed at her desperation. She'd never reacted to a man like this so quickly. God, she needed to get laid.

Maybe if she hadn't been distracted, she would have seen them and been able to avoid the group of kids on skateboards that came flying around the corner. When she attempted to dodge them, she cursed in embarrassment as her ankle gave out. Arms flailing in the air, Willow began to fall, her head hitting the trash can and...

Am I flying?

Large hands caught her and placed her gently on her feet, holding her steady.

"You okay?"

They both looked around at the kids who were rapidly calling out apologies and wisely hightailing it out of there.

Shaking, Willow took a deep breath and ran her hands over her body to make sure her pants weren't ripped.

"Shit, thank you," she said, rubbing the back of her head. There would be a nice lump there soon. "How did you catch me so fast?"

He shrugged. "I work out."

"No kidding," she replied without thinking.

He let out a little laugh as Willow wobbled on her ankle and stepped out of his hold.

"Seriously though, thank you. God, I'll probably need another stupid ultrasound." Willow glanced over at the clinic and cringed. The sonographer was still leaning over the counter, chatting. When she turned back, she found those silver eyes narrowed at her.

"Did that man harass you? I'll—"

"No. Nothing like that," she replied quickly, surprised by his response. "It was just a long wait, and I'm impatient."

He nodded, looking unconvinced.

She wobbled some more. "Hey, listen, I better put this on ice. Thanks for catching me." Willow gave him a grateful smile, straightened her handbag, and began limping away.

"Wait," he told her, barking out the order and surprising her again. "You can't drive like that."

He had a point. She could feel her ankle swelling and her head beginning to pound. Her house was only a few minutes' drive away, but it was still unsafe for her to be behind the wheel.

Willow looked around, considering how safe it would be to leave her car if she ordered an Uber.

"Sure, I'll..." She turned, swayed, and once again, the man steadied her.

"Let me give you a ride home."

What? Oh, hell no.

"No, that's not necessary."

Nor was it wise. Her body, despite the accident, felt like a volcano about to erupt in his presence. Every time he spoke, a vibration ran through her.

"I'll book an Uber." Willow pulled out her phone and wrapped an arm around her middle. Despite the inferno raging within her, she could feel the chill of shock setting in.

The other guy ended his phone call.

"You saving damsels in distress now?" He smirked, then raised an eyebrow as Silver Eyes removed his jacket and laid it over her shoulders.

"I'm giving this *damsel in distress* a ride home. Give me the keys." He held out his hand and tipped his chin up toward the building in front of them. "I'll be back by the time he's done."

He? Who was "he"?

The jacket was warm and had a deliciously masculine scent she wanted to melt into. She let out a little groan, and may have wiggled into it a little. Still, Willow considered herself street smart. She hadn't survived living in Los Angeles all her life by getting in vehicles with strangers.

"I'm not in distress." She shrugged off the jacket and began to hand it back, quietly mourning the loss of the delicious scent.

She would not be accepting his offer of a ride home nor getting in a vehicle with him. He looked like the strong, protective type, but that didn't mean she could trust him. Or his pecs.

He pushed the jacket back in place. "You hit your head and can barely stand up. Let me help you, woman."

Woman?

Oh, so it was like that, was it?

She knew exactly the type of man he was. Protective, yes. But also dominant and bossy. Probably incredible in bed, but a complete control freak outside of it. Unfortunately, she had a love-hate relationship with those kinds of men. They turned her on, but she hated being controlled.

Or have I just never met a man mentally stronger than me?

"Like I said, I'll just book an Uber."

"No, you won't," he growled. Like, an actual growl.

Startled, she looked up from her phone, a chill running through her. "What?"

Something felt wrong.

"It's not safe," he said.

She narrowed her eyes, glanced at his friend, then laughed to lighten the situation. "I don't even know your name. You're a stranger. I appreciate you catching my fall, but I am not getting into a car with a stranger late at night."

Okay, so it wasn't that late, but still. Did this man think she was stupid? This was Los Angeles, for goodness' sake. Getting into a car with someone who looked like he had a gun stashed in those tight, hot pants was stupid and irresponsible.

I don't think that's a gun.

Willow began removing the jacket, but again, he stopped her.

"Frank. My name is Frank."

His friend coughed. She glanced at them both with narrowed eyes. "Your name is *not* Frank." She really hoped she hadn't just offended him. But seriously, *Frank?*

"Okay, fine, it's Brayden. Now you know my name, so let me drive you home."

"So now you're just making up names and expect me to jump in your car? No, nope, nada. Not happening." She stepped away, removed his jacket, and looked around for a place to put it.

"Bray, what are you doing? Let the human go and let's wait for Vincent."

Human? And who was Vincent?

He took the jacket from her, gripping her hand while holding her gaze deeply for a moment. Willow felt mesmerized and frozen. Then he turned to his friend.

"No. Tell him I will see him tomorrow before the sun comes up. I won't need the vehicle."

"Oh, fuck."

The presumptuous, sexy son of a—

"Come," Brayden said, his silver eyes determined as they sparkled in the artificial light.

Her mouth fell open as he reached down and lifted her into his arms with such speed, she never saw it coming.

"What are you doing?" she gasped.

"Close your eyes." His voice was husky as he stared down at her.

"Wh—"

"Close your eyes. It'll be easier."

She couldn't explain why she did, but she closed them, and felt her whole universe shake.

CHAPTER TWO

Brayden read the woman's mind, found her name and address, and then teleported to her property.

Humans didn't transport well. For most of them, having their DNA broken down and put back together was a first, so it made them feel nauseous.

Very few ever experienced it more than once or twice, since any who learned about the vampire world had their mind wiped or were turned because they were a vampire's mate. Or on the exceedingly rare occasion, because it served both parties if they joined the race.

He placed Willow on her feet just outside her front door.

"What the—"

He tilted her chin and transfixed on her pupils. They began to dilate as he spoke.

"I drove us here after you *gratefully* accepted my help." He grinned. "We've just walked up to your front door and..." He stopped himself short of telling her she would invite him in. Just.

So basically, he was a saint.

Brayden dropped her chin and waited as her mind rearranged the memories. Slowly, she looked around and up at him. "Thank you for the ride home. I appreciate it."

He smiled, amused by the sudden shy blush that hit her cheeks. Her long lashes lowered, standing out against her smooth skin.

Willow was beautiful, her face untouched by surgeons. She wore little makeup, with long brown hair which flowed in layers down her back. His fingers itched to weave through it. Human females didn't have the same sexual potency that vampires did, yet he found it exceedingly difficult to look away from her. His fingers twitched. He ached to touch her again.

Clenching his fists to stop himself from taking what he wanted, he nodded. "My pleasure."

She stepped inside, turned, and stared at him.

"Invite me in, Willow." He punched his hands into his jeans' pockets, spread his legs wide, and waited. He could scent her attraction to him, plus he'd caught snippets of thoughts as he'd tracked her address. Respecting her privacy, he hadn't lingered for long, but it had sent thrills through his body.

He glanced down at his jacket, and she startled. He had shoved it back into her arms when he'd picked her up.

"Oh, here, sorry." She handed it back quickly.

Brayden took the jacket, capturing her hand as he did. He repeated his instruction. "Invite me in."

Despite the step she'd climbed to get into the house, he was still staring down into her green eyes. He allowed his dominance to wash over her, and felt his pants tighten as her body quivered.

Willow drew in a shaky breath. "Why did your friend call me a human?"

"Are you not?"

She was courageous, questioning him. He was twice her size and could crush her with his hands, not that she knew that. But even if he'd been human, he could have easily overpowered her. A low growl began in his stomach at the thought, and he quickly pushed it down.

She was right not to accept a ride from a stranger.

From the moment he'd seen her in the medical center, his body had reacted. Clenched. She drew him to her like a moth to a flame.

Standing next to his second in command with a hard-on for no apparent reason was hard to explain. Not that the guy would care. They'd known each other for a long damn time, and they'd seen each other's cocks plenty.

Willow's lips twitched. "Of course I'm human. You two are weird."

Without the jacket, he noticed the sun-kissed glow of her skin across her shoulders. Soon, he was going to run his fingers across them on his way down her body.

She was much shorter than his six foot four and would fit under his arm nicely as he folded her against him. He nearly salivated at the thought.

"Well, he's weird." He smiled.

Willow turned, switching on a light. He didn't need it, his vampire sight allowing him greater visibility in the evening, just as a feline had. She chewed her lip when she turned back to face him.

"I want to have sex with you."

"Jeez, beat around the bush, why don't you?" She laughed nervously.

"I never do. I want you, and the blush on your cheeks tells me you desire me also." He stepped forward, forcing her back.

Brayden didn't need her permission to enter the house, as many vampire myths portrayed. He'd just hoped she would invite him in.

It didn't matter. His cock needed to be inside her, and that was that.

The pull was enormous, unlike anything he'd ever encountered. What that meant was probably worth some consideration, but right now, he needed to scratch this unyielding itch.

"Yes," she said, placing a hand on his chest, fire erupting from her touch. "But I'm not just going to put out."

"No?" he asked, shutting the door behind them. He took her hand and kissed her palm, enjoying the first taste of her along with the little gasp in the back of her throat.

Willow pulled her hand back and walked into the living room. His eyes burned as he took in her small but supple frame, then he noticed her slight limp.

A few drops of his powerful blood would fix her in a matter of minutes. In fact, it would cure her of any pain or disease she had. It would also trigger the change to becoming a vampire. A small amount wouldn't complete it, but it would connect them on a blood level, and he wasn't sure that was a wise idea.

"Would you like a drink?"

"Sure. Just water."

He had no intention to sit around and chat, but he sensed she needed to, so he would accommodate her. For a small amount of time.

Brayden sat at the kitchen counter while she poured the water. She then picked up an apple and bit into it, pouring herself a glass of wine as she chewed. Lastly, she placed a bowl of peanuts between them.

"Help yourself."

He took a few to be polite.

"I missed dinner, so I'm starving."

He ate a few more.

"Nice house."

"Thank you. It's my little oasis."

He really hated human small talk, but he was intrigued by her comment. Her house wasn't small by LA standards. It was a generous three-bedroom home surrounded by palm trees and a beautiful view out to the ocean.

"You work at home?"

"Yes."

"Are you single?"

Her eyes widened as she took a long swig of her wine before placing it on the bench. "Yes, you?"

He smirked. If only she knew who he really was, she would never have asked. "Yes."

Vampires didn't date; they mated. For eternity—if they were lucky enough to meet their lifemate. So no, he didn't date; he fucked, which had recently lost its appeal.

Until now.

"What's funny?"

Brayden stood and walked around the counter.

"You're exquisite." Reaching out, he cupped the side of her face in his hand. "How is your head?"

"It's fine."

His thumb caressed her cheekbone as the need within him built like a volcano ready to erupt. "Can I kiss you?"

"Why do you keep asking when you intend to just take what you want?"

His pants tightened.

Her spunk was amusing, yet he suspected it was a cover for her nerves. Still, he was impressed by her courage. There was a vulnerability and softness which called to him and brought out his protective nature. If she asked him to stop or leave, he likely would.

Probably.

Maybe.

Though he suspected it would kill him.

A small glint in her eye caught his attention. His cock twitched. There it was. Underneath her fear, the thought of him excited her.

She was right. He had no intention of waiting for permission, so he leaned down and touched his lips to hers. His intention had been to coax her open, but as soon as their skin met, the fire flared. His tongue plunged into her mouth, and he took complete possession.

She fell against his chest, melting as he wrapped brawny arms around her.

He pulled her harshly up against his body, wishing—not for the first time—that they were both naked. She moaned as one of his hands slid up the back of her neck and held her head.

Pulling apart, they both panted.

"Jesus," he said, feeling as surprised as she looked before he took her lips again, much harder this time.

She returned the kiss with vigor, her tongue dancing with his as if desperate for life. Both lacked finesse as their mouths consumed each other.

She pulled back.

"Is your name really Brayden?"

"Yes," he confirmed as he brushed hair off her forehead, his eyes dark with lust.

"Okay."

A single word. They both knew it had nothing to do with his name.

He lifted her into his arms for the second time tonight and carried her into the bedroom.

CHAPTER THREE

Willow wasn't sure how she'd gotten herself into this position, yet here she was, lying on her bed. Naked.

More to the point, in between her legs was the most gorgeous man she'd ever laid eyes on. Oh, and good lord, he knew what to do with his tongue. And teeth. And fingers.

"You taste...divine," Brayden mumbled as his finger slipped inside her, his tongue circling her sweet, sensitive spot.

She was dying to run her hands over those giant tanned shoulders which were propping her legs up.

She should be ashamed of letting a man she didn't know into her house and, well, her pussy, but she damn well wasn't. She gripped the sheets and arched her back as a wave of pleasure spread throughout her.

"That's it, let go and..."

She came, her core clenching around his fingers. It had been so long since she'd experienced such pleasure; she felt dizzy and disoriented. But he wasn't done. Brayden's tongue lapped her cream, then suddenly, he was above her, blocking out the light and totally dominating her with his size.

He kissed her, gazing into her eyes as if she were the most magnificent thing he'd ever seen. No one had ever looked at her this way before.

She flushed, feeling deliciously sexy as this god of a man pushed off his jeans and positioned his cock at her entrance. Willow glanced down and swallowed. He was big, incredibly big.

Looking back up, she found silver eyes gleaming with need.

"Okay?"

She nodded. "Yes."

Grabbing his cock, he pushed in. Slowly. She let out a soft moan, and he kissed her lips.

"I know, baby, and it'll be yours in just a minute. I want to savor this."

Willow ran her hands over his shoulders, down his arms, digging nails into his solid biceps. With a mind of their own, her hips lifted and took more of him inside her.

"Shit," he gasped, eyes closing as if in pain.

"More," she begged.

Brayden gripped her hips, his face transformed with desire as those silver eyes blazed down at her.

"Tell me what you want."

He pressed in a little further, then pulled out. She cried out in frustration, but his mouth stole hers as he ran the head of his cock around the moisture of her pussy.

"You. I want you deeper."

"I want to hear you beg."

He pushed in a little further this time, his eyes darkening with his own need. She dug nails into his skin.

"Now, Willow."

His dominance overwhelming her, she cried out, "Please, I want you to fuck me."

His cock plunged deep within her as he flung his head back and groaned loudly. Willow cried out at the fullness of him in her body after nearly two years of celibacy. She felt him freeze.

"Are you alright?"

"Yes, keep going."

"You're hurting." His eyes narrowed.

"Move, dammit."

Growling, he gently moved until he felt her body adjust; then, he fully sheathed himself within her, his eyes locked on hers. Like a lightning bolt had struck them at the same time, their eyes widened at the sensation of their connection. She looked away, uncomfortable with the intimacy. It was intense, the burning desire flowing through their bodies fighting to overflow.

Brayden sped up, pumping in and out, in and out, as she met his every move with her own. He clenched her hips, taking control now, his thumb reaching to tweak her clit.

She cried out. It was too much. He was too much. Her body had never responded to a man like this. Her breaths ragged, she clung to his arms as if he was a lifeline.

He groaned.

"Fuck, Willow."

Pulling out, he suddenly flipped over and pulled her on top of him.

"Oh, no!" she cried, hands on his pecs, halting him. They'd forgotten something important.

Brayden shook his head, knowing what she was going to say.

"I'm clean."

"Me too, but babies."

He leaned up and kissed her. "I can't, so it's all good."

He couldn't make babies? He didn't seem upset about it.

"Oh, I'm sorry," she said as he lifted her back onto his cock. She groaned in absolute pleasure as he pulled her down against his chest, ignoring her apology.

"You feel so fucking good. I could stay inside you all night."

Before she could respond, he took possession of her mouth, gripping her backside with both hands and thrusting with great speed. All she could do was hang on and enjoy every sweet moment as another orgasm swept through her body. This time, Brayden came with her, the squeeze on her hips harsh as he looked at her in awe.

"Willow."

Her name, so delicious on his lips.

They rode the wave for a few moments until she collapsed on top of him. Eventually, she could croak out a small, "Wow."

It had been a long time, but not long enough that she didn't recognize fantastic sex when she had it.

After cleaning up, he surprised her by pulling her into his arms and running his hands down over her buttocks, tucking a leg between his.

"Can I stay?" he asked.

She remembered he'd said he wasn't going home until sunrise. Even if she wanted him to leave—which surprisingly enough, she didn't—she knew he would stay. His dominant nature was powerful. She saw it in his eyes, felt it in his whole being, in the way he held her and touched her.

Brayden wasn't leaving; he had no intention of doing so. It didn't matter whether she wanted him to or not. He had decided he wanted her. But for how long, was the million-dollar question. Right now, though, she didn't care. She felt deliciously content and safe in his arms, something she hadn't felt in a long time.

"Yes."

Closing her eyes, she sent a prayer out to her angels for the strength to survive the moment he left. Because he would. People always left her.

"Sleep, gorgeous. I'll wake you before I go."

CHAPTER FOUR

Brayden watched Willow as she lay sleeping in his arms, his cock twitching and ready to go again.

Her tightness had been a surprise. She wasn't a virgin, he wasn't naive to believe that, so it must've been a while since her last sexual encounter. The thought both pleased him and gave him pause. Her body would need more time before they could go into round two.

He might not be human, but he'd been alive for a long time, long enough to know females needed time to adjust to a new sexual partner.

Then there was the emotional side. The act of sex created a chemical reaction in the human body which was often mistaken for love. The effect was stronger in females, but not exclusive. He sensed Willow's strength, but in her eyes, he'd seen her vulnerability. He would be careful that she didn't get attached. There would be no happily ever after for them, just fucking fantastic sex.

So why the fuck was he lying there, holding her in his arms? He told himself it was because he needed to have her again. A lie.

He peered down at Willow once more and felt a weird shiver run down his spine. Images of the moment he would say farewell filled his mind, and a low growl suddenly built in his throat. She wriggled and opened her eyes.

"Go back to sleep," he whispered.

As she settled again, he lay back against the pillow, drawing in a deep, silent breath.

What the fuck?

Reaching for his phone, he opened his messages. It was the middle of the night, his equivalent of daytime. It was unlikely he would sleep. He could be doing one hundred more productive things right now—many things were expected of him—but for once, he didn't care.

Lying here, enjoying the warmth of Willow's body and breathing in her sweet vanilla scent was exactly where he wanted to be.

Vincent is pissed.

His eyes narrowed. He didn't like having Craig's voice inside his head while he was in bed with this naked female. The thought itself was hilarious, given the number of females they'd shared in their lifetime.

Tell him to fuck off.

Yeah, I'm not doing that.

He didn't need to. Brayden would do it himself.

I'll be home before the sun.

Roger that.

His brother, Vincent Moretti, King of the Vampire Kingdom.

While Brayden had enjoyed life as the second prince, and far more freedom than his brother the heir, that was now changing. His life was now far more important than it ever had been. Recently, he'd learned to value freedom more than ever.

Vincent had become king, as was his birthright, with Brayden heading their security—or as they referred to it, the Royal Army. Naturally, he was the more dominant alpha, something not discussed openly nor promoted; however, it made him the right male for the job.

As captain of the Royal Army, he reported to the king, as did every living vampire, but as brothers, they were close and respected each other's strengths. Vincent was a strong leader with the wisdom to allow Brayden control, never questioning his loyalty as a brother or royal. The death of their parents, the former king and queen, had bonded them more than ever.

Everything had been going swimmingly for over a hundred years—especially since Vincent had mated Kate, their queen—and a few little Vinnies were all they needed to put more space between the throne and Brayden. Then what do you know, the king became ill. Which was crazy; vampires didn't get sick. Yet here they were. The king had some undiagnosed illness they were trying desperately to cure, no one more so than Brayden. He didn't want to be king.

Ever.

He was a warrior, not a politician. He hated the games Vincent excelled in. There was always some dickhead vamp attempting a coup or threatening to overtake the throne, with one group getting noisier: the Russo family.

Which was where his team came in.

While the king was doing all the smooth talking, he would send in one of his well-trained teams to assess the risk. Sitting on a throne talking was not the way he dealt with things.

So here they were in California, hoping these treatments by a human doctor they'd found would help. They weren't. No one knew if he had a week, a month, or a decade. So unless Kate provided an heir to the throne before he died, Brayden was it.

He loved their queen. She was graceful, strong, and compassionate. Every day he watched her pain as her mate, his brother, faded more.

And everyone else watched him. Why? Because they believed they needed to protect the last heir of the

Moretti royal family. It was a fucking joke. He was the most powerful vampire alive. A fierce alpha.

He shook his head silently against the pillow.

They all knew he didn't want the job, but what choice did he have? Sure, he had a reputation as a playboy, footloose and fancy-free, but he wouldn't abandon his family and his responsibility when the time came. He just wanted space while he had it.

Vincent, on the other hand, didn't agree. He thought Brayden should spend time with him now, learning the ropes. He hadn't appreciated Brayden's recommendation to spend more time in bed with a different set of ropes and his queen. The guy had no sense of humor.

It had been a dark joke, given the two royals hadn't yet produced any little vamplets, a sensitive subject they'd danced around until now.

Since birth, Vincent had known he could one day become king, and had been groomed for it. Their parents had been immortal, but there were ways to die.

Exposure to the sun, for one—but that wasn't worth thinking about. Nearly all of them had seen someone burn to ash in front of them. The horror, the smell, and the noise were the thing of nightmares.

While their healing abilities were much more advanced than the humans', a stab to the heart would require removal of the weapon and blood from another to heal in time to live. Assuming the person who stabbed you wasn't playing, they probably were unlikely to offer their blood.

Lastly, the good old-fashioned beheading.

Their parents had died by choice. By severing their heads, the decision had been permanent. It was a moment neither Vincent nor Brayden would ever forget.

Extraordinarily, little else could kill a Moretti. The royal blood was the most pure and powerful of all vampires, a highly guarded secret which made killing a member of the royal family near impossible in battle. It also made healing faster and shared some of its potency with the receiver, temporarily. Vincent was the only one with the strange illness, and no one knew if or when he would die. Brayden was expected to prepare.

LA and this doctor had been their last hope. After six months, they had tried everything. Soon, they would return home to Maine, and it was likely he would soon become king, losing his brother and his freedom.

Brayden turned and nuzzled into Willow's hair. He ran his large hand down her soft back. In her sleep, she leaned into his touch. He smiled, closed his eyes, and dozed.

A few hours later, he awoke, conscious that the sun would soon rise.

He had to go.

Willow was lying on her back. He leaned over her and placed a gentle kiss on her lips. She wriggled, surprised by the touch, making him grin. Softly, he cupped a breast and ran his thumb over her nipple. She moaned, her legs opening for him.

Fuck. His semi became a throbbing hard-on.

Dammit. He glanced at the curtains. Still dark.

"Hey, gorgeous."

"Mmmph."

He grinned. "I need to leave."

One eye opened. "Now?"

He ran his hand down her body, between her legs. "Yes. I don't want to." She arched into his touch and he cursed.

Another glance at the curtains. Still dark.

Fuck.

She reached out and ran her fingers over his lips. He snapped with his teeth playfully and pulled her digits into his mouth. She giggled. His chest tightened and his forehead furrowed.

What was he doing?

Another glance.

Fuck it.

He pulled her underneath him, nudged her legs apart, and pushed inside her. She cried out, clinging to his arms as her wetness soaked his cock.

He groaned, shuddering.

His concern over the time had been unfounded. He would not last. Prince Brayden, the infamous playboy and host of the most outrageous vampire orgies, was about to blow in under thirty seconds.

Pleasure pulsed along his cock as Willow tightened around him. He'd never felt such pleasure. Pounding with as much grace as he could muster, mindful of his strength, he erupted inside her.

Breathing into her hair, he said, "You are so fucking sexy. My cock is addicted to you."

"Words every girl is dying to hear."

He grinned. "Well, I've never said them to anyone else, if it's any consolation."

She shook her head, offering him a smile. "It's not, but nice try."

Okay, so it wasn't his best compliment. Despite the smile, he could tell by the way she lowered her eyes that he'd upset her.

Unfortunately, time was not on his side. Through the curtains, he saw the night sky lightening.

He kissed her nose and went to the bathroom. When he returned, she was sitting up with a robe on. He could see her swollen breasts through a gap, and like a moth to a flame, he kneeled on the bed and pulled the material apart, leaning in to put one in his mouth.

Willow placed her hand on his head and threaded her

fingers through his hair. God, how he wanted to stay and play all day. When he lifted his head, he saw the desire in her eyes burning.

"I didn't mean to upset you, Willow, but you can't lie; your body is on fire for me as much as mine is for you."

"Yes, but..."

He ran his hand down her body and pushed two fingers inside her. "Yes?"

"Ahmmph..."

"I've just been inside you and you still want more, am I right?"

Eyes glistening at him, she chewed on her bottom lip, attempting not to cry out. He rubbed her clit, glancing at the curtains.

He was out of time.

"Come. Right now. Come on my fingers," he demanded, pushing his alpha energy through her.

"OhfuckohGodBrayden." She climaxed and cried out over and over again.

"Good girl."

Pulling his fingers out, he licked them while she watched. "Now, I want you to look after this beautiful pussy today. Touch yourself when you think of me, but don't come."

She gazed back at him, drunk with pleasure and desire.

"When..."

"I'll ring you. And I'll know if you have come, so no cheating. Tell me you understand the rules."

She nodded.

"Say it," he demanded quietly, firmly, as he pinched a nipple.

"I understand," she panted, looking dazed.

He stood and dressed, Willow watching him as he

folded his cock into his jeans.

"Wait for my call."

She nodded, looking deliciously flushed and ready to be fucked again.

Damn sun.

He walked outside and teleport to their home ten miles away. Punching the code into the door, he let himself in just as the sun rose behind the hills.

"Fuck!"

His skin sizzled from the burning beast, and his cock instantly deflated. Then a voice he really didn't want to hear boomed.

"That's about as irresponsible as you can get, Brayden."

"Hello, your majesty."

Brayden turned to look at the tall man standing in the hallway. The one who looked very much like him.

Vincent scowled.

"Fuck you."

CHAPTER FIVE

Willow woke up again a few hours later, feeling like she'd had the best dream of her life. Except it hadn't been a dream. Her body was on fire, and not exactly from a fever.

Despite having four or five orgasms in the past twelve hours, she was still wet and in need of release.

"Play with your pussy, but don't come."

Brayden had given her instructions, and she had agreed. She laughed. As if she would let him tell her what to do with her body. As if he would know. He'd been playing with her, obviously. Building sexual tension. It was just a game.

Her hand ran down her stomach until she reached her moist entrance. Grabbing her breasts, she pinched her nipples and closed her eyes, imagining Brayden licking her pussy.

It felt so good.

She was so near, so ready for release, when suddenly, she froze. She wasn't allowed.

What?

Heat flared at her core as she moved her hand away. Clenching her thighs together, she rolled over on the bed and grabbed a pillow.

"Goddamn him." Frustrated, she threw the duvet off and had a shower.

By midmorning, she'd finished a few of her deadlines, so she stepped outside to soak up the sunshine. Her long, floaty dress billowed in the light breeze as she lifted her face to the sky.

She sat down at the table and considered what she would do for the rest of the day.

Play with your pussy throughout the day.

Her nipples hardened at the remembered instruction and sent a thrill of pleasure through her. She looked around. Her home was very private, but not completely. Most people were at work, but she felt naughty and she liked it. Lifting her skirt, she ran a finger over her panties. He body reacted, moisture escaping and making them wet.

She pushed a finger underneath the fabric and gently rubbed her clitoris. An ache grew, arousal building. As she pushed a finger inside, she heard a car turn into the road.

"Do not come." She stopped, her body throbbing with need as she heard those words in her head.

Late afternoon, she found herself back on her bed, her panties on the floor and the vibrator in her hand, rubbing her clit. She'd been unable to concentrate on any of her work, so she had decided to ignore Brayden's little game and relieve herself. He didn't own her body.

Just as she was about to push the vibrator inside, the phone rang. One glance and she saw it was an unlisted number. She knew who it was.

Coughing to clear the desire rich in her throat, she pushed answer. "Hello."

"Willow," he said, voice equally gravelly. "Tell me what you are doing?"

Just his voice made her want to come.

"I'm..."

"Are you wet." A demand, not a question.

"Yes."

"Have you been behaving?"

"Only just."

She shook her head. This was silly. She needed to get back to work and snap out of this sexual haze he had her in. A change of subject would help. "Are you at work?"

There was silence.

"Are you wearing panties?" he finally asked.

Her body clenched. "No."

"Where are you? Tell me."

She sighed, giving in to the building need within her. "On my bed. I have my vibrator. I'm going to come; I have to."

She heard him groan, and took some pleasure in his own suffering. "Push it inside you."

God, she nearly came just hearing his words. Doing as he told her without argument, she moaned loudly.

"Turn it on."

She did.

"Move it in and out of you."

Brayden's voice got darker and deeper as she gasped and moaned.

"Brayden, please."

"No. Don't come, Willow. Remember the rules."

She continued to slide the device around, the friction becoming unbearable.

"Now turn it off."

"No!" she cried, tightening her pussy around the device.

"Now, Willow."

She cried as she obeyed him, turning it off and placing it on the bed beside her.

"I'll be over at 6:00 p.m. Be ready," he said, voice strained.

The call ended, and she lay there panting, wondering what "be ready" meant.

CHAPTER SIX

The confrontation with his brother, the king, hadn't gone too well.

After he'd followed Vincent into his private quarters, he'd demanded to know where he had been.

"Since when do I need the king's permission to get laid, Vincent? I am the prince."

"I don't need you to fucking tell me who you are, Brayden," he'd yelled, arms crossed.

The guy was slightly leaner than Brayden, an inch shorter. Regardless, he was a powerful, tall, and strong king. He had a presence about him that left no doubt he was their ruler.

Brayden respected him. Hell, he loved his brother. He just hated this goddamn situation.

"Perhaps I need to remind you of your role as captain of the Royal Army. Leaving your king without warning for a piece of ass, seriously?" He shook his head.

"Craig had things in hand, and you had three other vamps upstairs with you. You were well protected. Don't disrespect me, brother. I know my team and my responsibilities."

Vincent turned and sighed, sitting down behind his desk.

"Look, I know we're all disappointed this treatment isn't working, and no one more so than me. Do you think I want to leave my fucking mate?"

Okay, now Brayden felt like an ass. Still, he crossed

his arms. This was also his damn life they were talking about. A future he didn't want.

"Can't you do vampire IVF or something? Seriously, get shagging and create a goddamn heir, for crying out loud."

It was a low blow, but they frustrated him. The look he got was deathly.

"I'm going to pretend I didn't hear you say that." The king picked up a pen and idly twirled it.

"We've managed to keep knowledge of my illness contained to our trusted inner circle, but I don't know for how much longer we'll be able to. Once it leaks, we're vulnerable. We must see you stepping up. When we return to Maine, you will. No arguments, brother. The time has come."

Brayden sat in the large armchair opposite the desk.

"It'll be fine. It could be years, decades, before you cannot lead. If it happens, I'll learn the ropes. Regan can assist if...you know, you die suddenly."

Regan was the king's advisor, and he had been their father's advisor when he'd been king.

"No, Brayden, you won't. You do not know what I do each day. Father groomed me my whole life, for hundreds of years. There is a lot you need to learn."

He groaned.

"Jesus, Bray, you think you can just wing this?"

Yeah, he did, but he was still hoping he wouldn't need to, also known as denial. He wiped a hand over his face.

"Is this why you have found a human to play with?"

Yes, it was, and he was eager to get back inside her. "She's no one's business." He stood up. He'd had enough. "Vincent, you are my king and my brother, and I respect you, but you do not tell me what I can do with my life beyond my royal duties. Stay out of this."

The king's lips pressed together as disappointment lined his face.

Brayden took his royal responsibilities seriously. Never had he pushed back with such rebellion. He was a strong and independent prince who ran their army and supported his king. He would step up when required, but not today. Not if it took him away from Willow.

"Just answer me one question," the king started as Brayden reached for the door handle. He nodded, not turning.

"Why her?"

He squeezed the handle. *Why her, indeed?*

"It's nothing to do with her," he lied and left the room.

Brayden watched as the sky darkened, tapping his foot, before he stepped outside. He would not waste time taking a car to Willow's, not that he usually traveled by vehicle. He intended to spend every minute with her tonight.

He flashed to her street, ensuring he hadn't been seen, then wandered up to the house.

He smiled, knowing the sight that would greet him on the other side of the door. He'd asked her to be ready, and he was curious how she would translate that.

His cock hardened. He adjusted his pants before he knocked and waited. She made him wait, and he liked it.

The door finally opened, and standing in front of him was a goddess in a white sundress. Nothing overly sexual about that, except this one was usually worn over a bikini. Sheer enough to hint at what was underneath, but not see-through.

He could see her nipples pressing against the fabric, hard as fuck, and it was clear she was not wearing panties, especially as she smiled at him and turned so he could see the back.

"Come in," was all she said as she walked off.

"Hello, gorgeous." His voice was dark and seductive.

Suddenly, she stopped and turned. He came to a stop in front of her, his hands outstretched to touch her, but she stepped away.

"Where are we going tonight?"

"Where?"

"For our date. Where are you taking me?"

Oh. Date. Right. Yeah, he'd been thinking bed, then bed, then bed, then maybe a few other spots in the house. Then bed.

He wouldn't say that out loud. Not because he wasn't in charge but because she deserved to be wined and dined, and he wanted to do this for her.

"Out. For dinner."

"Okay."

He leaned in. "But you're not wearing this."

She blushed, and he smirked. There was no way on fucking earth he was letting her leave the house wearing this dress so other men, or women, could see her bits. His protective nature was kicking in big time, competing with his cock for dominance.

He spun her around, pulling her back up against his chest.

"Tell me how wet you are right now."

"On a scale of one to ten?"

He licked her neck. Oh, how he wanted to bite and taste her. Shit. He had to get inside her before he lost control. In tormenting her, he'd been suffering as well. All day his balls had ached, wondering if she was touching herself. After the phone call, he'd pulled his cock out and squeezed the fuck out of it, fighting the urge to ejaculate. He hadn't. He wanted to be inside her when he did.

"Answer the question," he growled.

"Twenty."

"Good." Brayden lifted her and took the three steps to the sofa, bending her over. He lifted her skirt, downed his zipper, and felt his cock flap against his skin. "Spread your legs for me, Willow."

He rubbed one hand up and down his cock, using the other to push his fingers into her pussy.

"Now you can come." He removed his hand and pushed his cock into her in one fell swoop, and they cried out simultaneously. He wrapped his arms around her, taking one breast while licking her neck.

"Jesus fucking Christ," he groaned.

She felt like an inferno around him, burning with desire. She clung to the sofa as he pumped and pumped, hardening further as her body responded.

"Oh God, oh God, oh God, fuck me, Brayden."

He pulled her up against his chest, flicking her clit, and they both came again and again until she could barely stand.

"I've got you," he said, carrying her into the shower.

An hour later, they were being seated at their table in the restaurant. The sparkle in Willow's eyes told him she loved the view. Boats were bobbing in their moorings as the moon, nearly full, cast a silvery glow across the soft waves.

"Can I get you any drinks?" the waiter asked Willow.

"I'm happy with water, thanks."

Brayden asked for a carafe of water for them to share. As the man wandered off, Brayden gazed across the table at Willow. She was glowing in the after-sex haze women got. It had certainly subdued her sassy nature somewhat, and he couldn't help feeling smug.

"What?" she asked in a whisper.

"You look beautiful." He smiled wider.

A blush appeared on her cheeks. "Thank you."

She had dressed, after their shower, in a mid-length black dress which hugged her breasts and hips seductively.

"I love knowing what's underneath."

"Well, you chose all of it."

He grinned at the memory of lifting the lacy black teddy out of her drawer and requesting she wear it. Thoughts of those three little snaps being easily popped open so he could slip inside her during their evening caused a tightness in his pants.

She shook her head, grinning.

"Are you saying no to me, Willow?"

While she had smiled playfully, the thought she might say no to him didn't sit well. If he wanted her, he would have her. He'd never wanted to dominate a female like he did her.

"Yes. I am." She arched an eyebrow at him in challenge. "Let's eat, talk, and get to know each other."

He withheld the growl in his throat. She wouldn't deny him. Her body was his, she just didn't know it.

They placed their orders, and he lifted his glass to his lips, awaiting the questions he knew she'd ask. The same all females asked. The same he couldn't answer regardless of the way he felt about her.

"So, where do you live? Your accent is odd; I can hear a Southern twang and some East Coast."

Originally, he was from Europe. His mother had been Italian. Or, at least, from what now was Italy. His family was old. Incredibly old.

"We lived in South Carolina, and now Maine." He nodded, keeping it brief.

"And yet you have a tan."

"Thanks to my Italian grandfather," Brayden responded.

He had a mountain of lies and excuses he could feed her, just as all vampires did. It was how they fit into the human world.

"Ah, which explains your good looks."

A smile reluctantly hit his lips at her compliment. It wasn't the first and wouldn't be his last, but hearing it from her was just sweeter.

Her questions continued.

"So how long are you in California for?"

This was the million-dollar question. It could be days or months.

"Unsure. We moved the business earlier this year, but there is talk of returning to the East Coast. Possibly soon."

He watched her reaction, but she simply nodded and took a sip of her drink before she looked out at the sea.

She took another sip of water.

He took a sip of his.

She sighed loudly. "Are you not going to ask me questions?"

He took another sip.

"No. I know all I need to know. You are beautiful, funny, and sexy."

"Don't you want to know what I do during the day? Or what I like or don't like?"

He sat back. "Okay, what do you do?"

"I work in media."

"What's your favorite color?"

Internally, he was rolling his eyes at the stupid questions. Brayden knew they were important to her, so he played along, which struck him as odd because he usually didn't.

"Blue. No, white."

"Which one?"

"White."

He nodded while trying to conjure a better question.

"Are you married?" she suddenly asked.

"No. You asked me that last night."

"Are you in a relationship?"

"No," he answered again, patiently. Suddenly a thought hit him, elevating his heart rate rapidly. "Are you? Do you have a boyfriend?"

"No."

Great. One less murder on his hands to feel guilty about.

"Why the need to ask me again tonight?"

Dabbing at her mouth with a napkin, Willow leaned in and whispered, "Because you disappeared in the early hours of the morning, have zero interest in knowing anything important about me, and seem more concerned with how wet my pussy is."

His pants tightened inappropriately.

"Is it?"

She narrowed her eyes and sat back as the server placed their meals in front of them.

Brayden took a mouthful of his Scotch fillet and chewed, watching her and awaiting more questions, but they didn't come. With each lift of her fork, he felt her energy slipping away from him. She ate all her chicken cos salad, sipped her water, smiled at him, and stared out at the beautiful view.

She had decided he wasn't for her.

He knew women. After hundreds of years of observing them, pleasuring them, he knew women. He knew the calm look they got which hid the sizzling emotion underneath that screamed *fuck you*.

He'd get the boot as soon as they had their next private moment. She would decide between their meal and the car ride home if they would have goodbye sex. He'd change her mind if she decided not to, which seemed arrogant, but it was true.

Of course, the power was his. All she wanted was for him to share more of himself with her. If he did, he'd need to let her into his world, which would be dangerous for them both. Lethal for her. He'd hurt her, eventually. Today, tomorrow, in a month—it didn't matter because it was inevitable.

Brayden was leaving; he would likely become king while Willow continued her human life and met a man whom she would marry and have children with. They would need to have sex to do that. His jaw clenched at the thought of a man between her legs, lapping at her pussy, taking what was his.

Whoa.
She's not mine.
Not mine.
Not, not, NOT mine.

He glanced across the table and saw her blush. Turning to see what she was looking at, he found a group of men, likely having a business meal, chatting. One of them was staring hungrily at her.

"See something you like?" he asked darkly.

Willow had already looked away shyly, but now she glanced up at him. "What?"

"You want to fuck him?" Brayden's jaw clenched as he fought to contain his fangs. He was ready to fly across the room and rip the guy's throat out.

"Of course not. He was just checking me out."

"Not on my fucking watch." He emptied his glass and stood. "Let's go."

He waited for her to stand, put his hand in the small of her back, and lead them out of the restaurant. The lucky guy would never know he'd been one step away from his last breath.

When they were some distance away, Willow turned

and placed a hand on his chest. "Brayden, stop!"

His heart thumped in his chest and his eyes sizzled as he glared down at her.

"We just caught each other's eye. It was harmless. You all but admitted you only want to fuck me, so why the jealousy?"

Yeah, Brayden, why the jealousy?

"If we weren't in public, I would rip your fucking dress off and fuck you right here, right now," he growled, gripping her hips.

She shook her head. "Take me home."

Mother-fucking-fucker.

She just turned around and walked away from him.

Forty million minutes later, after a silent drive home, he pulled into her driveway and parked her car. Willow gathered her bag and opened the door.

"There is no other woman," he spat out. "I have a demanding family and a family business. Responsibilities."

She turned and looked at him.

"So? Many people do."

Brayden gave her the elevator pitch they'd perfected and adjusted for modern times. It was vague enough to not require details, and had the added benefit of explaining their great wealth.

Willow would never be exposed to any of it, save what he flashed around. He wanted her to have the best he could offer, but no, anything to do with his family, the Moretti royal family, was off limits to Willow. She would not be going anywhere near them.

"It's a huge amount of money and responsibility."

"Whoa, so you're mega rich."

He nodded. "Like I said, enormous responsibility. Relationships are hard for me to fit into my life."

"So you just don't bother?"

"No."

Why lie. He had nothing to offer her other than sex, and only for a few more days at that. Anything longer and women wanted to see your place and know more about you. Things Willow was already asking about.

Brayden sighed. He knew what he had to do. He got out of the vehicle and walked around to her door. Willow stepped out and stood in front of him.

"Come on. Let me walk you to the door."

She sighed and took his hand as they walked up the long path. At the door, he gripped her hips and leaned down, kissing her gently. "I'm sorry."

"I am too." She lowered her eyes. "I guess I misread what we shared last night. So stupid."

A pain shot through his chest. Goddamn, he wanted to lift her in his arms and promise her the world. Just not his world.

"No, hey," he said anyway, lifting her chin. "Don't do that. I just..."

"I know. I heard you. Business and your family are your priority," she snapped. She was getting defensive, and he was glad. Angry Willow would bounce back. "I guess this is a good thing. I don't settle for second or third fiddle, anyway."

Fuck, she was amazing.

"You deserve to be number one, absolutely."

She nodded. "Well, then..."

She took her car keys from him and turned away. She stopped and looked down. His eyes followed. It was his hands holding her hips; he wasn't letting her go. She looked up at him in question as his own flared back at her with the possession of an alpha vampire, those visions of her moving on with her life playing like a movie in front of him.

"Brayden."

"You deserve to be number one," he repeated, his voice strained.

"Yes, you said. Can you please let me go?"

NO!

What?

Fuck.

She placed her hands on his forearms and tried to loosen his grip. There was no way any human could budge him. Very few vampires could, if any.

"You need to let me go."

"Do I?" he growled. He heard her heart begin to beat faster. Much faster.

"You're scaring me."

"I'm not sure I can, Willow." He reached around her and opened the front door, despite it being locked, and pulled her inside the house.

Confusion lined her face, but he couldn't explain what he was doing—to her or to himself. He pulled her handbag off her shoulder and dropped it on the floor.

"What are you doing?"

He slammed his lips down on hers, then pressed her against the wall. There was nothing sexual about this; it was pure and potent possession. He grabbed her head in his hands, stared at her as they both gasped, then plunged into her mouth, devouring her, tasting her, owning her.

Panting, they pulled apart and he breathed her in. Her scent, her energy, her essence.

"I can't," he said, voice thick with gravel.

"Then go." Her eyes were wet with both desire and sadness.

"No, I can't go."

She shook her head, confused.

He suddenly released her and began pacing the living room. What the hell was wrong with him? He'd never had a problem walking away from a woman before, never in hundreds of years. He turned and looked at her, really looking at her, stunned.

Was she his mate?

Willow stood with her arms wrapped around her waist, unmoving. Her hair was rumpled, her mouth taut, and her eyes were darting around the room. She licked her lips.

No. He would know. His eyes hadn't changed yet, in any case. That was the confirmation he'd need.

"I think," he said, wondering how on earth to phrase this. "I think I just need more of you."

She raised an eyebrow. "You...you think you need more of me? Like I'm a can of coke or something?"

He put his hands on his hips, watching as she picked up her handbag and stormed into her bedroom. Okay, well, it had sounded better in his head.

If only he could explain. He understood her point, but if only she could see it from his point of view—which he couldn't ever explain.

Ever.

Oh, hey. So, I'm a vampire. No big deal. It's unlikely I will ever love you, unless you're my mate, which you're not. And on that note, my mate's going to show up one day, so even if I could have a relationship with you—which I can't because the vampire king, my brother, is dying, so I'll have to become king soon—when she turns up, I'll have to break your heart, anyway.

But I still think I need to have lots and lots of sex with you for a few days. Then I should be okay.

"Don't come in here!" she yelled from the bedroom. "See yourself out. I'm saying goodbye from here."

The fuck she was.

CHAPTER SEVEN

Brayden ignored her and stepped into the bedroom doorway.

"Willow," he said in warning.

"Please, just go. We both want different things. The sex is amazing, but I'm not a consumable you can use until you're done."

She tried not to stare at the dark and sexy man standing with his bulging arms crossed. His swirling silver eyes pierced her with his frustration. Her body heated regardless. As if in reaction, those eyes suddenly narrowed in question, then heated, his pupils flaring.

"There's one thing we both want, though, isn't there, Willow." She shook her head, trying to deny it.

He took a step toward her. Moisture pooled in her panties. She looked down and saw he was hard.

"Let me have you again, and then you can decide."

She could barely hear his words as her nipples hardened. He was a foot away from her now. "Perhaps you just need to find someone else to have sex with?"

"No." He shook his head. "It's you."

"You should leave."

"Take off your dress."

Lost for words, her mouth fell open then shut.

"I want you." He unzipped his pants and tore off his shirt. "You're mine, Willow. I said, take off your dress."

She kept staring, her body an inferno of need. Fighting what she wanted, she shook her head, squeezing her eyes shut. "No, Brayden."

Her nipples were hard, the drum of her core thumping with the need of his touch. When she opened her eyes, she took in the large, now naked body in front of her.

He stood with his legs apart, cock jutting out as he stroked it.

"I can't keep doing this," she whispered.

"You have three seconds before I take what is mine," he growled low.

Her body flared with a powerful desire she'd never felt before. She wanted to be possessed, wanted his strong, dominant hands on her. Wanted to be controlled by this man.

Knowing there was no way she could deny him, she unzipped her dress. It fell to the floor, and she stood in the black lace teddy and black heels he'd chosen for her hours earlier.

Brayden took a step forward and gently nudged her onto the bed.

"Lie back."

He kneeled and undid the snaps, placing her legs over his shoulders. Watching her, he ran his fingers through her folds, then licked her. Her body roared. His thumb edged closer to her rear, and she gasped.

"Relax, baby."

Willow knew what he was going to do, and she wasn't ready. She'd never done it before. "I'm-I'm not sure."

"Do you trust me?"

She didn't. He wanted to take her places she hadn't gone yet, which she knew required trust. She sat up on her elbows and looked at him, chewing her bottom lip.

He nodded briefly. "You will trust me someday."

Lowering his head again, he continued sucking,

lapping, and flicking his tongue until she lost control. He didn't give her the release she wanted; instead, he stood and pressed into her. One thrust, two, and he filled her completely.

She cried as he threw his head back and clenched his teeth.

"Willow, Jesus."

He laid over her, pulling her legs around him, claiming her lips. She dug her nails into his arms, encouraging him to go faster. Brayden licked and bit her bottom lip, a small grin teasing her. She groaned, arching into him, and his smile faded.

He pounded hard and fast as the fire built in intensity within them. Deeper, harder, desperate, they clung as she tightened around him. A million stars exploded within as she combusted.

Finally, she opened her eyes and found a pair of silver ones bearing down on her, intense and blazing.

He placed a hand on her cheek. "Give me a week. Just one week."

The need in his voice was one she felt instinctively was out of character for him. He had a powerful alpha-like energy about him. Bossy, demanding, and jealous. The request threw her.

It was his eyes, however, which spoke to her. They burned into her with a depth she'd never felt from anyone. She knew this relationship was not going anywhere. She knew she would hurt at the end. Yet, her heart felt connected to this man in a way that demanded she follow it.

What could a week hurt? She already knew it was going to be hard to say goodbye to him.

Great sex for a week with a protective, gorgeous man who made her laugh and have multiple orgasms? It was hardly a chore.

"Alright, a week." She nodded.

Brayden took possession of her mouth, and she pushed on his shoulders.

"But"—she held his gaze—"I want you to let me into your life, not just have sex."

"Willow," he growled.

"That's my offer, or nothing."

Brayden dropped his head into her neck. Her heart cracked, wondering what was so very wrong with her that he didn't want her in his life. He sat up suddenly. "It's not you, Willow. It's my complicated life."

"Are you a mind reader?"

"Kind of." He sighed. "God. I don't think I can walk away from you anyway, you beautiful little witch."

"So, that's a yes?"

He nodded. "During the day, I work. In the evenings, I am yours."

She smiled.

Brayden carried her to the shower, and they stood under the water facing each other.

"Mine for a week," he said, running a soapy hand over her back, repeating the words as if they were a mantra.

Back in bed, wrapped in his arms, Willow could barely keep her eyes open. She remained aware, however, that she was risking her heart by allowing Brayden to stay in her life. Even if just for a week.

She guarded her heart powerfully, a heart which had only just begun healing, and yet, somehow, this domineering and sexy man had pushed into her world and burst it open.

There was no way this would end well. She'd deal with it when the time came.

CHAPTER EIGHT

Brayden left Willow a few hours later, knowing she was in a deep sleep and needed the rest.

He arrived back at the enormous property with mixed emotions; joy at the idea of spending a week with her, enjoying her body, and trepidation in allowing a human into his world.

The fact was, he couldn't.

He flashed into his home and changed. He could never bring her here, where dozens of vampires wandered around. She would be safe with him, but there would be no hiding who they were.

Even sex with her was a risk at this point. The way it felt when he entered her, the noises she made, caused his cock to get so damn hard it was becoming near impossible to keep from baring his fangs. He'd nearly bitten her twice last night.

There was no way he would risk it.

One bite, and the vampire change process would begin. The blood link would connect them and that was appealing, his need to protect and dominate her making his cock twitch. Of course, it was much more complicated than that, but it would expose who he was, and he'd have to wipe her memory and leave her.

Or he could change her and keep her. But that was something he would never do.

When he let her go, she would be free to mate with another man. Anger flared within him just thinking of it.

Shaking his head, he pushed away the thoughts, frustrated by the way they consumed him.

He had no fucking choice. One day very soon, he'd have to let her go. But not today.

No, not fucking today. Or tomorrow.

He'd written his cell phone number on a piece of paper and left it beside the bed, something he'd never given to another female.

While vampires could speak telepathically with each other, it was only possible with those you had swapped blood with. That took trust. Or dominance.

For example, with Craig, it was easy. They had a powerful bond, a trust that had formed from a history neither of them could change.

With his next tier of command, he had demanded it. While it still required trust, none of them would be in their roles if trust hadn't existed from his part or from any of them. They all desired to serve him and the king.

As blood brothers, the Moretti princes had connected the moment Brayden was born. Their blood was potent, creating an immediate telepathic bond.

Now Kate shared their blood as their queen, and she too could connect with them. She was a Moretti.

Willow would wake up to find the note in a few hours. He smiled, knowing it would make her happy. It also pleased him to know, if she needed anything, she could reach him. Though he wouldn't be able to go to her if it were daylight, and that bothered him.

He shook his head.

In a week, he had to let her go. With an imminent move back east and his ascension to the throne, he'd soon be distracted and forget all about the beautiful human. Once home, Brayden could have all the females he wanted.

They would be treated as concubines unless it was his

mate. Then it was a whole different matter—the path to becoming queen was a complex and serious endeavor. Rich in tradition, like all royal families, when a female was identified as a king's mate, they were taken under the wing of the family and groomed for their new position.

Vincent and Kate had been in a unique situation when they bonded. He'd just been crowned king in the wake of their parents' deaths, and she had been a young vampire already a member of the court. She had escaped much of the tradition due to Vincent's denial of her as his mate until he couldn't any longer. It had been a source of much amusement for Brayden and Craig. Less so for the queen herself.

He cringed mildly at the memory.

While Kate was his queen, as second in line, Brayden remained her senior. Brayden's position was his birthright, one which would only change should his brother produce an heir of his own, and then only once the child reached its one hundredth birthday.

While there was some speculation as to the reason for the lack of heirs—as in zero—from the royal couple, vampires didn't reproduce at the same rate as humans or animals, so the expectation had not yet peaked. Now though, with his brother's declining health, he hoped they were mating like rabbits to produce a little vamp or two.

Even if it didn't mature before Vincent had to step down—or worse—Brayden could take care of the role in the meantime. It was the best option. He was unable to produce an heir until he met his mate. There were no accidental pregnancies in the vampire world—females could only get pregnant once they mated and their cycles kicked in. And thankfully they couldn't impregnant humans, so there were no half vampires running around the world.

If the royal couple were able to get pregnant, it would mean there was an end date to sitting on that damn throne.

As in, not for-fucking-ever.

He felt sick to his stomach. All he could see was an endless future with carefully chosen whores, paperwork, and politics. Yawn-fucking-yawn.

His role for hundreds of years had been as captain of the Royal Army. He had no desire to change that. He excelled in it and was born for it.

Even before their father's death, he'd been in his role, while Vince was the one pushing papers around the desk. He didn't disrespect the kingly duties; they were simply different. The brothers were close, and while they'd disagreed on many things over the years, the tension between them right now was unique. It had never occurred to him he would become king.

Brayden stepped out of his rooms and made his way across the courtyard while the sun remained hidden from view.

"Bray," Craig said, the guy's voice deep.

"Hey."

"Where you been? Let me guess, living it up between those juicy breasts." He grinned.

Brayden growled and felt his fangs slip out from behind his lips.

"Jesus." Craig's brows drew together, and he took a step away. Not much surprised the dark and dangerous vampire.

Brayden coughed, clearing his throat, trying to pretend it hadn't happened.

But it had. Shit. He rubbed the back of his neck.

"Dude, have you...?"

"No. Fuck. No. Nope." His reaction had been

reminiscent of a bonded male. Thank God it had happened in front of his trusted friend and not anyone else. "Keep this to yourself, you hear me."

Craig held up his hand. "Sure, just keep it on the down low or..."

"I hurt the human. All I'm doing is making sure she's okay," he snarled. It was a lie, and they both knew it.

What hung delicately in the air between them was the fact that as a royal son, it was expected he brought his soulmate into the family immediately. If Vincent got even a sniff of who she might be, he would demand it.

And it would be forever.

It was said to be for their protection and immersion into their culture as the mating unfolded, but that was bullshit. As the mate of a royal member, you became the possession of the royal family because you could breed. It was about survival and longevity of the royal blood. Simple as that.

Kate had already been a vampire and a member of the royal court, so there had been little fanfare in that regard.

Brayden imagined Willow being dragged into his world, and felt sick. She'd be terrified.

His mother had been one of those possessions, the choice taken away from her. Frances, his father, had already been king, and she just a young, virginal farm girl. Not a gentle man, his father had taken her and turned her against her will.

It was said she had screamed and cried for one hundred days and nights. Eventually, she had forgiven him, been crowned queen, and birthed the two princes.

During the nearly one thousand years he had shared with his mother, Guiliana had told him of the lingering sadness she always felt at losing her humanity. She would speak of the sunshine on her skin, of bright blue days spent splashing in the sea and making sandcastles. They had taken the choice from her.

The resentment he'd seen flashing across her eyes when they spoke privately had not sat well with him. For a long while, he had harbored his own resentment toward his father, until his mother had asked him to forgive and let it go.

He had, but not until he'd made a vow to his future mate; should she be human, the choice would be hers completely. Brayden would never force the change.

Of course, there were consequences in doing that. If said mate walked away, their memories were taken from them, and for the rest of their life, they would suffer unexplainable heartache, one likely to be explained away as depression by the human medical doctors, and medicated. Or worse. He'd heard the stories of suicide and broken hearts. Literally, humans suffering heart attacks.

Vampires only had one mate. If you were lucky, you met them early on in your long life. In Brayden's case, he had filled the time getting lots of practice in among the human and vampire races. Nothing like meeting your mate with a bag full of experience, he figured, all of which was a load of rubbish. He loved sex, as did most vampires.

So, while the human's life was filled with anguish, depression, and unexplained heartache, the vampire also suffered.

Their selfless choice of letting their mate go came at a cost. They would never love again. They remembered every single detail of their mate and the love shared between them. Theirs was a long life, and the memories never faded, the loss deep and painful enough to send even the strongest vampire into a despondent darkness.

Still, forcing someone to give up their humanity and

watching them hate you for eternity? He pictured Willow with that look on her face and shivered.

Not that she was his mate. Just as an example.

The bonded connection was for eternity, and mates could communicate through telepathy and call for each other through the blood bond.

He had faith in his mate, whoever she ended up being. She would choose him. It would be fine. His challenge would be when he finally met them, keeping their relationship a secret so they could do things in their own time. Heck, it could happen any day now or in two thousand years.

With more eyes on him as Vincent's disease progressed, it made things more difficult. If he were king, it would be near impossible.

He shook his head and slapped Craig on the back. "Come on. We're late for the meeting."

They wandered across the courtyard talking shit, which suited him just fine. He knew his longtime friend and second in command would have his back and give him space. For now.

It was no biggie. Willow had agreed to a week of delicious sex, and he was going to enjoy every single day. He just had to figure out how to show her his world...without showing her his world.

Right now, he had to pull up his big boy pants and be the king's brother.

Or more accurately, Prince Brayden.

They walked into the hall, which acted as their royal throne room. It looked more like a corporate boardroom set up for a video conference where the event planner had mistakenly ordered two misplaced chairs.

The two red and gold thrones sat at the front of the room facing a long rectangular board table. Vamps milled around the room, pouring glasses of blood and talking shit.

His soldiers stood guard at the door in their black Moretti uniforms, looking like ninjas. The royal logo was visible on their chests. Trained to protect the royal family, the soldiers would kill or maim as necessary without conscience.

"My lord."

The one he was looking right through, lost in thought, nodded to him before he glanced away. He gave the guy a brief nod and wondered what Willow would think of him being a referred to as a prince or lord. She'd likely laugh.

He felt the queen's eyes on him, but as he turned, she glanced away, smiling at something her mate said.

"There you are, Brayden!" the king boomed. Truly, the guy only had one volume. "Let's commence now that the prince has graced us with his presence."

Usually he gave some smart-ass comment, but today he simply took his seat and crossed his arms behind his head. Vincent squinted his eyes at him for a moment, then continued with all the kingly stuff.

Brayden held two positions during these mind-blowingly boring weekly sessions: prince and captain of the Royal Army.

Craig, his second in command; the king's secretary, Seraphina; and the king's advisor, Regan, who had also been their father's advisor, sat to his left. On the opposite side of the table were the commercial team made up by the communications director, Murphy; the foreign affairs lead, Martin; the head of business, Amelia; and the lead legal counsel, Philip.

Living in a human world meant they needed to play by their rules to some degree. Their commercial team managed their business dealings and investments, even if it meant manipulating memories and human global records to keep their existence a secret.

On the wall, a screen lit up, and their Europe, Asia, and Australasian teams appeared on the digital tiles.

The usual weekly order of business was discussed: activity in the regions, security concerns, commercial and financial updates the king thought the wider team needed to be aware of, exposure concerns, and finally, the event calendar.

"We need confirmation of the royal ball, your majesty," Sean, the head of Europe, stated.

"What is the date?" Vincent looked to Seraphina.

"It's five weeks away, so if your majesty is ready to make a decision, we can prepare the ballroom."

The king looked around the room. His eyes landed on Brayden's, who quickly glanced at the queen as his own eyes widened in question. She narrowed her eyes in response, then returned them to her king with a small smile.

What the hell?

"We return to Maine in a week. Proceed with plans at the castle."

Brayden froze, his stomach dropping. With a dry mouth, he attempted to remain calm, knowing they could all hear his increased heart rate.

"Wait a minute. When was this decided? I thought we were cancelling this year. I'll need to rearrange security. I don't..."

"Leave us," Vincent demanded with a quick glance at the screen and room.

With nods and mutters of *your majesty,* the video stream disconnected, and the room's occupants were reduced to the royal inner circle: Regan, Brayden, and the royal couple.

As the others left the room, including his soldiers, he stood and stretched his legs.

"Sit down, Brayden."

"No, thanks, I asked a question. When was this decided?"

Kate stood up and placed her hand on his arm. "Just now. We're all finding out at the same time as you. No one is blindsiding you."

He glanced over at his brother. "So, you're giving up?"

He nodded.

Fuck.

He looked down at Kate, and through gritted teeth, said, "Get into your bedroom and make a fucking baby. Please!"

She shook her head sadly and walked back to the throne. Yeah, he knew they'd all heard. Regan knew all the family secrets, as he had since his father had been king.

He was the only outsider trusted.

"Prince Brayden, if I may, you are well suited for this role if, or when, the time comes. I have absolute faith in you," the old vamp said.

He glared at Vincent.

"I don't want the damn crown!" he yelled and saw the hurt on the king's face. "I'm sorry, brother, but between losing you and taking on a life I'll despise, you cannot expect me to be happy about this!"

The room went quiet. It was the first time he'd shared his raw feelings. Yes, he hated the idea of being king, but nobody had considered that he was losing his brother. He'd already lost his parents in the most devastating way, and now this.

He wasn't a snowflake, for God's sake, but death was unnatural for vampires. He was losing his entire family.

He heard Kate catch a sob in her throat.

"Oh, shit." The king pulled Kate into his arms and

frowned at him. Brayden didn't begrudge his reaction; any mated vamp would do the same if his female were hurt.

"Sorry."

Vincent shook his head in response, as if to say *don't be*. His eyes held his for a moment, acknowledging his pain, neither of them sure how to deal with it.

Brayden kicked the floor with his large black Nike.

"Seven days, Bray. We leave in seven days." Vincent released his mate and sat back in his throne, running a hand through his short brown hair. "Go play with your human, have your fill, then we return to Maine and begin your training."

Brayden died a little inside.

He turned and walked out of the room.

CHAPTER NINE

"All good, captain?" Craig pressed off the wall and strode alongside him.

The sun was now high in the sky, so they took the internal route back to their rooms. It was the longer way, but meant they didn't turn to ash, which was helpful.

If the cloud cover was thick enough, vampires could go outside during the beginning and end of the day. It was the direct sunlight that fried them. Literally.

And like the circadian rhythm in humans, where they rose and slept with the sun, the opposite was true for vampires. The moonlight gave them energy and the sun brought on lethargy.

"Besides having a fuckton of work to do now?"

"Yeah, there's that. I'll rally the team."

Brayden pressed his hand on the security panel to open his apartment door, then shoved his foot into the gap.

"It's getting late. Give the SLCs a heads up, and get some sleep. I'll do a full briefing with them later."

Craig reported directly to him and had a team of four senior lieutenant commanders—the SLCs—who they'd both personally trained over six hundred years ago when he'd offered the guy the top job. He trusted every single one of them with his and the king's life.

Craig gave him a mock salute. "Roger that."

"And commander"—he held his friend's stare for a long moment—"don't ask me questions about her again.

She's off limits. You got it?"

The guy swore and shook his head. "Brayden, you—"

"No. I'm pulling the prince card."

Craig went still, then nodded. There was a clear and formal structure to the Royal Army, but Craig and Brayden were friends. As close as brothers in many ways. They had been through some major shit together.

The guy was dark and dangerous, one of the reasons why Brayden had chosen him for the role of commander. Speaking as a prince and silencing the guy was a dick move, but well within his rights as sovereign. He knew it would raise suspicion, but he was out of patience after that damn meeting.

Spending time with Willow before they departed was now a priority. Second to the king's protection, but a priority nevertheless. And fuck the one-week agreement. Brayden intended to spend every minute he could with her. He'd question his motives later. Much later.

"The security won't be a problem," Craig said, his lips tight.

No. It wouldn't. Craig and his team could pull it together with their eyes closed.

"I know." He laid a solid hand on Craig's shoulder and bade him good day.

Yeah, he heard the muttered curses as he closed the door. Turns out it was possible to frown and smirk at the same time.

Craig was right to be suspicious. Brayden wasn't a shack-up-with-a-female-for-a-mini-relationship kind of vamp.

Occasionally one came along who he enjoyed on a more frequent basis, but his role as prince and captain always came first. The time he was spending with Willow was being noticed, he realized that.

And setting those boundaries with the king and Craig? Yeah, that was drawing attention.

As commander of the army, it was Craig's job to protect the prince. He fully expected Craig to ignore his warning, not out of insubordination but from loyalty and commitment to his job.

He'd do the same to him.

Still, he'd said it all the same, and knew Craig would balance his request as a friend and his need to do his job.

He didn't envy the guy.

He pulled his phone out of his pocket. It had been burning a hole in his pants all morning as he thought about Willow messaging him. Eagerly turning it on, he watched the screen. Nothing.

Oh.

Brayden glanced at the clock on the wall. Eight thirty. He smiled. She was likely sleeping in after their active night.

Or was she?

He lay down on his enormous bed, after downing a pouch of blood, and stared at the ceiling. He looked around the room and took in the custom-made blinds which were fitted throughout the property to keep the light out while they slept. Voice-activated lights lit the corners of the room, giving a hazy, calm ambience upon his instruction.

Brayden suddenly wished Willow was there, tucked against his body, or ideally, under his body. Hell, even over his body. His cock twitched.

Why hadn't she messaged him? Had she changed her mind? He picked up the phone again.

"Lights on," he instructed before he dialed her number. Explaining a moody bedroom scene would be a little hard at this time of the morning.

"Hello." Her face appeared on the screen, and his

chest relaxed about fifty percent.

"Good morning, gorgeous," he said, his voice husky.

"Oh, hey!" She grinned. "Are you at home?"

He nodded and wished like hell he could kiss those beautiful lips.

"Did you see my note?"

She nodded and blushed. He may have added some details about what he was going to do to her body tonight.

"I meant the phone number." He smirked.

More blushing.

"Yes. I was going to message you in a few hours. I didn't want to come across as too eager, but you beat me to it."

Yeah, he had, hadn't he? Too fucking bad. Did he feel desperate? No. She needed to know how he felt.

"Oh, baby, you know I'm eager. There's no hiding how much I want you. All of you."

She shook her head in faux exasperation.

"All right, before this becomes video sex, I have to prepare for a meeting at nine."

He smiled, loving how his words impacted her. She would be thinking about him during her meeting and all day.

"See you tonight."

"Shall I come to your place?" she asked hopefully.

Shit, no. As he imagined all the chaos her showing up in his world would cause, an idea came to him.

"I'll pick you up. I'm taking you to the ballet."

It had been well publicized that the New York City Ballet was in town, and he had tickets. Well, he didn't have them yet, but he would in a few hours. He had a feeling it was the sort of thing his pretty human would love.

"You do? For the Nutcracker?" Willow's face lit up.

His instincts had been spot-on.

"Mm-hmm." He nodded, feeling like he'd just taken down superman—which, had the guy been real, he totally could.

He smiled at his skill in sidestepping her request to see his home while enchanting her.

"And can we go back to your place afterward?"

Fuck.

"One step at a time, princess," he replied, inwardly groaning. "I've got to go. See you tonight."

Turning the lights off, he lay back down and let out an enormous sigh.

CHAPTER TEN

Willow changed into a third outfit—or was it forth?—and finally landed on her emerald-green dress.

She loved the ballet. It had been years since she'd been, and had spent far too much time during her day looking up reviews and images of the show.

A quick spray of perfume, a giddy twirl in the mirror, and she went into the kitchen.

It had been radio silence all day from Brayden. After his FaceTime call this morning, she had wondered if he was going to be one of those stalker boyfriends.

However, he wasn't her boyfriend.

Boyfriend for a week.

Lover for a week?

Whatever she called him, he filled her tummy with butterflies, like the seven million having a dance party in there right now.

Just the thought of opening the door to see the gorgeous silver-eyed Adonis standing there sent shivers down her spine. The sudden knock made her jump, and her heart missed a beat.

"Willow?" he called out loudly, sounding panicked. She opened the door and he stepped in, grabbing her arms. "What's wrong?"

Startled, she looked up at him. "Nothing, why?"

He scanned her face and body.

"What?" she repeated just as his lips landed on hers. He pulled her against him. God, he felt incredible. She steadied herself, gripping his shoulders and relaxing, melting into his powerful hold. She moaned, the kind you let out without meaning to when you sank into a hot bath.

He released her lips and looked longingly at her. "Yeah, that." Taking a step further into the house, he closed the door.

"Why did you think something was wrong?"

Brayden shook his head and waved her off. "My bad. I thought I heard something. So, are you ready? My God, you look beautiful."

She smiled as warmth hit her cheeks. They did that every time he complimented her. Hand in the small of her back, he guided her outside.

He'd hired a limousine for the evening. Willow climbed in the back and accepted the glass of champagne Brayden had poured. While she took a sip, he ran a hand up her thigh, into dangerous territory.

She turned to look at him, her eyes hooding. He dipped his head and kissed her long and passionately.

"I missed you today," he said, voice low.

Her hand landed on his six pack, and she glanced at his lap before looking back up at him. Silver dilated eyes captured hers, unreadable in the moment.

She grinned, and he suddenly grabbed her hand. "Hey, I wasn't going to do anything."

"Perhaps not, but if you did, we'd miss the ballet," he said gruffly. "I have no control around you."

She glanced down at her hand and raised an eyebrow at him. "I don't know; you're doing pretty well."

He moved her hand away from his body and sighed. "Only because I promised you more than just sex. If I had my way, my face would be between your legs, and you'd be coated in this champagne."

Her body flushed instantly with desire, moisture

pooling between her legs. She wanted him; she had wanted him all day. Now the thought of him licking the golden bubbles from her pussy tipped her over the edge. She needed it like her next breath. In fact, she couldn't breathe.

Mouth open, she licked her lips and looked longingly at his strong jaw, dark bristles, and full red lips.

"Breathe, baby." He took her chin. "I'll make sure you're pleasured tonight. First, we see the ballet."

The limousine pulled up outside the venue as he kissed her harshly. She didn't want to leave his arms; she needed him now. He was like a drug. Her body craved his touch, his ability to coax the delicious pleasure from her core.

"I need..."

"I have a surprise for you. Come." Brayden held out his hand, guiding her into the building and along a hallway. In her haze of lust, she suddenly found herself in a private box looking down onto a most beautiful stage.

"Push this button here if you'd like service, sir."

"Thank you. That's all for now," Brayden said as he stood looking at her, not taking his eyes off her.

Willow turned and looked around their box. There were four seats at the front, elevated on platforms, for viewing the ballet. Around them were two sofas and a small table with another bottle of champagne and two flutes.

Brayden stepped up to her and gripped her hips. "We have fifteen minutes before the show starts." The music was already loud around them. "You decide how we use them, Willow."

Brayden poured them glasses of champagne and waited patiently for her to decide. Willow took in his strong, solid frame, and peered out toward the theater.

She felt like she was in a fog.

Fifteen minutes? Idle conversation or...

She dropped her bag onto the table, sat down on the sofa, and slipped off her panties. Brayden silently watched her, his eyes dark with desire as he took sips of champagne.

"Lift your dress around your waist and spread your legs," he commanded.

Feeling deliciously naughty, she did as he asked. He tipped his glass to his lips again and adjusted his pants.

"Touch yourself, Willow."

A groan slipped from her lips. She ran her fingers over her thigh and down over the wet flesh. She tried to coax him to her with her eyes, but he simply stood there watching her, those silver eyes burning.

Her finger circled her clit, the pleasure blazing from her body. Willow sucked in a breath as he kneeled in front of her and grabbed one of her legs, nudging it wider, and gently poured the golden liquid over her. Leaning in, he ran his tongue along her inner thigh, gripping her hips to pull her closer to his face.

As he plunged his tongue through her folds, sucking and flicking her clit with his thumb, she whimpered. "OhGodohGod, fuuuck."

"Wait, Willow. You'll come when I tell you."

Two fingers pressed inside her as she fisted Brayden's dark curls, his rough face rubbing on the inside of her legs. Those fingers fucked her as he sucked her clit, his tongue doing magical things to her most sensitive area.

She couldn't last much longer.

"Now, baby."

Suddenly her mind went blank, and ecstasy flowed through every cell in her body, stars filling her eyes. She swallowed her scream as his mouth covered hers, the taste of champagne and her juices on his lips extending her pleasure.

A few hours later, the ballet finished, and they walked through the glamorous foyer of the theater. Willow felt like she was in a dream as Brayden held her close, his hand in the small of her back.

The bulk and height of his body in that black suit and crisp white shirt had women staring openly and men shooting glances. He looked down and winked at her. Oh yeah, he was fully aware of the attention, and looked completely comfortable. What he didn't do was revel in it. His fingers pressed into her back and gently squeezed as if to say *I'm with you, and you are mine.*

Her mind flicked back in time to a time when a different man stood beside her. Always a foot away, never completely committing to being with her, they could have appeared as friends or siblings to any onlooker, and that was just how Mike liked it. Despite living together for over two years, he had kept his options open.

Things had been different when Willow decided to play by the same rules. She had formed a girls' evening every two weeks, going out with friends to parties or a local bar. He hadn't liked it and had demanded she stop. She'd mistaken his interest and control for affection, both of which vanished quickly once the social group disbanded.

Mike had also stubbornly refused to take their relationship to the next level, so when her friends started having babies and getting engaged, she had become more and more depressed, until one day, her friend Brianna had met her for lunch at work and had one of those tough love conversations with her.

"'Low, you know I love you, and Mike's a pretty

decent guy," she'd said. "But I think you are after different things."

"He'll come around," she'd replied, hating herself for being *that* girl.

Three weeks later, at a house party, she'd gone in search of her handbag in one of the bedrooms and found Mike with his dick inside some redhead. She'd fled in tears, and once home, she had packed his bags and thrown them onto the lawn.

He hadn't come home.

Willow had sat on the shower floor crying for hours. She knew it was over and could never take him back. Strong instincts told her this wasn't the first time he'd cheated. In hindsight, there had been signs. His work Christmas party and the overly friendly office girl, the regular evening work meetings, the long text conversations he'd have with his *friends* where he'd smirk and get irritated when asked who he was talking to.

In her heart, she knew he hadn't been the one, but she'd fallen into the trap many women her age had: an expectation to quickly find a man, settle down, and reproduce before it was "too late." *Better two years than ten*, she figured the next morning when she watched him pick his clothes off the lawn.

Fortunately, Willow had owned the majority share of the house, so within three months, she'd bought him out.

Shaking her head to clear the memories, she realized it had been at least two years since she'd subconsciously decided to give up on men. Which was why this arrangement with Brayden suited her. She got to enjoy the sexual intimate delights with a drop-dead sexy man, but there were no expectations and no risk of getting hurt.

Aware of her every move, Brayden ran his hand over

her hip and nudged her closer. "What's going on in that beautiful head of yours?"

Before she could answer, an irritating voice called from across the alcove. "Willow!"

She tensed. Oh no, no, no. She painted on her best fake smile as Debbie Parkerson strutted over with her husband, Henry, in tow.

The irritating couple just loved to gossip and outshine other people, yet because of their wealth, they always appeared at every show and party in town. Henry worked for Google and Debbie was an interior decorator to the rich and famous.

"Oh, hi," she forced out as Brayden snorted.

"Look at you! You're just glowing. Oh my, is this Prada?" The woman eyed her dress and glanced at Brayden coyly. She wasn't interested in the dress in the slightest, label aside. In fact, if Willow hadn't been with Brayden, the woman would've snubbed her.

Gritting her teeth, she made a quick introduction. "Brayden, these are Debbie and Henry Parkerson."

Henry held out his hand. "Henry."

The two men shook hands as Debbie ran her eyes over Brayden's body. Willow wanted to slap the woman.

"Lovely to meet you," Debbie drawled, flashing her pearly whites and holding out her manicured hand. Bless his beating heart, Brayden simply shook it and turned to Willow, pulling her tighter against him.

"Did you enjoy the ballet?" he asked.

"Yes, it was just lovely. We're looking forward to seeing the Russian Ballet in a few weeks, aren't we, darling?" She barely glanced at her husband before leaning in and whispering, "I get tickets from my high-profile clients, you see. They're famous."

"How nice," Willow said, glancing about for an excuse to leave.

"I didn't see you inside. We were in the front row. Were you further back?" The snide comment was obviously condescending.

Brayden leaned forward a little as if to whisper, but he didn't. "No. We were in a box."

Willow bit her lip to stop from laughing as Debbie's mouth fell open then shut, her lips pressed together. A moment later she composed herself, that sharp, calculating mind working fast. Her eyes narrowed, and she inspected Brayden.

"Well, you seem like a well-connected man. How interesting."

"Not at all. I own it," Brayden said.

Now Willow's lips parted in surprise. Before anyone said anything further, he said goodbye without excuse and led her outside, leaving a gaping Debbie in their wake.

The fresh air hit them as they stepped outside.

"Wow, impressive." She smiled.

"I figured she wasn't a genuine friend." Brayden pulled out his phone. "I didn't text our driver, so we'll have to wait a few minutes."

Willow leaned against his body, soaking up his warmth while he leaned against a pillar, texting.

"No, she's definitely not a friend. I feel sorry for Henry."

Putting the phone away, he pulled her into his chest, wrapping her in his powerful arms. He nuzzled into her hair. "Don't. The guy's a fool. They're two peas in a pod; I've seen it many times."

She nodded knowingly.

"Now tell me what you were thinking about before they interrupted us. You were tense."

She turned to look into his eyes.

"Oh. It was nothing about you."

"I know, but I'd like you to share."

Willow didn't want to tell him what a fool she had been. Having someone cheat on her wasn't exactly a moment she was proud of.

"Just a flashback to an old life."

She felt Brayden tense against her. "A man."

"Yes."

"Do you still love him?" His voice was taut.

She turned in his arms and smiled. "You ask some heavy questions for a one-week lover."

He didn't smile back. Instead, he held her gaze and whispered in a low voice, "Answer the question, Willow."

She sighed. "No. Definitely not."

"But?"

"He hurt me. A lot." She shrugged. "Now, let's change the subject."

Brayden cupped the side of her face and kissed her lips gently. "He wasn't the right man for you. You have a greater destiny."

She smiled. "Let me guess, this destiny is in your bed tonight?"

His eyes darkened. "In *your* bed, gorgeous. And yes."

She frowned and was about to ask why they couldn't go to his place when they were interrupted again.

"My lord! I didn't see you there."

Willow turned just as a man bowed to Brayden.

What on earth?

With his arm, Brayden moved her behind slightly as if to protect her from the man.

"Oh, hey," Brayden replied with an unusual lack of enthusiasm as the man looked nervously between them.

"Of course. Sorry to interrupt my...sir."

He all but scampered away as the limousine pulled up to the sidewalk. Brayden ushered her inside, gave her a small smile, and stared out the window as the vehicle began moving. His hand held her thigh.

"Did I hear him right? Did he just call you *my lord*?"

CHAPTER ELEVEN

Brayden gritted his teeth.

It wasn't like vampires didn't circulate in public, so he hadn't been completely surprised at seeing one of his kind. In fact, there had been a few of them at the ballet.

This one, however, was a member of the Royal Army, and as the prince and dominant royal, he should have sensed him. Willow was more of a distraction to his senses than he'd realized.

The young vampire had looked surprised to see him in such an intimate hold with a female and had reacted. Every vampire wanted to see the prince mated, just as humans loved seeing their princes and princesses marry. It was the way of people.

Craig.

Yes, sir.

Thomas saw me with Willow tonight. Make sure he doesn't talk.

Leave it with me.

Vampires were all well versed in the appropriate manner to address the royal family outside their world. Around humans, Thomas should never have acknowledged him first, and certainly not referred to him as my lord or captain.

It raised questions, such as the one on Willow's mind right now.

Craig would deal with it. There would be no punishment, simply a reminder of the rules. He knew of

Thomas; he was a good kid taken by surprise by the sight of his prince with a human female.

Brayden ran his hand through his hair.

None of it was a big deal. It wasn't like he was a goddamn virgin. No. What had him reeling was whether Thomas had seen him sparkling; not the boy-band-Bieber type of sparkling but the ethereal sparkle all male vampires exhibited when in a highly protective state.

Their bodies released a unique chemical which interacted with the oxygen in the air and created an electrical charge that surrounded their bodies.

Brayden shook his head. He'd always thought it looked ridiculous, while female vampires thought it looked fabulous. Humans couldn't see it, nor could the male sparkling like a fucking Christmas tree.

It didn't mean the female, or male, was your mate, but it was a strong sign. The race believed it was a warning to predators; a bonded male was deadly when in protective mode.

As a dominant alpha, being protective was in his nature, but he'd never sparkled before.

Yet, as Willow had shared the story of her former partner and his desire to snap the guy's neck grew, he suspected he looked dressed for a fucking Disney show.

Did that make her his mate?

No. He would know.

Bonded males formed a black ring around the irises of their eyes. It could form slowly or appear suddenly, depending on the relationship. Just like human relationships, some happened faster than others, and so did the mating bond.

"Did he call you *my lord*?"

Fuck.

He really didn't want to lie to her.

"Ah..."

"Brayden?"

He turned in his seat and took her hand. God, she was beautiful.

"The guy works for us. It's a family business joke." He fake smiled.

"So why do you look so pissed?"

He waved a hand in front of him, all *no big deal*. "It just reminded me of a job I didn't finish today."

Willow sat back, buying his story, and he felt like a prick. Crisis averted. Sure, he could have erased her memory, but too much, and it really messed up a human mind.

Once they arrived, Brayden shut the door behind them as they entered Willow's house.

"Thank you for a romantic, and sexy, evening." She smiled.

"It's not over yet. I believe we have some unfinished business." He brushed his hand over her hair and pulled her against his body.

"Oh?" she asked innocently.

He tugged gently on her lower lip with his teeth. "I want as much of you as I can get this week."

Brayden saw the flicker in her eyes. He could have ignored it, but for some reason, he needed to know what that meant. Not by reading her mind, but he would if necessary. He had a strong desire to be inside her body *and* her mind. He wanted to know everything about this human.

"Talk to me."

"I am." Willow smiled. He watched as she physically shook off the thought with a little shake of her head.

"Don't do that. What's going on?"

She shrugged her shoulders and let out a little laugh. "No idea. Perhaps I'm hungry or something."

"Willow," he scolded.

"It's nothing." She sighed. "Look, I don't have any experience with this casual dating game, but I don't think spending every night together is how it works."

Brayden watched her eyes as they darted around nervously, and the way she chewed her bottom lip. Finally, she looked him in the eye.

"Perhaps a night apart." She nodded like this was a two-way conversation. "To keep things casual. Yes, I think it would be best for me to sleep alone."

A thump landed in his chest.

"No," he growled.

She blanched and raised an eyebrow at him. "Wow. Looks like we both need it."

"What?" he asked, narrowing his eyes at her in confusion.

"I said, it sounds like we both need some healthy boundaries." She began to pull out of his arms, and he tightened his hold. "This is feeling super intense. Let's call it a night, and I'll call you tomorrow."

Brayden's heart thumped loudly in his chest. The thought of leaving her alone in the house, of her sleeping without his arms wrapped around her, and the possibility of someone else being there with her, made him want to tear something apart.

The predator in him rose to the surface. His fangs ached. Slowly, he drew in a long, deep breath.

In a week he'd leave the state and Willow could do as she pleased. A growl began deep in his gut. He pushed it down and coughed.

"That's not our agreement."

"We didn't agree on any details." She frowned and stepped toward the front door. "Come on, let me see you out."

Brayden had never been dismissed in his life. He was a fucking prince!

"No."

Exasperated, she frowned at him, walked into her bedroom, and dropped her bag on the bed.

He followed.

"Willow, explain to me what is going on here. I don't understand."

She let out a huge sigh and put her hands on her slim, sexy hips. "Goddamn you, Brayden, I like you a lot. Too much. I just need a night to myself to get my thoughts and feelings under control, all right?"

He stared at her. A part of him wanted to grin like an idiot at her confession while another knew he should turn and leave. She was right. They should contain their feelings. He was leaving the state, and she would carry on with her life without him.

Because he was just standing there staring at her, she flung her hands up and cried, "So that at the end of the week I'm not some emotional, clingy woman, *capisci*?"

"You speak Italian?"

She frowned. "I've just been completely vulnerable with you and all you want to know is if I speak Italian?"

He grinned. God, she was beautiful when angry.

"So, do you?"

"*Sì*, now go home!"

"Technically, most of that was English." He grinned until he saw the anger in her eyes flare. He held up his hands. "All right, I'm sorry."

He took a step closer, his expression now serious. Sensual. "But, Willow, you have to know how sexy you are right now."

"You...what?"

He took another step. He was a predator, after all. He knew this dance.

"Sexy. Gorgeous. Passionate. It's pouring off you."

She was a little breathless, and his lips curved as he

began to hear her heart speed up. It was natural for her to be wary of his nature, even if it was a subconscious reaction of her body. Even as he knew he'd protect her with every inch of his being, it thrilled him to hear her react to his animal nature.

He took another step.

"Stop."

Another step. "I told you, Willow, you're mine. For the week."

She swallowed. "I need...space."

"You need me. You need my body," he said, an inch away from her. "And I need your body. There's more than one of us in this relationship, *principessa.*"

"I'm not a princess," she barely said.

"So you do speak Italian?" Smirking, he cupped her cheek.

Her eyes were burning as his lips landed on hers firmly. When he released them, he took pleasure in her breathlessness. Then, taking complete control, he scooped her up and placed her on the bed.

CHAPTER TWELVE

Willow felt Brayden's lips on her forehead moments before he climbed out of bed.

All night long, he'd held her tightly, possessively, after hours of pleasure. She hated to admit it, but it was exactly what she'd needed. Her nature was to pull away, so this was new for her.

It didn't change anything. In a week their affair would be over, and she'd grieve the loss of their intimacy and the man himself. The more time she spent with him, the more her feelings grew.

How she'd last, she didn't know. All she could do was take it day by day.

She'd expected his dominant nature to turn sexual as they hit the mattress last night, and he hadn't disappointed her. Afterward, lying sated, she'd felt his hard cock up against her stomach as their legs entwined.

"It's yours whenever you want, Willow," he'd said against her hair.

She let out a sigh, remembering the feeling of his arms around her, feeling safe and cherished. It was somewhat confusing. Wasn't a casual fling supposed to be less intimate?

"Go back to sleep, beautiful," he said, snapping her back to the present moment. She rolled over and watched him dress. His strong back and shoulders slipped into his white shirt. Solid thighs disappeared into long black pants. The well-tailored suit looked as good in the early dawn as it had last night.

Leaving his shoes off, one knee on the bed, he leaned over her.

"Anyone ever tell you, you're terrible at following instructions?"

Willow grinned and ran her hand through his dark curly hair. "Anyone ever told *you* just how sexy you are?"

Of course, millions of women would have. How could they not?

His lips landed on hers as an arm slipped under her, arching her up. The weight of his body increased in a delicious way that made her wish the covers and his clothes would vanish. She groaned against his lips, and felt his body react.

"God, woman," he moaned. "You are very goddamn hard to leave."

She gazed at him hungrily. "So get back into bed and be late to work for once."

Brayden glanced at the blinds, then shook his head. "I've got to go, beautiful." He kissed her firmly before staring at her for a long moment. Finally, he said in a dark and husky voice, "I'll talk to you in a few hours. Go back to damn sleep."

She smiled.

When she woke up a few hours later, she dragged herself into the shower and out the door. She had an important meeting in the city with a potential new client. The lead had come via her best friend, Brianna, who worked at the software company.

"You're here!" the redheaded beauty said, enveloping her in a hug. "Whoa, you look amazing. What are you doing? And how is your ankle now?"

Blinking for a moment, Willow had to stop herself from sharing her beauty secret: multiple daily orgasms.

There wasn't any shame in what she was doing, although Brianna had some strong morals. No, Willow wasn't about to start talking about her sex life to her closest friend whose husband had been killed twelve months ago.

Stationed in Afghanistan, Christian had been just weeks from returning home to her when his unit had been hit by an IED. The bomb had been planted on the road they were traveling on, and detonated. It had completely devasted Bri and his family.

The shock had worn off and her friend had received therapy, but there were some things in life you never forgot or got over completely.

"Hmm, you know, supplements, lots of water, exercise. The usual." Plus thirty-five orgasms in the past three days. No biggie. They sat down in the café downstairs from her offices.

"And my osteopath adjusted the treatment after seeing my ultrasound results, and it's made a big difference already." She wiggled her foot with a grin. "No stilettos for me for a while, though."

"You never wore them anyway." Brianna laughed. "So, are you all prepared for the presentation?"

"I think so. You said they wanted something disruptive to reach their younger target market, so that's what I'm giving them."

Brianna grinned and sipped her latte. "Awesome, you're going to rock this!"

She wasn't fooling anyone. Willow noticed the dark shadows under her eyes. She reached across the table and laid her hand over hers.

"Hey, how are you doing? Like, really."

Her friend shrugged and looked away into a void. "You know, some days are easier than others. I have so much anger and sadness, I'm not sure what to do with it."

She nodded and gave her friend space to keep talking.

"I just wish I'd had his baby and hadn't agreed to wait until he returned stateside. He pushed, you know. I'm so angry at him. At myself for agreeing."

More nodding.

Willow wished she could take the pain away, but grief was a solo journey, and everyone had to do it their own way. She could be there for her, though, and ensure she didn't fade into a dark place. There came a point where it was unhealthy to keep being angry and not forgive life.

"I know, honey. Are you going to the therapist still?"

"Yes, but all he keeps saying is I should release my anger and start forgiving. How? How can I forgive?" Her eyes filled with tears. "I want to yell at someone, you know. But who?"

"At whoever you want. Me, God, Christian, the government, life. Have you tried?" The look in her friends' eyes said she hadn't considered it, followed by a confirming shake of her head.

"No." Brianna squeezed her fingers. "I know you've been through this, and I appreciate your support."

It wasn't the same—grief never was. Willow had lost her parents in a car crash just weeks before her twenty-first birthday. The funny thing was, they'd been talking about getting a divorce, and now in a twist of fate, their souls were resting together, assuming what she knew about the afterlife was true.

She hadn't been all that close to her parents, who had both been intellectuals. College professors, they were more interested in her school grades than her feelings. The problem was, Willow had a high emotional intelligence, and they had found her overly emotional, while she had found them cold.

She knew they had loved her, in their own way, but it hadn't provided her with the love and sense of belonging she desperately wanted. What all children needed: emotional connection.

The pattern had inevitably repeated in her romantic relationships, and despite years of therapy, she wondered if she could have a loving connection with anyone.

They had left her financial security from two life insurance payouts, their LA home, a condo in Hawaii, and stocks. Willow was in a fortunate position for someone so young.

Still, despite all that, she'd choose to have her parents back in a flash. The pain never went away, but it dulled, and she had learned to forgive life for its unfair choices.

"Yeah, same but different. No pain is the same, Bri." They had always supported each other, and never compared their pain. That wasn't what friendship was about. She leaned back and finished her coffee. "Girl power forever, remember."

The two of them had gone to high school together and to Stanford University, where they'd both studied communications. While Willow had ended up building her own freelancing agency, Brianna had stepped into the corporate world.

"Girl power forever." Her friend smiled sadly before shaking herself. "Okay, show me what you have before we go up?"

Willow opened her laptop. "Oh God, yes. Feedback, please!"

Usually, she would have gone over it the night before with Bri, but Brayden was filling up her life right now.

When they weren't having delicious sex where he completely dominated her, he was making her blush and laugh. It was unlike any other relationship she'd been in.

"Hello." A finger tapped on her hand.

"Oh, sorry."

"Alright, what's going on?"

"Hmm?" She aimed for vague, but Brianna knew her too well.

"Oh my God, you have a man!" she said loudly before clapping a hand over her mouth. "Sorry, I'm just so excited for you."

Willow looked around them and faux laughed at a few people. "Bri," she chided. "No, I don't. Stop. We are not talking about this."

Her friend leaned forward. "Because my husband died? God, Willow, you don't need to become a nun to protect my feelings."

Well thank God, or she'd have been failing in the friendship department for the past few days.

"I don't care. Still not talking about it. It's nothing anyway," she said, and pointed to the screen. "Now let's go through this. We have ten more minutes."

After a long stare, Brianna frowned, knowing she was right. Willow expected to be drilled afterward. As they headed upstairs to the meeting, Willow's phone beeped.

Aside from me, what's your favorite thing to eat? I'm bringing takeout tonight.

She let out a choking cough in the lift with her best friend and three strangers. Still coughing, she typed a reply and put her phone on silent.

Turkish. Also...I'm not wearing panties.

Payback. She grinned and stepped into the presentation feeling fucking awesome.

CHAPTER THIRTEEN

Brayden gripped his cock tight. His girl was getting brave, and he had a whole bunch of mixed feelings about it, especially as they were leaving in just over six days. And yeah, he'd be spending those days with her, no matter their one-week agreement.

His girl.

He chose to ignore that and carried on.

Throwing his black jacket over the chair, he eyed his bed. He needed to get a few hours' sleep after running an intense security session with the SLCs and Craig.

He'd also had a big walk through the facility. Spotting Thomas, he'd wandered up to the vampire and his friends.

"Officer."

In comparison to them, Brayden was big. Really fucking big. At six foot four, he was taller, broader, and his royal blood pumped out a potent and powerful essence.

The guy bowed low. Really low. "My lord."

The slight tremor in his voice was all he needed to hear. He gave the guy a nod and wandered off, confident no gossip would leave his young lips.

He didn't care about royal gossip; it was part of being a Moretti brother. But drawing attention to Willow was another thing—keeping her safe was becoming a top priority for him.

A knock at the door snapped him out of his thoughts.

He reached out with his energy and felt the queen's.

"Kate, come in," he called out and telepathically unlocked the door. He turned and narrowed his eyes at her upon hearing the speed of her heart rate. "Is everything okay?"

She stepped in and closed the door. Looking as graceful as any queen in a flowing, knee-length navy dress, she sat in the chair he'd dropped his jacket on. "We need to talk."

Shit.

He stood up. "What's happened? Is he dead? Do I need to...?" He started for the door, but she held up a hand to stop him.

"No. Brayden, stop. I need to speak with you privately."

He froze.

"Sit."

Kate had no authority over him, even in her role as queen, but this wasn't royal protocol they were following here. She looked sober, serious, and scared.

"What is it?" He sat in the chair opposite her, the table in between them. It felt awkward. He wasn't sure why.

Kate clenched her jaw. "This has to remain between us. Confidential."

He frowned. He was a Moretti; his brother was king. They had no secrets—of great importance—between them, not to mention, it was illegal. "Kate, you know I can't do it."

"But you will," she said. "If you agree. If not, you will still never repeat this."

The hair on the back of his neck prickled. "You need to tell me what is going on right fucking now," he said darkly.

She squeezed her eyes shut, took a deep breath, and

opened them, giving him a piercing stare. She stood from her seat and began pacing. "What you said, about the baby."

"You're pregnant?" He stood, hopeful.

She shook her head. "No, but I could be."

"Then fucking do it."

Kate looked down for a second and back up at him. A chill ran up his spine.

"It's been one hundred and thirty years, Brayden. Perhaps it's the disease or whatever is wrong with him," she said, a mix of sadness and fury in her voice. "Or it could be me. We don't know."

He stared at her.

"You are right. If there was a baby, I would have something to live for. A child would relieve you of responsibility, in time, and I would be queen mother."

He continued staring.

"It must have royal blood."

More staring and the start of a stomach ulcer.

"Brayden..."

"Oh, fuck no. No, no, no, fucking no." He stepped away.

"It solves both our problems, you know it does," she said, waving a hand. "It would just be sex. Once. Then...then we just forget it happened, and everyone will think it's Vincent's. My cycle, it's..."

He stopped listening as she talked about how the window to procreate was open. He didn't know where to look. The bed? Fuck no. Her? Nope. The door? Yes, a better option.

"I think you need to leave. You're right; we will never talk of this again. Ever."

She took a step toward him. "Brayden, listen to me. Think of the bigger picture here. Don't you want to be free? You hate the idea of being king, and we both know he's weakening."

She was right about one thing. If their enemies, the Russos, got wind of the king's illness, it would make them incredibly vulnerable to a coup.

Every day the rebellion grew louder, demanding a democracy. He had no idea why, when they only had to look around them and see the shitstorm that looked like among humans.

The truth was, the rebellion was being driven by Stefano Russo, who desired nothing more than to replace Vincent on the throne. Democracy my ass. The guy was a psychopath.

He growled.

"He could still recover, and if I need to step up and become king, you know I will. I'm not an asshole."

She winced.

"God, I'm sorry."

"No, you're right. We've been hard on you. I know you'll do the right thing when the time comes."

She walked across the room and laid a hand on his arm. "We have this window of opportunity before his illness becomes more widely known and a pregnancy questioned."

He shook his head.

"As if anyone would ever dream this possible. Shit, Kate, I can't believe you're asking me to do this."

"For us both, Brayden. For the family, for the race."

His mind filled with images of lying to his brother, bedding the queen, and impregnating her. While it was unthinkable, he understood why she was asking.

Coming to terms with it was another thing altogether.

"It would be my daughter or son."

She nodded.

"I would never be able to claim it as my own."

She shook her head. "No."

"We'd be lying to everyone, as well as committing treason." Brayden ran a hand through his hair, disgusted with himself for even having this conversation.

"Think on it. We only have a few days."

They'd never be questioned. Spending time with the king and queen was something he did every day, thought Kate didn't visit his quarters or his rooms at the palace very often.

Kate was a beautiful female, without a doubt. Tall, graceful, with luscious breasts and curves any male would love to sweep his hands over. She was, however, his brother's mate, his queen and...ugh, as the thought entered his head, he flung his head back. She wasn't Willow.

Fucking fuck, fuck, fuck.

Was she his mate?

"God, Kate, this is insane," he cried. "I understand why, but I need to think on it. Go, please. Let me freak out in peace."

She turned to leave. With her hand on the door handle, she said quietly, "Don't take too long."

CHAPTER FOURTEEN

Stefano Russo stared out at the lush green Italian landscape laid out in front of him.

For thousands of years, his family had owned this land, and many others. Miles of rolling hills, respectable estates, and award-winning vineyards. They were wealthy, successful, and powerful.

Like all vampires, they paid taxes to the king. For what? The fuckers lay around in any one of their dozens of castles, flew in their private jets, cruised on their mega yachts, and ate from their fucking gold-plated everything that came from the money other people worked hard for.

Very rarely did he himself lift a finger, but that wasn't the point.

The Russos had challenged the Morettis for centuries. His father, Roberto, had died at the hand of the former king, King Frances. Granted, he had challenged the throne and known the consequences, but all three of the Russo sons had been there that night, as had Vincent and Brayden Moretti.

After seeing his father's head roll on the ground as the sword sliced cleanly through, Stefano had sworn to avenge his father.

As humanity evolved and grew more empowered, so did the unrest among the vampires. It hadn't taken much to pick on the more vulnerable ones and stoke the fires.

Soon, there was a noisy rebellion demanding a democracy with him as their leader. They believed he would free them of their taxes—fools—and that their quality of life would improve.

He himself was a cunning businessman among the humans, and leader of the vampire resistance. He, along with his brothers Luca and Marco, had promised the rebels—and yes, they had a Facebook group—a democracy where there was equal wealth, fair rules, and their voices heard.

With him sitting on the throne as king.

Fuck democracy. What the race needed was a strong leader. One who didn't let assholes like him be capable of freedom of thought and planned coups.

He let out a laugh.

Weak. He shivered in anticipation. The day the Moretti brothers would be weak was drawing closer.

He was playing dirty, but that's what it took to get the Morettis off the throne. They were strong and impenetrable with a powerful army. But not for long.

He had an inside guy now. A vampire close to the king, and trusted. It had been an ingenious idea.

His, of course.

Now that they had the king in a weakened state, Stefano was nearly ready to attempt the coup. It was just a matter of weeks now. The only part of the puzzle still left to solve was the vampire prince.

Brayden Moretti.

Lethal, powerful, and loyal to his family, it was whispered he was even more powerful than the king.

They were not strangers; they had known each other all their lives. Every year, the Russos attended the ball and other society events where they rubbed shoulders, showed mock respect, and sneered at each other.

Brayden had been there the night his father had lost his head, and had spent the rest of the night celebrating and fucking.

Some had said Stefano was bitter and jealous of the fucking huge vampire. They no longer lived.

The rebellion was no secret. He had known the moment the Morettis had tried to infiltrate his inner circle, and he'd allowed it, feeding them the information he wanted them to know. They had underestimated his intelligence, and would pay for that arrogance.

Stefano smirked. He loved the dance of power running through his veins. It sent thrills up his spine and to his groin. He rubbed his hand over his cock.

This year, he would sit on the throne and pump his cock until he creamed all over the fucking thing.

"I've sent the updated instructions to LA."

"*Eccellente!* Best we prepare our costumes for the ball, brother. Send in our RSVPs." He let go of his cock and grinned darkly at Luca, who had just stepped into the room.

Luca, a few inches shorter than his six foot three, returned an equally evil smile.

"What about the prince?"

"Keep watching him. He'll have a weakness; everyone does. Tell them to get closer to the prince," he instructed. "Even if we only take down Vincent Moretti this time, we'll be one step closer."

Marco walked in.

"And if the queen is pregnant?" his younger brother asked.

He snarled. "We kill them both. Seriously, do I have to do all the thinking? For fuck's sake."

Marco crossed his arms. "Really? We're going to kill babies now?"

"A king, Marco. The kid will be a king. Or queen. Whatever," he said, astounded by his stupidity. "What do you think we have locked away in the back rooms?"

"A remote control." Luca sniggered.

Well, at least one of his brothers had his head in the game.

"She's not a baby, for fuck's sake."

He ignored his pathetic brother, but not to the point where he overlooked him being a possible weak link in their plans.

"Go. Find out what you can about the prince. And send my tailor. I want to look my best when I take my seat on the throne."

He might even take one of his whores to America with him. Power made him horny as hell. It was unlikely the Americans would have anything worth fucking, so BYO it was.

CHAPTER FIFTEEN

After a few hours of fitful sleep, Brayden got dressed and stepped out the door. He'd dressed casually tonight for their takeout-and-Netflix evening. He wanted to see Willow relaxed at home and just hanging, as the humans said.

Leaning against the pillar, he waited for the sun to sink into the horizon. The shadow struck, and he began to exit the building.

"Brayden. A word."

Oh, Jesus.

It was the last person he wanted to see right now. "Can it wait? I have a date."

Vincent rolled his eyes. "Seriously? Your king asks to see you, and a female is more important."

He shrugged. "Bro, you know how it is. Chicks before dicks."

The king frowned.

Yeah, okay. He wasn't that young, stupid vampire anymore, but he seriously didn't want to face the king right now.

Oh God. Had Kate gotten a case of the guilts and confessed?

He hadn't agreed to anything, so if the queen had spoken out, he wasn't taking any blame. Aside from the fact that he should have marched directly to his brother and told him everything.

Right?

They were living in unprecedented times. Everything about this was completely fucked up.

"Fine. What can I do for you, my liege?"

"My office." Vincent rolled his eyes and began walking.

Don't freak out, don't freak out, don't freak out.

There was no way he knew. He wouldn't be this calm.

Totally normal. Totally normal.

The door closed behind them, and Vince turned, large hands landing on his hips. After a second, he sat on the edge of the desk and grabbed a hold of it with his hands. The king was tired. It grated on his nerves to see his big, strong brother fading like this.

It had started with dizzy spells, then he'd begun throwing up blood, and now he was losing his powers. Vincent could no longer port, which used a lot of energy, nor could he move as fast as usual. They all covered for him, keeping his illness confidential.

Aside from the queen and himself, only Craig, the SLCs, Regan, and Seraphina knew of his condition. Any sign the king was weakening would be dangerous to the throne. Over the centuries, many had tried to take over the kingdom from his father—no more so than the Russos, but there were always others.

Since Vincent's coronation not long after the death of Roberto Russo, who had challenged their father for the throne, there had been a growing rebellion led by Stefano Russo. They were based in Italy, and word of a coup grew every day.

Craig had vampires inside the operation sending regular reports, but Brayden had long since suspected they weren't getting the full picture.

Vincent's illness had been a huge distraction, and now that they were heading back east with plans for him to step up in the role of king, it was time they reviewed the risks. A change in sovereign was always a vulnerable time for a kingdom, but not for the Morettis.

What the Russos and the entire vampire race didn't know was the power of the Moretti royal blood. It was far more potent than any other vampires. The power source was an energetic one, gained from the allegiance of their people, a mystical source that had never been fully explained.

It was passed on by birth and by sharing their blood, and it gave them greater strength in all ways.

Kate, as queen, had undergone a full blood transfusion from her mate, Vincent, and was now a full-blooded Moretti.

It was their closest guarded secret. In fact, the only vampires alive with the knowledge were those with the Moretti blood: the king, the queen, and him as prince. All three of them had the potent blood running through their veins.

If they shared blood with another, which was rarely done, the receiving vampire would experience an increase in power. However, it was temporary, only until their own blood filtered it out.

Only a complete blood transfusion, such as what the queen had gone through, would allow it to become permanent, and a Moretti would only offer that to a mate.

It was the Moretti blood which had given them the power to hold the throne for eternity.

Anyone who attempted a coup by challenging the sitting king always failed. And they always would.

The idea of a democracy was ludicrous. One had only to look around the world to see democracy had its pros and cons, and with a powerful race like the vampires, who were fundamentally predators, it would never work.

Vampires were predators. Predators needed clear and strong rules, and one alpha who enforced those rules. It was no different than in the animal kingdom, humans included. They just weren't aware enough to acknowledge it.

Vincent, the king, was that alpha.

Brayden was a powerful alpha in his own right; in fact, more so than the king, though it wasn't discussed openly. Brayden had no interest in challenging the king for his position, and Vincent knew it.

The Moretti blood that ran between the brothers gave them power, yes, but it was steeped in loyalty. A loyalty that would see him protecting Vincent's rule no matter what challenge came their way: this mysterious illness or Stefano Russo.

Loyalty and a sense of selfishness. Brayden did not want to be king.

While a coup could happen at any time, they were weaker with Vincent ill, and he had to wonder whether this ball was really a good idea.

Vincent clung to the desk for support, looking jaded, and Brayden knew if he were challenged, he would fail. He gritted his teeth. That would leave Brayden with no choice but to take out the challenger, though rules dictated he couldn't intervene beforehand.

Fuck the rules.

"My mate," the king started. Brayden stilled, using every ounce of his strength to keep his heart rate and body calm.

"The queen."

Vincent sighed. "She's upset. Since your outburst—and wait, before you think I'm about to go off at you, I'm not. I understand. Both of you have a right to feelings about this."

Brayden stared as the king walked around the desk

and sank into the chair.

"I've been so focused on your succession that I haven't stopped to consider how you felt about losing me. I want to apologize."

Brayden shoved his hands in his jeans pockets. Vincent wasn't known for expressing his emotions, not that he was completely inept in this department. He loved his queen and wasn't shy about showing it. When it came to brotherly affection, they had a good, solid relationship, but they weren't huggers or anything.

"Fuck, Vince, don't do that, man. You're dying! Forget about me. I'll deal."

The fact he was slightly, ever so slightly, considering shagging the guy's mate made him want to shoot himself in the head.

Twice.

"I'm not sure Kate will. I need you to look after her for me, Bray. When I'm gone."

Christ, could tonight get any more fucking weird?

"Of course I will. She's family. She's our queen."

"Well, yes," he said, picking up a pen and tapping it on the desk. "I've been looking at our laws, and it's not clear what her position will be upon my death. Because, you know, we don't usually fucking die."

Brayden sat in the opposite chair, and the two brothers stared soberly at each other. And Vincent began coughing all of a sudden.

He pulled out a bunch of tissues, which always seemed to be in his pocket these days, and dabbed at his mouth. It came away coated in his blood.

Brayden's chest tightened.

"I'm fine," he said, and the lie hung thick in the air. "Anyway, we don't have an heir, and as you know, you'll take the throne." Vincent opened a large leather-bound book on the desk.

"There's no concession for this situation in our laws, and so in theory, it makes her role as queen redundant." He looked up at Brayden, eyes boring into this. "I can't and won't let that happen."

Brayden shook his head. "No."

There was no way he would leave Kate unprotected in the wake of the king's passing. He had considered this months ago and was going to deal with it, but the fact that Vincent had brought it up now gave him goose bumps.

Did he think the end was close?

"In line with human royal structures, I've decided to create two positions: *Queen Dowager* and *Prince Consort*. Both allow a position for the mate of the ruling vampire after their death."

Brayden nodded. Vincent was also preparing, he realized, for other kings and queens to potentially die.

Were they evolving?

Was their immortality weakening?

"You think I could be next?" The idea didn't scare him as much as he thought it would, until his mind flashed to Willow. As his body began to react—his chest clenching and back straightening—he shut down the thoughts.

Not my mate.

The king shrugged.

"I'm not sure. My responsibility is to my mate and to the throne. To you, brother. I have to make arrangements while I'm of sound mind and body."

This was so fucked up. Vampires didn't have these kinds of conversations.

"Fuck!" He stood up, punching his hand through his hair. "No matter what happens, I will protect Kate. You have my word. I will ensure she is protected, cared for, and all her needs met. She's a Moretti. Nothing changes that. I promise you."

Vincent looked down at the book and nodded. "Thank you, brother."

He was, at the heart of this, just a male hurting for his mate. The feeling of unimaginable frustration and anguish at leaving her behind and not being able to protect her was one Brayden could only imagine was tearing him apart.

Kate would step out of her role as queen and become queen dowager, and the vacant position would be held for Brayden's mate. Unless he fulfilled Kate's request and impregnated her. Then she would become the queen mother, holding the position until her child became of age. None of this was written into their law, and neither could he discuss it with the king. He would have to wait. Take it one day at a time.

Right now, he just wanted to see Willow.

Outside, the sky had darkened.

Brayden felt a heavy responsibility, heavier than the throne, land on his shoulders. What had earlier felt unthinkable, now began to feel like a necessity.

If he impregnated Kate, no one would question whether it was the king's child. Bonded vampires had no sexual attraction to anyone but their mate, so infidelity didn't exist in their world.

Once pregnant, her role in the royal family—*should* Vincent cease to exist—would never be challenged. In time, he could step down and watch as his child became the king or queen and led their people. While he'd never be recognized or known as the father, he'd still play a vital role in the child's life as uncle.

It was so messed up, yet so brilliant.

The question was, could he do it?

CHAPTER SIXTEEN

Willow threw the T-shirt on the bed and groaned. She was aiming for sexy and relaxed, but fifteen outfits later, she was ready to give up. Brayden would tell her to go naked.

She swept her hair into a messy bun and put the white top back on. On her bed was a pair of sweatpants and a pair of tight jeans.

The jeans won.

Not exactly Netflix attire, but they made her butt look sexy, so she slipped them on and took once last look in the mirror.

Knock, knock.

"Gorgeous," Brayden said as he pulled her against his lips after she had opened the door.

She heard the paper bag and looked down. From the delicious aroma, she guessed it was their Turkish takeout.

"You smell delicious," she moaned hungrily.

"If I had known hummus got that kind of reaction, I would have layered myself with it."

She grinned, took the bag of food, and stopped herself from responding. His ego was big enough.

"How did your presentation go?"

"Good, I think. I'll find out in a few days. I was so nervous, but having Bri in the room helped."

She'd told Brayden all about their friendship and her friend's loss. He'd surprised her by listening quietly while running his thumb over her knuckles affectionately and asking a few questions. Part of her resented the easy way they were together. Why couldn't she meet a man like this for a long-term relationship?

Perhaps it was easy enough to do when he was only spending a few days with her and there was a guarantee of sex at the end of the conversation. She was aware of how cynical that sounded.

"Loyal friends are valuable," he said, gathering the napkins and following her into the living room. "I'm sure you were amazing, and if not, you'll learn and incorporate them into your next pitch."

She loved that he was business-minded and they were able to talk shop. It was a complete turn-on. However, getting Brayden to talk about his day, in any detail, always fell flat.

Recalling her first impression of him, she began to wonder if this intimidating and powerful-looking man was mixed up in something criminal.

Whenever she pushed for more information, he'd brush her off saying his business was boring and would rather hear about her day. Did he think she was naive?

Willow had dropped it because in a few days, their affair would be over. The sobering thought had her glancing over as he bit into his kebab.

His forehead was creased and his eyes were everywhere but the TV. Something was on his mind. Looking back, she realized he'd only kissed her once and hadn't laid a finger on her since.

It was incredibly unusual, based on the full four days she'd known him. She rolled her eyes at her insecurity and picked up the remote, switching to Netflix.

"Any favorite shows?"

Dropping his plate on the table, he laid a hand along the back of the sofa. Not on her.

"As long as it doesn't start with *Housewives of...*, you choose."

"I can guarantee it won't." She smiled, turning on an episode of *Lucifer*.

"Nice." He moved over slightly and planted a kiss on her head.

Like. She. Was. His. Sister.

What the hell?

A while later, the screen began to load the next episode. Brayden glanced at her and ruffled her hair.

"Okay. Enough," she said, switching off the screen. "Who are you and what have you done with Brayden?"

He pulled back his chin and laughed. "What now?"

"You've been here for over an hour and haven't tried to have sex with me yet."

He relaxed and laughed some more.

"First, I don't *try* to have sex with you. I fuck you thoroughly, Willow. Second, the night is still young, *principessa*."

He kissed her nose.

"There! That! You kissed my nose. It's something you'd do to your sister."

"I don't have a sister."

"Wait. Are you going to break up with me?" she asked, mouth gaping.

"Don't be ridiculous. I'm getting my full week with you, Willow. Believe me."

His voice was dark and sultry, and the way he looked at her, full of desire and want, felt far more familiar. She relaxed a little.

"Then what's going on? I don't mind this snuggly version of you, I just—oh God, it's the unsexy outfit, isn't it? Too soon."

She couldn't stop herself. She was never this insecure, but he was so damn hot, and she was...so damn normal.

Even in jeans and a sweatshirt, he looked like a god. In fact, tonight he looked bigger than usual in the blue-and-black outfit. Had those shoulders and chest grown overnight?

He shook his head and pulled her into his arms and onto his lap.

"Willow, you'd look sexy in a paper bag." Pulling on her hair tie, he ran his hands through her brown waves and looked at her like she was an ice cream.

Now, that was better.

"I have some things on my mind, nothing else."

She sighed as his lips landed on hers, softly. As she opened for him, his tongue caressed hers sensually. He ended the kiss, and his silver eyes danced in a now familiar way before he blinked and they returned to normal.

"Want to talk about it?"

He glanced away and shook his head.

"No."

Fingers on his chin, she turned his face back to hers. "Stay with me."

A line appeared between his brows and his body tensed underneath her. "Have you ever had to do something you don't want to do? Something inexcusable."

"No. Do you really *have* to do it, or just think you do? Are there any other options?"

"Yes. And no."

"Then only you know what the right decision is for you."

He kissed the side of her mouth. "Unfortunately, this impacts many people. People I care about."

"I may not know you very well, Brayden, but I do not think you would do anything to hurt anyone you care about. It's not in your nature."

He glanced at her and squinted.

"I'm serious. You are very protective, and when you speak of your family, you have love in your eyes."

He cupped her cheek and began kissing her. Longer, deeper, harder. His hand snuck under her top and ran up her back, making its way around the front and cupping her breast.

Underneath her, his cock hardened. They both moaned. There was the possessive and passionate man she knew. Releasing her lips a moment later, he gripped her waist tightly.

"You mean more to me than just sex, Willow. I want you to know this."

She hadn't expected to hear those words from him. Her eyes glistened, and the corners of her mouth curved up.

Oh.

She was ridiculously happy to hear him say that, and she'd worry about why later.

"Hey, we don't have to do anything. I was just feeling insecure. Sorry."

"No, you weren't. I was distant, and you picked up on it intuitively."

Her mouth fell open. "Okay, seriously, am I on some reality show?"

"What?" He laughed.

"Either you're an AI prototype of the perfect man or I'm dreaming. Something's going on here."

He laughed. "I'll take it as a compliment."

She laid her head on his shoulder. Brayden was right, though. She had picked up on his emotional distance, except she'd made it all about her. It wasn't like her to be so insecure, and while everyone had their moments, she usually kept hers in check.

Surprised again by her reaction to this man, she found herself unable to stop.

"So, do you want to share more about this situation?"

He shook his head. "I can't. I'm sorry." Taking her face in his hands, he gazed seriously into her eyes. "Willow, I found out yesterday that we're heading back east in six days. I intend to spend all of them with you."

She opened her mouth. Closed it. It wasn't like she was counting the days, but if someone had asked, technically, it would give them two additional days together. But she wasn't counting.

"There will be a day or two I am busy, but afterward, I want...no, I'll need to see you." He glanced across the room, his eyes looking haunted.

Now she was really beginning to wonder what he was involved with.

"Bray, I'm not sure..."

"I need you. For the next six days, Willow, I want you in my life. I've got some responsibilities to fulfill that are...difficult."

She swallowed deeply and ran her fingers over his new stubble, wondering what he was getting himself into—or was already knee-deep in.

Some women liked bad boys, and while they were most certainly sexy, Willow preferred her bad boys in a romance novel, not in her bed. Had her initial instincts been right about Brayden and his friend?

"If this is something illegal, perhaps it's best you don't do it."

He let out a dark laugh. "Oh, it's far worse than illegal."

She pulled back. "What do you mean?"

He shook his head.

"Are you going to hurt someone? Please tell me you're not into bad things, Brayden." She tried to move off his lap, but he held her tight, eyes boring into hers.

"Honestly, if I do this right, the only person getting hurt will be me. It's so fucked up."

He let out a breath and his eyes darkened as they ran over her body. She saw the moment he shut down. His eyelids dropped and his large hand ran over her forehead, across her hair, and gripped it.

"I am not the nice man you think I am, Willow."

She sucked in a breath.

"You're scaring me, Brayden."

"Am I? Or are you excited?" Her core flared with heat, her panties becoming moist as his cock grew harder and larger beneath her. "Isn't this what you wanted? To have me desire you, touch you, and taste you."

Her breathing became ragged as he ran his tongue down her throat, stopping at her pulse.

"You have no need to fear me. I'll never hurt you."

He pulled her T-shirt off, exposing her favorite sexy bra. She was also wearing the matching panties and had shaved and dabbed perfume in all the right places.

His strong hands held her hip and back of her head. She loved his dominance.

"I thought about you wearing no panties today. You were very naughty texting me that."

"Did you believe me?"

"It doesn't matter," he said, suddenly lifting her up and laying her on the sofa.

His strength never failed to surprise her. She gasped as he laid his large muscular frame over her.

"Now, I'm going to punish you for that tease."

He sucked on her nipple and unzipped her jeans, pulling them free.

"Punish me?" she squeaked out, a flush of anticipation running through her body. Kneeling over her, he nodded then reached one hand behind him, ripping off his top.

Willow took a moment to enjoy the gift that was Brayden. His abdomen was tight and hard, with muscles that nearly defied nature. She reached out and ran her fingers across his soft olive skin and stopped as she saw the head of his cock peeking out. He grabbed her hand.

"You want that?" he asked as she licked her lips. She nodded, eager.

"I have some playing to do before you get it. As your punishment."

He undid his jeans, and it sprung free. Her body clenched with a need so powerful, she burned.

"Bray, I..."

He grabbed her wrist again and pushed both her arms over her head. "Do I need to bind your hands?"

She swallowed. It was probably best. His body was layer upon layer of raw masculinity that she had to touch.

Free of his jeans, she noticed Brayden held something in his hand. He spread her natural juices around her pussy, and licking his fingers, he looked up at her, eyes dark with desire as she arched into him.

Her hands reached for him again.

"Last warning, or I'll tie you up."

She groaned. "Fuck me, Brayden. I need you inside me."

He opened his hand. In his palm was a short string of large white pearls. She stared at them, then at him.

"I'm going to put these inside your nice, wet pussy," he said, rubbing his hand along her thigh. "Relax, baby." He dropped and began lapping at her, the feeling so intense and erotic she nearly came. He lifted his head and tapped her clit. "No. I'll tell you when you can orgasm, Willow. Now relax and open for me."

She gasped, the jolt and instruction stopping her.

Brayden lowered again and his fingers and tongue began moving around her folds, the delicious feeling causing all kinds of short circuits in her body and brain. Suddenly, she felt the foreign object enter her. It felt large but not uncomfortable. Just a pop and it was inside her. Her pussy contracted around it, wanting more.

"Yes, oh, good girl." Brayden kept with the fingers and licking, then another one entered her. "Oh yes. God, Willow, so hot."

Soon all five of the white pearls were inside her, filling her, every move she made creating waves of pleasure.

"Oh, my..." She groaned.

Brayden glanced up at her, running his tongue over her clit. "Next time, you will wear panties when you're not with me, won't you?"

He pinched a nipple and she groaned. "Brayden, please."

"Oh, we are just getting started."

He stood and her eyes widened. Where was he going? But he didn't go far. He moved to her side and gripped his cock. "Open your mouth, sweetheart."

He slipped his cock in and pulled her hair into a tight bunch. She sucked on him, moving up and down his shaft. Every inch she moved stimulated the pearls within her, sending flares of ecstasy throughout her body.

"Oh God."

Brayden held the base of his cock, pushing her head to go deeper. "Yes. God, Willow, that's it."

She was on the edge, so on the edge. Just when she thought she could handle no more, he surprised her again.

"Don't come," he reminded her, running a hand along her stomach, tweaking her clit, and lining his finger with her moisture only to lick it off. Her eyes begged his as he stared down at her with more desire than she'd seen in her life.

"God, you're gorgeous," he said, affection and lust filling his eyes. "You ready for more?"

She nodded. A sudden buzzing began within her, and she cried out, throwing her head back.

"Fuck, look at you."

Pleasure flooded her body, short-circuiting her brain.

"Fuckfuckfuckfuck. Brayden!" she cried as he shoved his cock in her mouth again.

He reached and began circling her clit. "Come for me, Willow. Come now."

As soon as permission was given, her body convulsed, arching into the pleasure of the vibration and stimulation from his fingers. She clenched, mouth flying open as powerful waves of pleasure blossomed through her. In complete surrender, she opened her eyes and watched as Brayden pumped his cock, spilling his seed into her mouth.

"My girl," Brayden said, moving into position between her legs. Slowly he pulled the pearls out, one by one, and each time, she let out a pleasure-laced moan.

"Bray."

Lying back, he pulled her on top of him and slid into her.

"Argh, fuck," he exclaimed in surprise. "God, you feel so damn good."

"I..."

"I'm going to fuck you hard, Willow. Are you okay with that?"

She nodded and he did. Hard and fast, he pounded into her, moving her with his hold on her hips. How he had the strength, she had no idea and didn't care. It was exactly what she needed. Every damn inch of him with total and utter dominating power.

They both came again before collapsing.

Brayden kept one arm around her lower back as they breathed laboriously together. He lifted her chin and kissed her long and hard.

"Never," he said darkly, "Never will I not want you, Willow. Remember, always."

His lips landed back on hers, totally owning her.

She didn't know what the proclamation meant, but she did know she'd be giving him those six days, without question.

CHAPTER SEVENTEEN

Brayden pushed through the double swinging doors into the security briefing Craig was heading up.

Mutters of *my lord* greeted him.

As his senior team, he'd told them it wasn't necessary when he was in his role as captain, but many of them had known him for centuries, so it had become habit as they'd worked their way up the ranks.

"Captain," Craig nodded in greeting.

"Sorry I'm late," he said unnecessarily. One thing he'd learned from his father was that respect was earned. He may be the royal prince and lead the warriors, but he believed in behaving in the manner you wished others to behave.

In this case, he was fifteen minutes late—fifteen minutes he'd lain staring at Willow while she slept looking like an absolute angel. He had known he was running late, but had found himself in an obsessive thought pattern. Was he using Willow as an excuse not to betray his brother with Kate, or was the thought of having sex with anyone but this human even more unthinkable than the queen's request?

"I've just distributed the relocation strategy file you approved earlier tonight."

He nodded and sat down, watching his team review it on their digital devices, fingers scrolling and heads nodding to no one in particular. For the next hour, Craig walked them through the plan, assessing challenges, and prepped the senior lieutenants so they could brief their own teams.

"Prince—ah, captain, you haven't put your departure date in here," Marcus said, lifting the device.

"No." He paused, took a deep breath, and stood. "I'll make the decision closer to the date."

Craig looked at the male quickly then back at Brayden, keeping his face blank.

"We can work around that last minute," Lance, one of the other four senior lieutenants in the room, said.

"Okay. Go brief your teams and let's get this show on the road. Tom, can you update the operations team?" Craig asked.

The tall, dark-skinned male nodded, making a note on his device. His mate, Lucinda, oversaw the housekeeping and kitchen team, so it naturally, and often, landed on him.

Brayden looked around at the males. They'd all worked together for so long, this was like clockwork. Yet things felt different. Very few people knew about the king's illness, but these males did. They hadn't asked anything, as no well-trained soldier would. And they *were* highly trained and deadly machines, each with their own strengths and skills.

It wasn't his decision to impart more knowledge about the king's situation, and it served everyone to know as little as possible. While he was prince and captain, the fact remained that Vincent was king. For now.

However, as captain, he was empowered to share information to ensure the good mental health of his team. He knew these men had no problem with him stepping into the role of king one day—they all loved and respected him—but they also loved their king.

"One last thing," he started. "This information stays

inside this room, do you understand?" Single nods all round. "The treatment hasn't delivered the results we hoped for. We're returning home, not because the king has given up but to consider other options."

"And for the fucking ball." Craig smirked, breaking the tension.

"Hey, I like the ball!" Kurt proclaimed.

"For the chicks," Tom teased, although it had been at one of the balls that he'd met his mate. That she was the sister of the Russos was something they were all cognizant of.

"Anyone know the theme yet?" Kurt asked.

"Victorian era."

"Top hats and skirts big enough to fit under. Excellent," someone else said.

"I prefer those little flapper dresses of the twenties." Kurt shrugged.

"They'd look good on you."

"Fuck off."

Brayden smiled, happy the team was in good spirits. He nodded to Craig, who dismissed the team. "Okay, that's a wrap."

The room emptied out as Craig closed his laptop and pushed a few buttons to shut off the digital projection on the wall.

"Who's organizing the jets?"

"I am," he said, and continued packing up, putting his equipment and files in a black shoulder bag. He pushed a pen through a black loop, positioning it carefully.

"What's up?" He knew Craig nearly as well as he knew himself. Something was off.

The male stood up to his full height and put his hands on his hips, considering him. Across the table, he stood nearly to Brayden's height and width, but not quite. Still, he was a big male, and with those piercing green eyes and tribal tats, he most certainly wasn't a metro man, as the humans called them.

No, Craig was all muscle and didn't beat around the bush. When triggered, those fangs came out, and he was a mean-looking motherfucker. He was also strong as fuck. It was his loyalty and ability to lead that had secured his position as Brayden's second in charge all those centuries ago.

That and their history. Not for the first time, Brayden wondered what Craig would be capable of if the guy had their potent royal blood. He still wouldn't have the kind of power Brayden had, but he'd be a wrecking ball, that's for sure.

"Not a fucking thing," he replied. "You?"

They stared at each other for a long moment. Craig was the only vampire on the planet he allowed to speak to him that way.

"Do you have your period or something?" Brayden put his jacket on and started walking toward the door. He sighed when the guy didn't respond. "Ask me what you want to know, Craig."

"You won't fucking answer."

"I will."

"All right. Is she your mate?"

He froze.

"I rest my case."

Brayden clutched the door handle.

"Forget it. I need your head back in the game, and before you kick my ass for that comment, you need to know something. You're being watched."

Dropping the handle, he turned, fury building in his veins. "I'm sorry, what? Who. Is. Watching. Me?"

Craig closed the space between them and stopped a few feet away. "They're not just watching you, Brayden. They're watching Vincent, Kate, and your girlfriend."

He grabbed the guy by the front of his shirt and lifted him off the ground. Craig didn't flinch.

"Why the fuck are you just telling me now? Who are they?" he growled, his eyes glowing with the power of the Moretti blood. When Craig glared at him, he released his grip and let him drop back to the floor. "Tell me."

"Russo's males," he replied, tugging his black uniform back down. "One followed you after you left last night. I followed his port energy and found him standing outside Willow's house as you went in."

"What did he do?"

"Watched the house for a few minutes then left. He wasn't aware I followed him." Of course he wasn't. Craig couldn't be seen or traced if he didn't want to.

"Why didn't you arrest the fucker?"

"For what? Sightseeing? Protecting the prince?"

Brayden's fangs made an appearance.

"You think I wouldn't have acted should I had cause? Fuck you, Brayden."

He looked into the eyes of his friend and retracted his fangs. Fuck, he'd been an asshole lately. He had a few good reasons though. One, he'd had to accept he would become king; two, the queen wanted him to fuck her so she could get pregnant; and three, he strongly suspected the human he was banging was his mate.

None of which was casual watercooler conversation.

Also, if anyone called what he was doing with Willow *banging,* he'd rip their throat out.

"Fuck! I apologize," he said, shaking his head and turning away for a moment.

Craig simply nodded. And that would be it. The centuries of history between them would take more than a butting of heads to break.

"There's more." Brayden gritted his teeth as Craig continued. "Regan asked me to double the queen's security."

Brayden tensed momentarily, then forced himself to relax. There was no way anyone could know about the discussion between him and the queen yesterday. No matter what happened, it was one secret he would be taking to his grave. If he ever had one.

"I want eyes on Regan." He pulled his phone out of his pocket, but stopped. Looking at his commander with narrowed eyes, he gave him a direct instruction. "In fact, they need to be yours. The queen's security stays as it is. If he tries to dictate any security changes again, direct him to me."

Craig nodded and walked back to his bag, picking it up.

"She's not my mate," Brayden said quietly, finally answering the male's question. He sent Willow a text as he spoke. "She's important to me, but she's not my lifemate."

"Are you sure? Because you were sparkling like a firecracker a minute ago."

He turned back for the door. "Like I said, she's important."

He heard Craig groan behind him.

Even if she were, he couldn't destroy her life. She deserved better than having her life ripped away from her like his mother had.

Fuck, he had no mental capacity right now to think about that.

Right now, he had a queen to deal with.

CHAPTER EIGHTEEN

Kate rolled her eyes at her mate.

"Not on your life, sunshine."

Vincent laughed. "Sunshine would end my life, so another reason to consider one."

"I am not getting a vibrator. You're still here and functioning fine, thank you very much." She wriggled in his lap and felt his body confirm her statement. He slid his hand up her thigh, under her dress, and she slapped him playfully. "Stop, someone could come in."

"I'm the king, what the hell are they going to do, tell me off?" He laughed. "Plus, you know I can lock the door, just as you can, from here."

Kate had planted herself on Vincent's lap after finding him seated in the large chair behind his desk. She'd been going stir crazy since speaking to the prince. How could she have done it? How could she not?

Admitting to herself that she had done it partly due to self-preservation was hard, but the truth was, she was terrified of losing her mate. She loved him more than life. To produce an heir would mean the world to him. Vincent had always wanted children, though he never said so to anyone outside their relationship.

Both had suffered from guilt for their lack of procreation yet chided the other when it rose to the surface. Producing vampire children was not easy; they didn't breed as abundantly as other animals on the planet. It was a rarity, which is why their population was low. However, after one hundred and thirty years and still no heir, it wasn't looking hopeful.

Such things were not talked about openly, but it was a concern for the race's long-term existence. Just another thing the resistance pushed back against. They thought a recruitment program to change humans was a bright idea.

Fortunately, the king was highly opposed to it.

Kate was now in a fertile window, and they had been making love frequently, but these days, it was done with little expectation it would result in a child.

She knew it was a long shot with Brayden, but should they be successful, it would change everything.

Whether the prince was willing and whether the two of them could follow through on the act was another story. The prince was a wildly attractive vampire, yet the thought of sex with someone other than her mate made her sick to her stomach. That was the way of mates.

"So back to this vibrator, do you think they come in extra-large? Because obviously—"

"Oh my God, please stop talking about this."

"We could get a custom one made." He grinned, and she raised an eyebrow. "What? They could make a mold of my cock and then you'd..." He caught sight of her expression and grew quiet. "Too much?"

She nodded, eyes lowered, heart clenching at the thought of losing him.

"Sorry, my love." Vincent pulled her closer and nuzzled into her neck gently.

"Please don't give up," she said in a small voice. As if on cue, the king started coughing, and she handed him a ball of tissues to soak up the blood.

If only it were as simple as replenishing it with her own, she would do anything to keep him alive. Slowly his powers were fading, his movements slowing. It pained her to watch such a powerful male suffer, especially since he was supposed to be immortal. Heck, they all were meant to be.

For those in the know, keeping the situation contained had been a priority. Word of a potential coup by the rebellion grew every day, and if the king were challenged today, he would lose.

Brayden wouldn't. He was the most powerful vampire among them. They would lose the king, but it would mean the Moretti bloodline would be safe.

Safe enough for her to bring an heir into the world.

She hated that this was happening to the vampire she loved, to his beloved brother, and to her. Together, the brothers were a great team, with Vincent as the diplomat and Brayden as the muscle. Vincent had evolved his father's reign, and the race was now thriving under his lead. Modern times and modern thinking had been contributing factors. The only thing the Moretti brothers disagreed on was Brayden's belief they needed to take a stronger stance against the resistance.

She suspected that was about to change.

"I'm trying my best, darling. For everybody."

Kate nuzzled into his neck, allowing herself a rare moment of weakness.

"Hey, did you guys...oh, fuck. Sorry."

Kate turned to see Brayden standing in the doorway looking apologetic and beginning to back out.

Shit.

She tensed.

Vincent glanced down at her in question, and after a moment of panic, she realized what he was asking.

She nodded.

He rubbed her arms as he called to his brother, "Come in, Brayden."

"I'll come back."

"I doubt it. You are rarely here." The king scowled.

"I'm here enough. Don't start, brother, we have more important things to discuss."

Kate moved to the seat next to the king and smiled as he took her hand. His thumb rubbed over her knuckles unconsciously.

"Is there something wrong?" She wasn't worried he would betray her; he loved the king. He might not agree with her crazy request, but he wouldn't hurt Vincent.

"I'm being followed by some of Russo's men." He crossed his arms. "I don't quite know how or why, but I think Regan has something to do with it. We're investigating further, but I wanted you to know. Limit what you share with him."

"Don't be ridiculous."

"Trust no one, brother. He asked Craig to double Kate's security."

Vincent frowned. "Why?"

Brayden nodded thoughtfully as if this confirmed what he was thinking. "Then it wasn't at your request."

"No, for what purpose. She is not in any danger."

Brayden nodded. "Craig is going to monitor him."

"So everyone is following everyone."

Brayden rolled his eyes at the king and walked to the floor-length windows, gripping the top of the frame with his hand. The windows in all their properties were coated to protect them from turning to ash. Handy, but daylight still drained them rapidly if they did not sleep, just as night did with humans.

"Pretty much," he replied. "I'll bring more information to you as soon as I hear anything. We need to be more alert. Something feels very off about all this."

The king stood.

"Why is Regan interfering with the queen's security, in any case?" Irritation turned to anger as he spoke.

Kate watched Brayden turn to the king, relieved his

brother had finally begun to take this seriously. "It's an interesting question."

The king frowned.

Kate placed her hand on his arm. "Regan is probably just overstepping his boundaries, as he's prone to do."

"Possibly, but Brayden is right to be cautious. I want to be kept informed. Immediately. I don't give a fuck who does what around here, when it comes to the queen, I get told first. *Capisci?*"

The prince nodded. Then he glanced at her, just a little, enough to know...yes, she should go to him. Her chest tightened, heart pounded, and there was nothing she could have done to stop it.

"What's wrong, my love?" Her mate was attuned to her heart just as she was to his. Brayden glared at her and she winced.

"I just don't want this to upset you or make you any more ill." It was a half-truth. "Let the prince take care of it."

Vincent shook his head. "If my advisor is up to something, Kate, I need to know about it. Especially if it involves your safety."

"Do not confront him, Vincent. Give us time to watch him and the others."

The king nodded.

Brayden began to walk out.

"Have you finished playing with your little human now, brother?"

Kate could nearly hear the prince's teeth grinding.

"Her name is Willow."

Vincent's face remained blank, though she knew him too well not to notice the flicker of interest in his eyes. Like her, he had noticed subtle changes in the prince. Brayden might think he was fooling everyone, but he most definitely was not.

This woman was important to him. There was every reason to believe she might be his mate, and no reason to believe she was.

She would check his irises again when she visited, though the fact that he appeared to have agreed to her proposal gave her pause.

Surely, he wouldn't go through with it if he had bonded.

Then again...how could she?

CHAPTER NINETEEN

Brayden lifted his phone again and checked for a response from Willow. Nothing.

It was nearly midday, and he needed a few hours' sleep. He didn't know when to expect the queen; it could be any time. Until he did, he needed to stay here.

And afterward?

Could he return to Willow and act normal? Would he ever feel normal again?

"Fuck it." He sat up, leaning on the headboard, and dialed her number.

Ring. Ring. Fucking ring.

"Hello!"

The sound of her voice calmed him. "Hey," he said, all husky. "Switching to FaceTime."

"Oh hey...oh hey!" she repeated as his face appeared on screen. "Where are you? It's all dark. You okay?"

Oh, right. He hadn't thought this bit through. He was also shirtless. What good reason would he have for lying in the dark in the middle of the day? Jesus, he was losing it.

"Migraine," he said. Thank goodness for human TV.

"Damn, I get them occasionally. Do you have medicine?"

Medicine?

Nope, and he didn't have the information of what they used stored away, so please don't ask, he silently prayed.

"Yes. I'll live, but I wanted to see your face before I crashed."

A smile spread across his lips as a blush hit her cheeks. God, she thrilled him. The way she reacted to his voice, his body, his mind—it was beyond anything.

"You are so sweet."

Yeah, fuck, he was not sweet in the slightest.

Warmth spread through his chest at the way she was looking at him. "I've never been called sweet before, Willow."

The blush deepened and she chewed her bottom lip. His cock stiffened.

"I don't want you to be sweet all the time."

The delicious moment hung between them until it became awkward. Like full-of-feelings-and-sexual-need awkward.

He coughed.

"Are you feeling okay today? After last night?"

He'd been hard on her body. She had loved it, but he suspected she would be sore today. God, he really wanted to be with her right now, taking care of her.

She nodded, not shyly but in an intimate way only the two of them understood.

"I'm all right. I was in the bath soaking, which is why I hadn't responded to your messages."

His body relaxed at the explanation, and he mentally reminded himself to kick his own ass. What a pussy. Then he realized it wasn't insecurity but a need to ensure she was safe.

Fine, not a pussy. Thank fuck.

"Do you need anything?"

"No. I'm fine, Bray, honestly. You get some rest and take care of your migraine."

His body tensed with the need to port to her and hold her. To gently make love to her or simply massage her.

Instead, he ran a hand through his hair and sunk down into his bed. God, how he wished she were in his arms and they could just lie and talk all day.

It never felt like he had enough time with her.

"I'd rather you were here."

Whoa.

Where the fuck had that come from?

It was one thing to think these emotional thoughts, another to say them out loud.

"Same."

More of the staring.

Speak, for fuck's sake.

"Well..." He coughed. "Yeah, I'll get some rest and head over. If..." He'd been planning to make an excuse for tonight, assuming Kate turned up, but now he was so fucked up in the head about everything he didn't know what to do.

About anything.

"If you don't feel up to it, stay home. Or I could come to yours?"

Nooooo.

His heart literally skipped a beat. It could never, ever happen. He watched Willow's beautiful, hopeful eyes poke dents in his heart.

"I'll text you later to tell you how I'm doing, okay, beautiful?"

She nodded, giving him a small smile at his nonanswer.

"Bye," he said, soaking up every little inch of her as she blew him a kiss and ended the call. Brayden slammed the phone on the bed, frustrated, his fangs extending.

What the fuck?

He sat up, touched his fangs, pricked his finger, cursed, then licked to seal the wound.

Now, this was new. Not the fangs, he'd had those since birth. His powerful and aggressive reaction to his female was new.

His?

Goddamn it.

He teleported into his bathroom because walking was too slow in a moment like this. He had to know.

Just fucking look.

Taking a deep breath, he peered into the mirror.

Yes? No? Maybe.

Heart pounding, he couldn't tell if he was imagining a fine, thin line appearing around his irises, or if it was real.

Jesus fucking Christ.

He needed to figure this out fast. Walking around with shades on like U2's Bono wasn't going to cut it.

The knock on the door and the tiny body which slipped inside without his permission made his blood go cold.

Kate picked up on his reaction from a room away and didn't try to pretend otherwise.

"I feel the same."

CHAPTER TWENTY

Regan pulled the briefcase out of the wardrobe and proceeded to unlock the three different padlocks.

The sad part was that he didn't need them. No one would ever suspect him of having such an item on his person. He was the king's advisor, as he had been for the king before. He had loyally served both kings for over one thousand years.

Until recently.

Shame spread through him.

It wasn't by choice. Like any bonded mate, his loyalty was to his mate. It was nature. It was the way of the vampire.

Never in his wildest dreams had he imagined he'd be tested like this. If he'd thought there was another way, he would have gone with it, but they'd taken his mate, Selena, and daughter, Lily, while they were in Italy visiting relatives.

They being the Russo family. Stefano Russo, leader of the vampire resistance.

As their father had done over one hundred and thirty years ago, in 1891, Stefano and his brothers were now making their move for the throne. This time, however, they were not doing it with honor or following the way of their race. Instead, they were using him as their weapon, along with a poisonous substance Regan had to give the king each day.

At first, he'd thought it would be ineffective.

Vampires didn't get sick. But with each day, the king grew worse. Now, Regan had been instructed to increase the dosage.

They hadn't told him anything, but after months and months of overthinking it all, he suspected the Russos planned to weaken the king so they could infiltrate the castle and take the throne from him.

Regan wondered what they planned to do about the Moretti prince. Brayden was a powerful—some would say *the most* powerful—vampire.

If his brother was beaten in a challenge, the prince would immediately step into the role as king, a role he was mentally preparing for now, if reluctantly.

He'd known Brayden and Vincent since they were born. In fact, he'd go so far as to say he loved both the king and the prince; he certainly respected them. And so, he knew that once his involvement was exposed—and one day, it would be—Brayden would destroy him.

Regan would beg for his mate and daughter to be saved, and then he would accept his punishment. It was deserved.

He should have confessed the moment it happened, but how could he risk their lives? The Russos were rich and powerful, and had been planning this for over a century. He had no idea where they were keeping Selena and Lily; he was given photos of them looking terrified and hungry, and had to trust they were recent.

He hung his head in shame and placed the small plastic bag containing the powder in his pocket. All he had to do was deliver the king's evening tea with a dose stirred in. He always watched to make sure the vampire king drank it during their nightly briefing.

It was the perfect crime, and no one suspected a thing.

He opened the door to the kings' office. "Good eve,

your majesty."

"Regan," the king said stiffly.

He froze. Something had changed.

"Come in. Don't mind my mood. I'm just feeling more unwell than usual."

He knew that wasn't true, but it *was* about to be. After this double dose.

This is going to kill us both.

"Perhaps this will help, sire."

CHAPTER TWENTY-ONE

Kate stood staring at him like he was the Antichrist, and he supposed he was looking back at her the same way.

"This has to be the worst moment of my life," she said, turning in circles.

He walked to the bed and retrieved his shirt, which seemed ridiculous, given the circumstances.

"Um, thanks."

She flung her hands in the air. "You know what I mean."

Brayden nodded. "Before we—shit, I'm not sure we should do this." He ran a hand through his hair. "I just don't know. Hell, I'm beginning to wonder if we have a choice. Am I mad?"

The queen dropped her face into her hands and groaned.

He wanted to go to her, but it seemed wrong to touch or comfort her.

"I know, I know."

Brayden paced the room. Images of what they would soon do filled his mind, creating a churn in his stomach. This was wrong.

Humans said they found cheating immoral, but many of them still did it without any conscience. For vampires, it was different. To bed another when mated was unfathomable. To bed another's mate was unthinkable. To bed your brother's mate, despicable.

To bed the king's mate, suicidal.

And yet, here they were. The queen and the prince. Unable to look at each other, let alone follow through with the goddamned act.

He sighed.

Kate finally looked up at him, then away, then back at him, then away. "So, my cycle is...yeah. We can, so let's...God, let's just get this over with."

Heart pounding in the back of his throat—somehow, it had made its way up there—he tried to speak.

Couldn't.

Tried to move.

Couldn't.

Did he really have a choice? Of course he did. He could let his brother die without an heir, take the throne, and be the king for eternity. Which he really fucking didn't want to do it.

He looked at Kate, nodded, and stepped toward her.

He had to do this. To provide her with a child the world would think was his brother's. Assuming he could, it would bring joy to his brother and the kingdom around the world. An heir to the throne when they came of age.

"Okay."

She swallowed. Nodded.

"So, we do this now?" he asked.

"Yes."

He looked around at his room, wondering if he should have prepared for this moment. How did one prepare for something this fucked up? What was he going to do? Lay rose petals and light candles? Fucking hell, this was a nightmare.

"I'm really not sure how to do this?" He glanced at the queen. "And before you crack a joke, you know what I mean."

She slumped on the bed.

"I mean"—he sat beside her—"do you want me

to...shit, I don't know...kiss you?"

Kate looked up at him and a tear fell down her face.

"Oh man, please don't. You're making me feel like an asshole. This is hard for me as well."

"Sorry, I know. God, I know," she said, wiping the tear away. "Okay, let's just be really clinical about this."

He nodded. "Yes. Right. Good idea."

What did that even mean?

He dug through his mental manual of the birds and the bees. Facts: she needed to be wet; he needed to be hard.

"So, we take care of ourselves?" he asked.

She glanced at him.

"I mean...I can help. If you want," he added, not sure that was true.

"Sure, yeah, maybe. Can you please turn the lights down more?"

It made no sense because they were vampires, but even the low light didn't feel comfortable for such an occasion.

Brayden removed his shirt and pants and deadbolted the door. He turned as Kate untied her dress and placed it on the chair next to the bed. Without looking at him, she lay on the bed and removed her bra.

Fuck.

He climbed on the bed, sitting up against the headboard. She glanced at his boxers then up at him.

"Give me a moment." She nodded in response and slipped her fingers into her panties.

Jesus, were they really doing to do this?

Brayden watched the movement under the silk. He gripped his cock and began stroking it until it got hard. He was a sexual being; it wasn't difficult for him to get an erection, though it certainly didn't mean he was happy about it.

His chest tightened as he tried to block out any rational thoughts and his conscience. He knew the argument for and against what they were about to do—what they *were* doing—and the decision had been made.

This would all be over soon. Except it wouldn't, would it? The memory would last forever. A child would remind them every day.

He heard Kate's heart rate increase, and slid down the bed to lie flush with her. Laying a hand on her stomach, he slowly moved his fingers up toward her breasts.

Their eyes met.

Suddenly he froze.

Those eyes. The wrong eyes.

Hell, he'd had sex with hundreds of females in his long life.

Blue eyes, green eyes, brown eyes, red eyes. He'd seen them all. Lust, passion, desire for power, desire to control, desire to be controlled, and desire to lose control.

Millions of eyes.

The problem wasn't that they were Kate's, although yes, that was all kinds of fucked up. No, it was that the eyes staring back at him weren't Willow's.

Fuck.

What if she was his mate? If she was, he'd be betraying her as well, and somehow, despite his love for his brother and his allegiance to the crown, this was worse.

He scrunched his eyes and flung his arm over his face, groaning. "I'm sorry, Kate."

She'd already climbed off the bed, and by the time he opened his eyes, she was dressed.

"Hey." He needed to say more, to explain.

"Stop. I'm surprised we got this far, to be honest."

She looked down at the floor before glancing back. "Thank you for trying, Brayden. Let's never speak of this again. To anyone."

"You have my word."

The door closed behind her. Brayden let out the biggest sigh of his life.

"Fucking hell."

Could he have followed through if it weren't for Willow? He'd never know. Right now, Brayden had one big reality to face.

He stepped into the shower to wash away the near sin, and afterward, he would have a few hours' sleep. Then he needed to figure out the rest. Fast.

CHAPTER TWENTY-TWO

"So, you think the green?"

Willow tipped her head from side to side as if it would change the look of the color samples in front of her. "Honestly, I like them both." Brianna threw a few more color cards on the table, and she inwardly groaned. "Okay, now my brain is going to explode."

"See. This is impossible."

Her friend slumped back in her chair. Willow smirked. For three months, Brianna had been deciding on paint colors for the outside of her house. This wasn't their first review of the damn color swatches she wanted to burn. Not the first, not the third, and not the fifth.

There had been progress today, though: Brianna had decided on a version of white. Seriously, how many kinds of whites could there be?

The answer was millions, apparently.

Looking for something to say other than *please poke my eyes out*, she landed on: "What does the painter say?"

"I fired him."

She choked on her glass of lemon water. "He hasn't even started painting yet."

Brianna nodded slowly. "That's right," she said, as if the reason was obvious.

Willow shook her head. "You fired him because he hasn't started?"

"No, because he was disagreeing with everything I said before we even got started," she replied as if she was being completely reasonable. "So clearly, it was never going to work."

Willow stood up and refilled her water.

"You know what, I do like the green. No, wait, the blue. Except it's so..."

Willow tuned out.

Bri had been planning the paint job with her deceased husband, and had an unhealthy attachment to the task. She had to let her work through it on her own.

One glance out the window and she saw it was getting late. It was the first night since meeting Brayden that she was unlikely to see him, and she felt odd. Like she had a hole in her chest. In another week, he'd be gone, and life would be back to normal.

"Are you staying for dinner?" Willow asked.

Brianna shook her head. "No, I'm meeting the twins, so I should get going. Hey, why don't you join us? They're off on holiday next week."

The twins were two hunky gay guys they'd befriended a few years ago. They were a bundle of laughs, and after Brianna's hubby had died, they'd all formed a kind of family unit.

Right now, Simon and Mark were both single, so it would just be the four of them. Willow hadn't seen them in nearly a month, so after a quick glance at her phone to see there were no messages from Brayden, she decided to join them.

"Sure. I'm in. Text me the restaurant details."

Brianna tilted her head. "Everything okay?"

"Oh yeah, I was just trying to recall if I had any deadlines tomorrow. All good."

It was a stupid thing to say, given it was Saturday, but she occasionally worked on the weekend, being a freelancer, so fortunately, her bestie bought the little white lie. A quick hug, and Bri was gone, taking her evil paint samples with her.

Willow looked at the phone again and sighed. She really shouldn't be getting this attached, but she was. In truth, she felt she was falling for Brayden.

A night apart to clear her head was a smart idea. She quickly showered, threw on a white sundress with a blue blazer and matching heels, and stepped out the front door.

And right into a tall, muscular warm body who caught her in his deliciously strong arms.

"Going somewhere, gorgeous?"

CHAPTER TWENTY-THREE

Brayden grinned as he caught Willow in his arms. He hadn't smiled all day, yet less than a second in her company, and his face muscles were getting a workout.

"Oh!"

He loved how flustered she was. Suddenly his face fell. "You're dressed up. Are you going out?"

If she said she was going out with another male, he'd be ending a life tonight. No question about it. He felt his fangs aching.

God, things were really escalating.

"I thought you were still unwell, so I accepted an invite to dinner."

They stepped back in the house, and he pulled the bag off her shoulder. Her eyes followed the bag, then looked back up into his eyes.

He lowered his lips to hers and let them gently and seductively open hers. When he slipped inside, all hope at going slow disappeared.

She was like a drug. Passion fired within him like the fourth of July fireworks. He grasped her head, her body, pulling her up against him, her pebbled nipples pressing through their clothes. The little moan which escaped hit the spot, and his cock went from excited to completely invested in the outcome in a split second.

This female undid him.

"Hi," she said when they finally had to stop for oxygen.

"Bedroom," he instructed huskily.

"I can't." His eyes darkened at her refusal. She touched his bicep and squeezed. "I have to go, or I'll be late. Why don't you come with me?"

"That's what I was trying to do," he growled into her hair.

"Stop it." She giggled.

"You don't want me to stop, Willow. How long do we have?" He stared heatedly at her so she knew he had no intention of stopping.

She glanced at the clock on the wall. "Twenty minutes, but traffic..."

He flipped her around and pushed her up against the wall. "Stop thinking, I'll get us there on time. Now, panties off."

While she followed his instructions, he undid his fly and removed his shirt; it would only get in the way. His cock sprung free.

"Brayden, be gentle."

He ran a hand up her thigh, lifting her dress. "I will, baby."

He kissed her neck, forcing his needle-sharp fangs to stay put. She groaned and arched back into him. He had to be so careful from this point on. If he bit her, it would trigger her change, and he was not fucking doing that.

Cock firm in one hand, he pushed Willow's legs apart with his foot. A few fingers told him she was already wet enough, so he lifted her and pushed inside.

"Oh God, yes," he cried. He needed this so badly. To feel her around his cock, to know it was her and no one else.

Willow clutched the wall while he rode her gently but with greed. He needed to go deeper. Slipping out, Brayden led them to the sofa. "Here, baby." She stepped into his outstretched arms, straddled his body, and sat down on his cock. Wet, slippery, and tight. "Fuck, yes."

Sucking a nipple, then the other, he rubbed her clit and watched Willow's face change as the ecstasy built up. Gripping her hips, he sped them up, pressing her into him to increase the friction and pleasure as she glided up and down his hard cock.

He knew she was ready. His cock swelled.

"Yes, fuck, Willow," he said as she let go and he simultaneously filled her with his need.

She collapsed against his chest, and he kissed her head, running his hands through her hair. He didn't say it out loud, but in his head, he said *I missed you.*

"You okay?" He probably could have been much gentler with her, but his need to possess her made it difficult. He was a vampire, so was already holding back his natural strength, and now he had to keep his fangs out of her skin. It would only get worse the more time they spent together.

"Worth it," she mumbled against his chest. He tipped her chin up to look at him, and delighted in how spent she looked.

"Your eyes!" she exclaimed, touching his face.

Oh crap.

Of course she'd notice his eyes. They spent a lot of their time gazing at each other like a fucking Hallmark card.

"Oh. Contacts. Different ones," he lied.

She nodded and lay back on his chest. Patting her bare bottom, Brayden reminded her they had to get moving.

Moments later they stepped outside, and Brayden pulled her into his arms. "Forgive me. You won't remember this in a moment."

He ported them to the Venice Beach restaurant and silenced her squeal with a kiss. Capturing her gaze, he rearranged her memory.

Forget that happened. We caught an Uber here and made it in good time.

No way was he wiping her memory of their sexual encounter. He wasn't crazy.

Willow looked around, then grabbed his hand. "This way!"

They headed toward the restaurant, and Brayden prepared himself for an evening socializing with humans, something he'd not done, aside from with Willow, for a long, long time.

"Hey!" a voice shouted out and a hand waved in the air. A woman with long curly red hair, who was sitting next to two men, called them over.

He pulled Willow to a halt.

"Willow," he said darkly. "Is this a double date? Are you being set up?"

She looked over at the table, back at him, and burst out laughing. His eyes narrowed at her. A bonded male was dangerous. Brayden dug deep for patience, knowing his human had no way of understanding what was going on with him.

"Hell no. That's Mark and Simon. They're about as interested in my vagina as a blind man in sunrises."

Or a vampire.

He instantly relaxed.

"Not a fan myself," he muttered and nudged her toward the table.

"Sunsets?"

"Much more my taste." He grinned, taking her hand.

"You're so romantic."

If staying alive was romantic, then yes, he was Mr. fucking Darcy. A round of hellos, introductions, and handshakes ensued as they joined the group.

"Please excuse my rudeness, Brayden, but helloooo,

Willow, you never told me you were seeing someone."

He watched Willow blush, and realized they hadn't discussed this. Likely she'd planned to have a chat during the drive over, but he'd taken the opportunity from her. The way she was glancing around the group, it was clear she was uncomfortable. He decided to take the lead, hoping he was doing the right thing.

"It's my fault. Willow didn't get my text saying I was coming over, so she felt obliged to invite me tonight."

Talk about a nonanswer.

"I doubt it. Our Willow never feels obliged," Simon quipped, sipping on his fruity cocktail.

Our Willow?

No. She was his.

"Brayden's only in town another few days," she said, offering her friends an apologetic glance and another nonanswer.

They were quite the pair.

Everyone politely nodded and smiled, jumping to their own conclusions.

Brayden would have moved on, however, the dominant bonded male in him was still stuck on Simon's comment.

He knew modern human women considered dominance as controlling and a potential danger, but he needed the world to know she was his. Because ripping the male's head off was not good dining etiquette, he slipped an arm along the back of Willow's chair and ran his thumb across the arch of her neck.

Brayden had ignored it for days, but now it was obvious. If a fellow vampire saw them together, they would know he was bonded.

Well, fuck.

"So, what's good here?" he asked, smiling at the group.

When he was asked the usual questions during the meal, he gave them his elevator pitch—the one that had changed and evolved over the years to fit into the human world.

Property investment was boring when you forgot to mention you were a vampire and owned castles on three continents, mansions in over one hundred and twenty global locations, commercial property, and an island.

"I hear you're painting your house, Brianna."

The swift change of topic had nervous eye darting around the table. Yeah, he knew he'd stirred up the hornet nest a little, but he wanted the attention off him.

"I am. Actually, I have some of the paint swatches with me if yo—"

"No."

"Nooooo."

"God, no, please."

Willow's friend took another bite of her fish tacos and shrugged. Brayden didn't miss the way she squinted before masking her pain. Or that Willow had noticed.

"Just paint the damn house, Bri. You can always change it if you don't like it," Mark said. "I've redone mine three times in the past five years."

"You're a decorator and change your style more than your underwear," Simon said, tossing his drink and waving for the waiter.

"It's true, you do." Willow laughed. "Anyway, change of topic please."

Brayden watched Willow reach under the table to pat her friend's hand. He wanted to help the girl, and when he got the chance, he would. She was clearly a good friend of his mate, and for that alone, he'd help her.

"Anyway, what gives with the Hawaiian shirts?" Willow asked.

"We're starting early. Oh, you don't know. We're

going to Hawaii on Monday."

"So lucky. I love Hawaii," she said dreamily. "Have you been, Bray?"

He shook his head.

Tropical islands weren't an easy place for vampires to visit, which was why they'd purchased and set up their own island.

"You love the beach, though, right?" she asked.

Brayden made a mental note that the ocean was important to her. Just like his mother. Guiliana Moretti had often spoken of her love of the sun and sand. His blood chilled. If she was his mate, Willow would hate him for taking that away from her.

"Yes. My favorite time is at night, just after sunset."

"I agree. Speaking of, how about we head down to the pier and get ice creams for dessert?" Mark proposed.

Willow grinned. "Yes!"

The cold around his heart melted as he watched her face lit up at the simple idea of ice cream at the beach.

Then she glanced at him, and the watery sparkle in her eyes sent a hint of unspoken emotions. Did she feel more than just a physical attraction for him? As his mate, she should. Like him, her feelings would be developing rapidly and be confusing.

The others walked ahead of them discussing flavors as he wrapped his arm around her. She tipped her head into his shoulder.

"Thank you for coming tonight."

"Where you are, I am."

"For another few days," she said as they reached the ice cream parlor. It was full of people looking to quench their sweet tooth and stay cool in the warm Californian night air.

"I plan to kidnap you and bring you home with me." He wasn't entirely joking. Brayden's smile widened as he watched her eyes sparkle with laughter.

"Do you now?"

He whispered against her lips. "Yes."

The others took their ice creams and sat down, and Brayden stepped up to the counter to order. As he was about to speak, out the corner of his eye, he saw metal.

"Hands in the air!" a voice yelled. In stepped a mask-wearing man holding a pistol. He pointed it at the young man who had been serving. "Nobody move and there won't be any trouble."

He waved the gun around, and Brayden wanted to snap the moron's neck. He pushed Willow behind him, her heart beat thundering in his ear. Sure, he could hear all the humans around him going into a state of shock—blood pumping, gasps, little cries. Yet it was Willow's heart rate that was front and center.

"Oh God," she exclaimed as she clenched the back of his shirt.

His eyes remained on the gunman, studying him.

"I said don't move, asshole," the guy yelled at him. Brayden nodded. If there was one thing a vampire did well, it was stillness.

The perp's eyes were covered in gauze, so the option of manipulating his mind was off the table. Damn.

"No problem. How about you let my girl go?" he asked calmly.

Brayden did a quick scan of the room. Only one guy. One gun. Two exits. Security cameras. They wouldn't be monitored.

A shitload of people.

He knew his vampire speed would allow him to reach the guy before he shot him, not that Brayden cared if he did. He'd heal. What he couldn't guarantee was a stray bullet wouldn't hit Willow. She was directly behind him, and would likely take the hit.

He wouldn't take the risk. She was too important.

Brayden realized at that moment how his life had irrevocably changed. No longer was the king his priority. His mate was.

"She stays put. You all stay put. Move again, I shoot."

Yeah, no, you won't, you little fucker.

If Willow was hit, he could save her life with his blood, but that would turn her. So no. He wasn't taking the risk. He'd made the promise to always give his mate the choice of becoming a vampire or not, and he was following through with it. No fucked-up junkie was going to change that.

"Just take the money and go," the shaking server said.

The gunman waved the gun between the young guy and Brayden. He suspected this was his first robbery, or he could be on drugs. It didn't matter either way—he simply wanted Willow safe.

The guy became fixated with him, his vampire size and presence likely intimidating the gunman. For once, his size wasn't serving him.

Willow gripped his waistband and he slowly wound his hand behind him, rubbing her back. "S'okay, baby."

"I said shut it." More wavy, wavy of the gun.

He'd had enough. Another sweep of his eyes, and he had his strategy. He caught the eye of the ice cream server and locked on.

Put the money into the bag. Slowly. Do it now.

All he needed was a distraction of a few seconds.

Craig, need you to port to me right now. Guy with a gun. Secure the shop and prepare for some memory rearrange.

Roger that.

A second later, Craig appeared beside him. Head-to-

toe black sweats, no shoes. He'd been working out.

"What the...!"

Ignoring the humans, Brayden gave his commander half a second to assess the situation before he gave him instructions.

He's mine. Move Willow and get the door so nobody leaves.

The server began filling the bag with money, and as predicted, the gunman's greedy eyes followed the green notes.

In three, two, and GO.

Brayden jumped the counter with vamp speed, whipped the gun out of his hand, and elbowed him in the face. He went down.

"Arrghh," Willow cried as Craig whipped her across the room.

Brayden jumped back over the counter and took her arms while Craig flashed to the door. He hated the look of terror on her face. Grabbing her chin, he spoke, "I promise to explain all this one day, but for now, sleep, baby."

She collapsed in his arms and he laid her gently on the ground. Craig had heard every word, despite the cries and screams going on around them. He'd have questions, but Brayden wasn't going to answer them tonight. Right now, they needed to finish cleaning up.

"My God, how did you...?"

And cue the typical human questions.

"Are you special ops?"

"If special means I want to drain your blood, then yes, ma'am." Craig smirked as the woman gasped. Brayden rolled his eyes.

"Stop fucking around."

Craig grinned wider. "Hey, just having some fun while cleaning up your mess, my prince."

He ignored the smartass comment. He wasn't the prince right now, though technically that wasn't possible. Craig was right; tonight, he was a friend helping him out of a mess.

"Just get on with it, Brad Pitt."

The guy snorted at their private joke and began to whip around the shop. In a few short minutes, they had wiped everyone's memories, and all fifteen of the humans were currently in a temporary trance.

Brayden grabbed the young server and raised him to his feet.

Forget any of this happened. When you wake, wipe the security tapes and carry on with your job.

Over his shoulder, Craig short-circuited the cameras. They'd done this a thousand times, and likely would a million more.

"You want me to clean this up?" Craig kicked the gunman. Brayden stared at the collapsed human. The sad reality was that the guy was probably desperate and hungry, trying to feed his family.

He knelt and shoved a hundred in his pocket. "Drop him a mile away."

"Gotcha." Craig looked around. "That it?"

Brayden nodded, then lifted Willow off the floor. "I need you to keep what you saw—"

"Don't fucking say it, Jesus, Brayden."

His jaw tightened. "I'm the prince, Craig. You know the repercussions for her." He watched his commander and friend lower his eyes and take in the human lying in his arms. His eyes followed. "I'm still getting my head around it."

Craig ran his hand over his short hair and let out a long breath. "Shit, man."

He pressed his lips together and nodded.

"All right, I'm out of here. See you back at the pad."

Craig ported out, taking the gunman with him.

Brayden looked around at the sleeping humans. He eyed Brianna slumped in her seat, and with Willow still in his arms, he walked over and crouched down until he was level with her empty stare.

It's time to heal your broken heart, Brianna. You still love your husband and honor his memory, but now you move forward and live your life. Paint the house, open your heart, and live.

Human life was so short. Over his lifetime, he'd seen so many people live and die in what felt like a blink of an eye. Even with his immortality, he recognized life was a gift. So many of them wasted their precious time dwelling on anger and pain. It did nothing more than extend their suffering. It made no sense to him.

Forgive and move on. Or kill the offender. But yeah, humans usually couldn't do that.

He placed Willow on her feet, arm around her, then said, "Awaken."

Around him, the room came to life. The server immediately swung into action and disappeared out the back to delete the footage. People resumed their all-important discussions about ice cream flavors, chatting away as if nothing had happened.

As he and Craig had dictated.

"What are you having?" Willow asked beside him. "I'm going crazy and getting double chocolate chip."

"I'll have the same." He kissed her nose, enjoying the view of her perky bottom as she stepped up to the counter to place their orders.

Brayden turned to check on Brianna. She gave him a little smile. Beside her, the twins were sucking on their fingers. Ice creams were melting at a fast rate all around them, and there were some confused faces. Yeah, he had thought about it, but it hadn't been a priority. Still, he smiled at the amount of high-speed licking going on.

He winked at Brianna and her smile widened.

"She looks happy," she said, nodding at Willow.

He followed her eyes and found his human laughing, conversing with a handful of people. They were joking about upsizing their ice creams or some such thing. His heart swelled.

"She is. And I promise she always will."

Something had passed between them when he'd healed her mind. Trust. A type of bond.

"That's all I need to hear."

CHAPTER TWENTY-FOUR

"Go to sleep, Willow."

"I can't." She flipped over for the hundredth time. "Maybe it was all the sugar."

"Maybe I need to wear you out some more."

"Ah no, I am quite worn, thanks."

Brayden had pulled her into the shower when they'd arrived home and taken his sweet time washing, kissing, and running his hands over her entire body. Only then had he slipped his fingers deep inside her core.

"Beautiful," he'd whispered against her lips and she had melted.

It had felt more intimate than with anyone she had been with before. He'd lifted her leg and slid his extremely hard cock into her, one hand on the tiles above her, the other on her hips as his silver eyes burned into her. He took her breath away.

Then he had begun to pump, pulling her against his pelvis to deepen his reach. It had been as if he owned her body, mind, and soul.

"Braaaayden," she had gasped, unable to look away from him.

"Come for me, baby." His voice dark and masculine. And oh God, she did. Her orgasm had been long and had rolled out in waves of pleasure.

Curling her toes, she could still feel the echoes of it throughout her body. She nudged her bottom into

Brayden and slid her fingers in between his where they rested on her stomach.

"Bray."

"Yeah, baby."

She could feel the words on her lips, and tried to hold them in, but they were like a prisoner facing an open door.

"I'm going to miss you. Like, really miss you." She frowned at the emotion leaking into her voice. He half sat up and leaned over her, arms on either side of her head.

"Hey."

"I'm sorry. I realize this wasn't the deal, but I wanted to tell you. No biggie."

She couldn't see his face clearly, but she felt the possessive way his body covered hers, the feel of his thumb as it rubbed the side of her face, his cock hardening. She sensed he felt similarly, if not quite as deeply. Now she'd broken the silence, and it had suddenly become awkward.

Trust her to wreck everything. She squeezed her eyes shut.

"Willow..."

She stopped him. "Can you just tell me how you feel about me? Then I'll stop talking. Promise."

"Where?"

"What?"

"Where do you feel it?"

She frowned. "I, well...I'm not sure." She didn't know where he was going with his questioning, but if it got him sharing his feelings, she figured she'd run with it. "My heart. No, my body. No. Here, in my gut. Yes, like instinct, but it's more than just a thought. It's tangible."

He kissed her lips gently.

"I feel everything you do, Willow. I feel a lot of things I never expected to."

Oh. She smiled. "Thank you for telling me."

She was grateful he had given her that gift. Soon he would leave to return to Maine, to continue running his family business weighted down by all his responsibilities. Her life was here.

It wasn't impossible. They could try long distance for a while, but it wouldn't be her that brought it up. It had to be him.

"How did you feel when you thought you wouldn't see me?" he asked.

She remembered the ache in her chest, feeling hollow, and how it had surprised her. "Sad."

He ran a finger down the arch of her neck. "How else?"

"I'm not sure what you mean," she said.

He palmed her breast then suddenly got up and walked across the room, leaving her feeling abandoned and her body needy of his touch.

She sat up abruptly. "What are you doing?"

"That," he said, pointing at her.

"What?" She looked down at her naked body, frowning.

Brayden stood on the other side of the moonlit room. The desire to climb out of bed and feel his touch was intense.

"That feeling. The one you're feeling right now." Willow closed her eyes. "Is that how it felt?"

She chewed her lip. "Yes."

He climbed back into bed, pulling her into his arms. The instant he did, she felt warm from the inside out. She sighed and snuggled into him. Great, he was her own personal drug.

"This can't be good."

"What if I told you I want...no, *need* you to want me more than anything else in your life?"

She knew he had a possessive streak, but the question still surprised her.

"I'd say it sounds like you want to take our relationship to another level."

He kissed her lips.

"Yes."

"Then we need to clarify what that is. I can't get hurt by assuming something you don't mean to back up."

He ran a hand over her cheek. "We will. Tomorrow. Your body is very tense after...a late night. You need to relax and sleep."

She snorted. It hadn't been that late at night. She hadn't figured him for a lightweight. "Fine. Tomorrow."

Pushing Brayden never worked, but she would make sure they had that conversation. He was right, though. Her shoulders were tight, and her ankle felt sore and achy.

"Maybe I'm getting sick."

"You're not sick, baby." Brayden's hand ran down the side of her body, over the arch of her hips, and nudged her legs slightly apart. Gently, he massaged her inner thighs, fingers grazing over her pussy.

"Not sure that's going to help." She raised an eyebrow at him.

Ignoring her, Brayden slid under the sheets and positioned himself between her thighs, his tongue taking over. She groaned, her head tipping back.

"Relax, baby, let me pleasure you into sleep."

Huh. No way she'd be falling asleep now, but who was she to argue with the talented man. His tongue lapped away, hands holding her thighs wide as he hit all the right spots.

All of a sudden, she felt something foreign. Cooler.

The vibrating began next. He had her vibrator. She tensed.

"Relax." He pressed it against her core as heat and anticipation flashed through her body. She'd never had a man use a vibrator on her before. His hand lay across her pelvic bone. "Open for me, Willow."

She relaxed her muscles as he pressed the buzzing device in. She cried out. "That's it, oh yes, good girl."

He expertly moved it in and out of her, trying different angles, stimulating her pussy, pushing her to the edge.

"I love fucking you like this." Brayden spun around and lay alongside her, continuing his penetration. Then he gripped his cock and guided it into her mouth. "Suck me off while I fuck you with the dildo."

She closed her lips around him, tasting his pre-cum. Groaning, she felt full at both ends as her mind faded and her body relinquished control to the large masculine man who seemed to be dominating her life.

"I need to be inside you." He groaned after a while, removing his cock and flipping around. Then he was inside her, the mood shifting from erotic to intimate. Tucking a hand under her head, breathing together as their rhythms aligned, he kissed her.

A moment later he threw his head back and cried out her name. She grasped his strong, muscular arms and let her body join in the ecstasy.

Collapsing to the side while pulling her on top of him, Brayden whispered, "Sleep, *mi amore*."

Willow nodded gently, aware he was still inside her, as she replayed those words over and over.

He'd just called her *his love.*

Not that she could speak Italian.

CHAPTER TWENTY-FIVE

Two nights later, Craig leaned his elbow on the bar and threw his beer back. The bottle clunked as he placed it back down, deciding if he should have another one.

In front of him, three women swayed their hips and tossed their hair to the deep bass music. He watched them with modest interest. In contrast, they were very aware of him. It was the usual reaction vampires of his rank got thanks to the energy they put out; sexual with a high degree of danger. Females loved it. And human females? Forget it. It was like moths to a flame.

He smirked and waved his hand at the bartender.

"You want another?" Craig asked the vampire next to him.

"One more," Lance said, emptying his beer.

Both were dressed in black jeans and boots. He had a vintage AC/DC T-shirt on which stretched across his chest, while Lancelot—who hated his nickname—wore a plain black shirt rolled up to his elbows. They weren't exactly gunning for the fashion pages this weekend, but neither of them gave a shit.

They clinked the Steinlager bottles at the neck and chugged down another long, refreshing mouthful.

Craig noticed the redhead glance his way for the second time, and he stifled a moan. She was hot in that corporate girl way, though it could go either way in the bedroom. Some turned into tigers, others were so fucking boring he found television more interesting.

And he fucking hated television.

"You going there?"

"Not sure," he answered honestly. She was sexy enough in her button-down shirt, extra button undone, and her tight black skirt riding up as she danced. Her long red locks waved around her back as her more-than-a-handful boobs bobbed.

The song finished. Panting, the girls headed to the bar.

Lance took a step away to make room for them, giving them a *no problem* when they thanked him. A few fluttering eyelashes, and they began to order their drinks. Lance glanced at him and grinned.

As the blonde with the short, bouncy hair turned, Lance stepped into her space and whispered something. She arched her neck to make eye contact with the guy, and her eyes glazed. Nothing made a woman all hot in the pants more than a tall, muscular man stepping into her personal space and towering over her.

That easy. Craig smirked as Lance looked over and winked at him.

The redhead swayed to the music and took a sip of her drink. She didn't look at him.

Oh, for fuck's sake. He drank his beer.

"Are you going to talk to me?!" she suddenly demanded.

Now we're talking—the girl had fire.

He grinned into his beer, then dropped his voice and said, "Well, I could, but it would only end up with me on top of you, so you decide."

The little gasp in her throat and the long swallow that followed were simply perfect.

"You think so?"

He slowly stood up straight, punched one hand into his jean pocket, and raised his beer to his lips. "Baby girl, I know so."

She shook her head and he could almost see the hairs on her body begin to vibrate in irritation. Defiantly, she took another sip of her drink. Rum. He could scent the black liquor blending with her musky perfume. It was a tantalizing, rich mix.

"Forget it."

"Nuh-uh. Come on, why don't you females ever admit what you want and then take it?"

He was in no mood for the I'm-not-that-kind-of-girl speech. If she were wise, she would walk away. As her mouth dropped open then abruptly shut, Craig couldn't take his eyes off her red wet lips.

What the hell?

She pulled all her hair over one shoulder with a huff, so it now flowed down over one breast, exposing her neck.

Bad, bad move, sweetheart.

His cock suddenly wanted in.

"Have you never heard of innocent flirting? Jeez. Men!"

He stepped into her space. "Don't bullshit a bullshitter. You want me."

She did. Her pulse was rapid, blood had rushed to her face, and he could scent the smell of her desire. Underneath, there was also a tiny hint of fear, which only added to his growing and unexpected arousal.

The female was smart to be afraid of him. He was a dangerous male. Size, height, and tribal tats aside, he was a predator, the worst and best kind, depending on who you were. He had a darkness in him that he kept contained.

Most of the time.

She glanced around at her friends, who were busy giggling and touching Lance every chance they got.

Shit, the guy might end up with them both tonight. Usually Craig played the game, but with everything going on back at the pad, he was feeling testy.

And cue the soft cock. Just thinking of what he'd discovered over the past few days since the prince had tasked him with spying on Regan took away the buzz.

He needed to speak to Brayden as soon as possible, but interrupting the guy when he was with his female was about as wise as shoving your head inside a fucking blender. So he'd wait.

For now.

He felt his patience snap.

"Come with me." He placed his hand in the small of the female's back and, ignoring her gasp, led her through the dance floor.

"Where are we going?" she asked, walking double time to keep up with his strides.

He didn't answer. There was no need. She knew. He knew.

In the back of the club, he pressed his bulky shoulder into the door of the disabled toilet.

"Are you kidding me right now?" she cried as he pulled the door shut. "I told you I was only innocently flirting, for God's sake. What is wrong with you?"

He leaned in, a hand on her hip, and tugged her into his hard cock.

"Last chance, gorgeous. You can either walk away or turn around while I fuck you."

Her breasts moved as she panted, furious; however, she stayed put. Her eyes darted around the white tiled room.

"You don't even know my name."

"Tell me," he said, impressed by her courage. He was an intimidating creature, and here she was, demanding respect.

"Brianna."

The corner of his mouth turned up as she wobbled on her feet and gasped as her palm landed on his rock-hard abs.

"Well, Brianna, are you going to turn around?"

She shook her head, and he raised an eyebrow.

"I want to know your name." Her demanding eyes bore into him. "And I want to face this way."

He let out a laugh. "Oh, human, so many demands. Do you really think you're in control here?"

She pushed against his chest, which did absolutely nothing.

"Yes, I do. I can say no at any point and you *will* respect that. Tell me your name."

He didn't know if she was completely mad or ridiculously brave, but goddamn it, his cock hardened further. He held her hips harder to stop himself from swirling her around and ripping up her skirt. She was right; he wouldn't take from her without her permission.

"You haven't said no."

"You haven't asked."

Shit. She had a point.

Craig stared down at the brightest green eyes he'd ever seen challenging the very core of him. One minute, they were breathing hard, both needy and fighting their desire. The next, he found his lips on hers. Harsh, angry, and totally owning hers. She moaned. He eased up, and she opened up to him, allowing him to slip his tongue inside. She tasted like rum and a whole bunch of goodness. Everything he wasn't.

Without realizing, he had pulled her legs up over his hips, and she was gripping his shoulders. He ran his hand down her back and over her tight, soft ass, the heat of her sinking into his skin.

Her bright red locks brushed his cheek as she

moaned. He opened his eyes and saw three tiny freckles to the side of her eye. What the fuck?

He abruptly let her go, sliding her down his body. Panting, they stared at each other. Brianna's eyes were dilated as fuck, glossy with desire and waiting for him to make the next move.

He looked around the bathroom and back at those freckles. Fucking freckles. What did they matter?

"Fuck." This was fucking wrong. He looked down into eyes that pleaded with him for more at the same time they challenged him. "Let's go."

He began to pull her out of the room, but she tugged on his hand. There was no way she'd be able to move him an inch, but the very fact she had tried brought him to a halt.

"Why did you stop?" The hurt on her face had him narrowing his eyes. "What did I do wrong?"

"Not a thing." He brushed her hair over her ears. "Keep away from assholes like me, you hear."

She stared at him confused, eyes full of moisture. He leaned down and kissed her gently, wondering when he had ever kissed a female in such a way.

"Let's go. I'm taking you back to your friends." Her muted nod and sad eyes nudged a spot inside him he didn't know existed. As they broke through the dance floor, he saw Lance with the two other women and...

Holy fuck, what was Brayden doing here?

"Bri!"

And Brayden's human.

"Hey. How do...?" Willow looked between the two of them, then back at the prince. "What's going on here?"

One glance at Brayden's face, and he knew this wasn't good.

CHAPTER TWENTY-SIX

What the fuck was Craig doing with Brianna?

Watching his mate—who didn't know was his mate—take in the state of Brianna raised his hackles. The girl was shaken and emotional.

Instantly, Brayden was pissed off.

Tell me you did not just fuck this female.

Craig defiantly looked his way and glared at him. *Who is she?*

Willow's best friend. Now answer the fucking question.

"Shit."

"Shit, what?" Willow continued with her questioning. "How do you know Craig?"

Brayden had spent every spare minute he had with Willow over the past two days. They'd been walking around the pier when he'd asked after Brianna. It had been his idea to pop in for a drink to check on her. The last thing either of them had expected to see, for entirely different reasons, was Craig.

Brianna turned to look at the guy, then back at Willow. "We met tonight. *Craig* was just escorting me to the ladies."

You didn't even tell her your fucking name?

It's not what it looks like. Okay, it is, but then...look, I didn't fuck her.

Craig awkwardly ran his hand through his hair, which was awkward in and of itself, given he was usually a cocky bastard. Brayden looked over at Lance, who was also frowning at the odd behavior.

"Oh, that's nice of you," Willow said naively.

"Yeah, I'm a knight in shining fucking armor," Craig spat out before gazing quickly at Brianna in concern. She turned away, but glanced back when Craig wasn't looking.

Brayden was getting whiplash. Something was going on here.

Dude, she lost her husband a year ago. Stay away from her.

Noted.

"Let's get some drinks," Willow said, looping her arm through Bri's and dragging her up to the bar.

We need to talk, Brayden. Now.

He looked over at Lance.

"Hey, Lancelot, look after the ladies for us, will you. We're just stepping outside for a minute."

A slap on the shoulder, and they walked outside into the fresh air. Brayden took a long, deep breath as they walked until they found a spot away from people. They could talk with telepathy, but two guys standing around not talking with a face full of emotion always looked weird.

"What's up? No, wait, first tell me what the fuck is going on with Brianna."

"Nothing, and there won't be."

Brayden waited.

"Yes, I took her out back to fuck her. In my defense, she'd been eye-fucking me for two hours. I didn't know she was Willow's friend. I kissed her, that's it."

"What stopped you?"

Craig had strong morals, but females didn't say no to him. He had the height, looks, sculptured body, and bad boy charm females turned to mush over. He'd been watching him in action for centuries.

"She turned me down."

Liar.

"Anyway, we have more pressing issues to discuss. My investigation."

Now he had his attention.

"You've found something?"

Craig nodded. "I believe so. At least, I think so. Is the king on any medication?"

Brayden recoiled at the question. Vampires didn't take medication. "No. What kind of medicine?"

The guy sighed and crossed his enormous arms. "Then we have a big fucking problem."

Craig told him how he'd been ghosting—a skill few vampires possessed which allowed them to be present and not seen by others—Regan one day while he was in the kitchens and had followed him along the hallway to the king's chambers, a route Regan took every day on his way to their meeting.

When Craig had been about to leave due to the confidentiality of the discussions which took place in the space, he had noticed Regan slow his pace. The old vampire had then sprinkled a powder into the king's evening cup of tea, stirred, and put the pouch into his pocket before continuing into the room.

"Shit, man. I honestly thought it was medicine the human doctor had recommended."

Over the past few days, the king's condition had worsened, and they were all becoming increasingly worried.

Brayden slapped him on the shoulder. "I know it doesn't feel like it right now, but I'd say you've just saved the king's life."

Craig shook his head. "It doesn't make sense. Nothing like that should affect him, or any of us. We're vampires, for fuck's sake."

He nodded, feeling as dumbfounded as his second in charge.

"Hell, I don't know, maybe Regan is trying some concoction to help, and we're wrong about him."

Craig shrugged. "Perhaps. Perhaps not."

"Shit, man, that old vampire has been loyal to the Moretti royal family for over one thousand years."

Craig nodded slowly. "Exactly, so why would he?"

Brayden looked up. "Have Selena and Lily returned to Maine? They went to Italy on holid—fuck me."

"Fuck."

Of course none of them had noticed. Like all of them, he'd assumed—actually, he hadn't thought about it for one damn minute, why would he?—that the two females had returned from their holiday and settled back into the castle. He vaguely recalled the queen asking about them months ago and Regan saying little. The thing was, Regan's mate and daughter visited Italy from time to time. It had been no big deal.

Unless they hadn't returned.

Brayden tensed and looked at Craig.

"It can wait a few hours. Kurt has eyes on him."

"Let's go inside. I don't like being away from my mate for too long," Brayden said. "Disappearing without explanation is not an option."

Craig grinned as they began walking.

"Fuck off. I refuse to wipe her memory every damn day."

"Yeah, it minces their brains. Speaking of, those colored contacts are bullshit, Bray. You think the king hasn't noticed? You need to tell him."

"Nope." No, he didn't. Right now, he needed to deal with the new knowledge the king was being poisoned.

"And keep your mitts off Brianna," Brayden added.

He heard the growl. "Yeah."

Just when Brayden thought one problem had been resolved, they walked into the bar and saw the way Craig and Brianna looked at each other. He let out his own groan. Christ.

Then Willow walked up, and all his problems vanished. He lifted his arm and she parked herself under it, wrapping hers around his waist.

"Hey, gorgeous." Their lips met, and hot lava flowed through his body. The little minx had refused to let him fuck her when he'd arrived at her house. She had said he had to wait until they got home.

"I got you another beer." She handed him the bottle and he took a long swig. He ran a hand over her bottom and nuzzled into her neck.

"I need you." Between his need to be inside his mate and the strong sense to protect the king, the predator in him was right at the surface.

My lord!

Fuck. His fangs were making an appearance.

Shit. Thanks, Lancelot.

Brayden, be wary.

I'm fine, Craig. Just...on edge.

A low growl whispered through his mind.

"We've been here less than an hour." Willow giggled. "Your gorgeous cock was inside me less than a day ago."

"Not helping, Willow." He groaned, adjusting his jeans.

Five long dances, three beers, and a whole lot of blah and blah later, finally the group was heading home. The desire to get his mate home safe and to feel her warmth around his dick was strong. Then he could deal with the rest.

"Where's your car?" Craig growled at Brianna.

Willow looked up at him in question, like he had all the answers. He gave her a small reassuring smile, which completely missed its mark. She was right to be worried. As his mate, she was immune to Craig's charm, so all she sensed was power and danger.

There was a reason why he was the commander of the vampire Royal Army, and it wasn't because he was next in line to be on *The Bachelor*.

"I caught a cab, so I'll hail one down on the corner," Brianna replied, half ignoring the guy. She reached out to Willow for a hug. "Night, Brayden!"

He gave her a brief smile and waved, his eyes taking in the interesting scene unfolding before him.

"Call you tomorrow, honey," Willow said as Brianna walked off.

His commander followed.

"Craig!" Brayden said with authority, inwardly cursing at himself for not using telepathy.

Lance looked between them. Willow tensed in his arms at the power rolling off him. Craig slowed and turned while continuing to walk in reverse. "Yup?"

Casual. No big deal.

Smart.

Brayden ordering him so publicly put them in a tricky situation. Craig had to obey him. They all did. He was their captain, yes, but he was also the prince twenty-four fucking seven. As captain, there were boundaries where his authority stopped. As prince? None. That was the thing about royalty.

Brayden had learned to walk the tight line of power and authority with his senior team, especially with Craig. So this was a tricky position for them both, since Brayden had given an order, and Craig had disobeyed.

Craig wasn't just a subordinate; he was a powerful and important member—and asset—of the Moretti team.

Someone Brayden trusted with his life. Rarely did his commander ignore an order. If he did, it was with good reason and done without undermining him in front of anyone else. They both respected each other immensely. And sure, the guy could take whatever female he wanted to bed.

Except Willow's best friend.

He watched Craig. Something had gone on between them, but he didn't sense she was in danger. In fact, it appeared the vampire was trying to protect her.

He had to drop it.

"Make sure she gets home safe." His face was one of authority. Willow relaxed in his arms and Lance looked away, comfortable with the direction of the discussion.

"I will." Craig nodded, a flash of gratitude in his eyes. Brianna glared at the guy and walked away. Brayden felt a pang of pity for him.

See you back at the house in two hours, he said to both vamps.

Roger.

Gotcha.

Lance wrapped his arm around both the other women, winked at Willow, and left. Brayden smirked, then tried to hide it when Willow looked up at him. "What?"

She narrowed her eyes. "You want to wait another twenty-four hours?"

No, he fucking did not.

He swooped her up into his arms and fought his laughter as she squealed.

CHAPTER TWENTY-SEVEN

Brayden and Craig stood outside the king's chambers, waiting.

And more damn waiting.

Vincent, hurry the fuck up! This is urgent!

The door flung open a moment later. "What the fuck is so urgent? I'm going through papers with Seraphina."

In the background, he could see the king's secretary shuffling said papers and one of Regan's legs. He had considered confronting the vampire himself, except he knew his brother. The king would want to deal with this directly.

Given he *was* the one being poisoned, it seemed only fair. Allegedly.

"We need to speak with you now. Alone."

What is it?

We believe we have discovered the cause of your illness.

"Leave us," the king said without looking away from Brayden.

The two vampires departed the room in haste, gathering up papers in handfuls and slipping past them with nervous glances. Brayden held the king's stare, not looking away.

Vincent turned, and they all walked into the room where they stood in an awkward circle of three. "Speak."

"We believe..." Craig started, then stopped.

We believe Regan has been poisoning you, your majesty.

I can't be poisoned.

We believe it might be possible, and that you are slowly being poisoned.

Why?

The only reason would be to weaken you to take the throne.

The king looked at Brayden, anger lining his face.

I watched him pour a substance—an unknown substance—into your tea earlier this evening. Then out loud, Craig asked, "Are you taking any medication, your majesty?"

Vincent gave a small shake of his head.

"Could the queen have ordered this?" Brayden asked, a degree of hope in his voice. Nobody wanted to believe they had a traitor in their castle, certainly not someone as close as Regan.

He watched the king's eyes as they momentarily looked distracted, and realized he was speaking to his mate. "No," Vincent finally answered, and walked around his desk to sit. He directed them to do the same. They didn't. The door flew open, and Kate marched in.

"What's going on?" she demanded. An awkward moment passed between Kate and Brayden as they locked eyes. They glanced away.

"Craig witnessed Regan slipping something into my tea," Vincent responded, looking as perplexed as Brayden had just a few hours earlier. Kate followed suit.

"Slipping what? A knife? You can't be poisoned."

"Look, I realize this is all theory, but unless Regan has a damn homeopathy business on the side, it's still fucking suspicious, don't you think?" Brayden said.

The king narrowed his eyes at the tone he used with the queen.

Whatever.

"Even if poison were possible, what would be his motive? He's been loyal to this family for centuries."

Vincent coughed, one of his phlegmy, disgusting coughs which usually resulted in one of them offering him a blood transfusion. Out came the tissues, reminding them all why they were here.

"Which is why we wanted to discuss the next steps with you, your majesty. We could search his chambers or confront him," Craig continued, getting straight to the heart of the matter.

The room went quiet.

"Kate, has Selena returned from Italy?" Brayden asked.

The queen glanced at the king. As both their eyes darkened, the room became thick with anger.

He nodded. "So I'm right. That fucking Russo piece of shit."

"Why didn't Regan come to me?!" the king roared.

A week ago, Brayden wouldn't have understood, but he did today. If someone had Willow, he'd do anything.

"They have his mate, Vince," Kate said quietly. She was friendly with Selena. "And probably Lily. My God."

"My own fucking advisor!" the king muttered between gritted teeth. "Fuck this, *cough*, get him in here!"

Brayden nodded to Craig, who marched out to do the dirty work.

He understood his brother's fury. For months, he'd been poisoned by someone he trusted.

"Kate, you need to leave."

Her head whipped around. "No, I will not!"

"Yes. I don't want you exposed to this or to be in any harm."

Brayden nearly smiled. The advisor was a slight

vampire. Even with Vincent's poor health, there was no way Regan could hurt Kate, especially with Brayden and Craig in the room. However, now with a mated mindset, he understood the irrational, protective behavior.

"Don't be ridiculous. I am not going anywhere. He's been poisoning you, for God's sake!"

The door burst open and Craig dragged a pale and terrified-looking Regan into the room. He flopped onto the floor and began crying.

"Stand!" the king ordered. Regan tried and failed.

Vincent glanced at Craig, who shrugged. "I didn't say a word to him. He knows why he's here. Guilty as charged."

More sobbing.

"I said stand!"

Brayden stepped forward and assisted the man to his feet.

"My lord"—he held out a shaking hand—"let me explain."

Vincent held out his own palm. "Quiet. You will speak when I tell you to," he boomed, and Brayden grinned at his brother. It was good to see him be all kingly and shit again. "Have you been poisoning me?"

Regan gave a little nod. A whimper followed, and he nearly collapsed.

"WHY?!"

"Theytookmymateanddaughterandaregoingtokillthem andididn'tknowwhattodo," he mumbled out at high speed. "I know it was wrong and I should have told someone, but they said they'd kill them. Oh God, they're going to kill them now."

Brayden let the guy fall to the floor and bawl.

"So they do have Selena and Lily?" Kate asked, crouching down, though staying a distance away.

The male nodded, clutching at his shirt. "Yes, have

they told you? How do you know all of this?"

"Where are they keeping them?" Craig asked.

"I don't know. They went missing during their visit to Italy six months ago. I've had a few photos sent to me by Luca Russo, but they may be old. They may be dead."

Brayden felt for the guy. If someone had Willow, he would...well, yeah, he would do anything, and fortunately, he had the power of his position and body to do it. Regan didn't. It didn't excuse his actions, but he kind of understood it.

"What have you been putting in the tea?" the king asked.

Kate walked over and helped the male to his feet, leading him to the long sofa off to the side. He turned to her, surprised by her kindness. He was met with an angry but compassionate face. The queen was no fool, but she was kind.

"Belladonna," he said. "It's a nightshade plant poisonous to humans."

"Also called the murderer's berries or beautiful death," Craig added, nodding. Of course he knew. The guy was a deadly warrior in every way.

"Yes." Regan nodded.

"I never tasted anything."

"No, it's a sweet flavor, and they instructed me to give you only small amounts."

Which brought them to the next important question. Brayden sat on the edge of Vincent's desk and crossed his arms.

"So the Russos are behind this? They have been supplying you with the herb and instructing you. Is that right?"

Regan nodded.

"Stefano Russo," Brayden said in disgust.

"They're going to make a play for the throne," Craig

guessed. "When?" He took a step toward Regan and knelt. "Look, I know you're scared, but you need to tell me everything you know. I will try to get your wife and daughter back, but you have to tell us everything."

Brayden's head was going one hundred miles an hour. "Who else knows?" he demanded. "Outside the Russos and now the people in this room."

They needed to keep this as contained as possible. Craig nodded, knowing where his mind was going.

"No one, my lord, just me. I couldn't risk my family."

It was highly unlikely they were still alive, knowing the Russos were a murderous bunch, but there was a small chance.

Craig stood. "There may be others who are spying. On all of us. I think it's best we continue on as planned so as not to raise suspicion."

Brayden stood up from the desk and nodded. "The ball. That's their game plan, isn't it, Advisor?"

"They haven't told me their plans, but the timing to increase the dosage this week does indicate that." He nodded sorrowfully. "I'm so sorry, my lord, your majesties."

Vincent had been quiet. Brayden turned to look at his brother. Their eyes met and they both shared a moment of sadness. This man had supported their father and the two princes upon his death.

"I cannot begin to understand the position you've been in, Regan. To choose between your king and your mate must be a sentence worse than death." The king coughed and wiped his mouth. "Whether I would have actually died from this shit or just weakened until one of the Russos took my head, I do not know, but nevertheless, this is still treason against the crown."

The room remained silent.

"I will not keep you wondering. Your time as advisor has come to an end. As for your life, it all depends on how you assist us henceforth."

The male looked pale as shit, and simply nodded. "I will do all I can. My loyalty has always been to the throne. To your father and now to you, your majesty. My mate and daughter, though...I—you have to understand."

The king nodded. "I do. Which is why I will spare your life. For now. The prince shall arrange for you to have a personal guard. For your protection and so we can watch and know your every move."

"Come, Regan, you need to tell me every fucking thing you know," Craig said and looked up at the king. Vincent lifted his chin, indicating Craig should take him.

"Wait," Kate said. "How do we get the poison out of his system?"

"I assume it's only a matter of time, as I had to give it to him frequently."

"Is it actually deadly to vampires?" she asked.

"I do not know for sure."

After they left the queen walked over to the king and threw her arms around him. It was an intimate moment, one that strangely involved him. Vincent opened his eyes and caught his glance.

Thank fuck Kate and he—God, he couldn't even think about it.

Just thank fuck.

"Brother."

"Your majesty." He grinned.

"Yes. Looks like I will remain your king."

Brayden laughed.

Thank fucking goodness.

"Don't get too cocky, Vincent," he said, his laugh fading. "You need to be in good health and prepared to face a coup. The royal ball is highly likely to be their target. Craig and I will review the information we've gathered and advise soon. Go rest. And can I recommend you start drinking whisky instead of fucking tea."

The king smirked as Kate laid her head on his chest.

He turned to leave.

"Brayden," the king said gently. The prince stopped in his tracks, a chill going up his spine. "You need to bring her home. When we leave. It's time."

His heart thudded in his chest and he hung his head.

Of course the king knew he had mated. With their Moretti blood bond, he knew. He had known all along.

I've been a fool.

He didn't respond as he walked out and shut the door.

Fuck.

CHAPTER TWENTY-EIGHT

The late afternoon cloud cover had allowed Brayden to venture out earlier than usual, so here he was, standing on Willow's doorstep knockity, knock, knock, knocking to no avail.

He wandered around the property to see if she was in the yard. Still no luck. The windows were all closed, and there was a stillness about the property. He listened. Willow was not inside, or if she was, she had no heartbeat. The moment the thought crossed his mind, he teleported inside, ghosting at high speed through the rooms. No Willow.

A sense of dread began to irrationally grip his chest as his overactive mated mind kicked in.

Am I being irrational?

The Russos had poisoned the king. If they wanted the throne, the next step would be removing Brayden, and what better way to do it than finding out who was important to him? He'd been watched; it wouldn't take them a huge amount of intelligence to figure out Willow was one of those people.

His chest rumbled as anger boiled within him. He pulled his phone out and pressed her name.

"Hello!" she cried, voice shaky and agitated.

"Where are you?"

Silence.

"Willow?"

"I'm out for a run, but I think, um, there's a guy

following me. Wait. I'm not sure."

His whole body froze.

"Where are you?" he demanded.

She told him her location, and he ported there immediately. He scanned the park and found her staring at her phone in confusion, calling his name. Brayden ran over and pulled her into his arms.

"Brayden! How the hell did you get here so quickly?"

Now she was safe in his arms, he scanned the park further for any threat. A figure flashed in the distance and disappeared.

"Shh," he said, rubbing her back. "First let me make sure you're okay."

"Thank God you're here. It was probably nothing, but I freaked myself out. How the hell did you get—"

He gripped her shoulders, interrupting her. "Willow, tell me what you saw."

After a slight hesitation, she pointed in the direction she'd been walking. "Down there. The path goes through some bushes, past a river. I run there most days, but I felt someone following me. I saw a man in a hoodie. No, wait. Ugh, I'm not sure."

Brayden gritted his teeth as he realized another vampire had likely manipulated her memories. The idea that if he'd been a moment longer something could have happened sent a cold shiver through his heart.

"Can you remember anything?"

Her eyes glazed over as she shrugged, then struggled to focus. Yeah, some fucker had gotten near her.

"Hey." More rubbing of her back. "You're safe now. Where's your car? I'll drive."

He wrapped an arm around her waist, and with one last scan of the environment, led her to the car. Inside, he turned to her. "Okay?"

She smiled and gave a little nod, but her eyes were

restless, darting around. Then they met his.

"How did you get here so quickly?" Her beautiful eyes were wide in confusion.

She zipped up her Adidas sweatshirt and put her seat belt on before she glanced back at him, awaiting his answer. He wasn't going to give her one. Not here in the parking lot.

However, it was now time she got all her answers.

"Let's get home and then we'll talk," he said, taking her hand. "Tell me how your day was."

As she sighed then launched into her day, he imagined telling her about his.

Mine was great. I discovered the vampire that's been our king's right-hand vamp for centuries has been poisoning my brother. But hey, some asshat kidnapped his mate and daughter, so he was in a pickle. If that had been you, I would have killed them, no question.

Anyway, it's my job to find them and bring them home safe, though they're probably dead. The vampires who took them will die at my hands if my instincts are right.

However, I doubt you'll be happy to know that I have killed. And will kill again. Or the fact that I have mated with you and will need to kill you to turn you into a vampire so I can spend eternity with you. No biggie. I'm sure my cock is worth it.

He groaned.

"I signed a new client and sent off some quotes. Pretty uneventful," she said as the groan escaped him. "Sounds like you had a bad one. What happened?"

"Nothing major." He shrugged. "Just some Human Resource issues."

"Oh God. Super stressful. That's why I freelance."

He glanced over and nodded, a small smile on his lips at her delightful and total ignorance of his dangerous life.

Once back in the house, Willow poured a glass of wine for herself, and handed him a beer. He'd gotten used to their nightly routine, and settled onto his stool at the kitchen counter. They chatted away until he pulled her onto his lap, nuzzling into her neck. "You smell delicious."

"I'm all sweaty."

"Like I said, delicious."

"Brayden." Hooded eyes glistening with joy blinked at him.

"Willow." His voice was dark as he cupped one of her breasts just in case gravity doubled.

"I missed you today."

"I miss you every damn day." He kissed her softly.

"You're leaving in two days." She sighed and gazed at him vulnerably.

He lifted her chin, scanning her beautiful face, burning the raw emotions into his memory. It could be the last time she looked at him this way, and he wasn't missing a damn thing. In a moment he was going to tell Willow who he was, and he'd have to watch the love and affection turn to utter fear.

No, I can't do it.

But he had no choice.

"You feel it too?"

"What?"

What were they talking about? Oh. Shit. He really needed to stay focused.

Her face fell.

"Yes. I do. Willow, please look at me. You have become particularly important to me."

Tears formed in her eyes.

"Shit, baby." He caught one escaping from her eye and gently wiped it away.

Who knew a female could soften the edges of such a hard male? While she brought out the possessive alpha in him and he would kill to protect her, he also turned to mush when he saw her in pain.

As those eyes full of emotion held his, they stirred up feelings of hope deep within his soul. Damn, he hoped like hell it wouldn't be the last time he was blessed to be held in such esteem by this beautiful female.

Lost in the energy flowing between them, the words just fell out. "I love you."

She sucked in a breath, and though he wasn't sure, he thought he'd done the same. "Willow, I love you."

Frozen in his lap, she imitated a goldfish, mouth gaping and closing.

"I'm *in* love with you. So, fucking much."

Oh my God, stop talking.

Her lips landed on his, and the next minute he was carrying her into the bedroom, their clothes flying off them.

No romance. No foreplay.

Willow pressed herself against him. He pushed her onto the bed, lay over her while he pulled her legs around his waist, then pushed in. Wet and ready. Tight and gripping.

"ShitmyGodIloveyoutoo." She gasped and arched her back.

Ignoring the inner dialogue that flashed ahead thirty minutes to her inevitable reaction to his identity, Brayden raised her bottom and pumped faster.

About twenty-five seconds later, he collapsed on her, panting.

A squeak under him got him moving his big body off her. Flopping onto his back, he pulled her to him.

Willow laid her head on his shoulder, drawing lines over his pecs as she always did, until the silence grew heavy and he knew it was time to talk.

He swallowed heavily.

Rolling to face her, he placed a hand on her cheek. His chest swelled as he took in her post-sex glow. Yeah, he thought, she's been royally fucked. Literally.

"You really love me?" he asked, needing to know her feelings were strong enough to carry her through what he was about to tell her.

"I do," she said with shy, downcast eyes. "I didn't want to tell you because it's so soon."

"I knew." He smiled.

"Stop."

He couldn't stop smiling. His mate was just adorable. Sexy, sweet, smart, and just a little bit sensitive. So this was what it felt like to be in love. Totally worth the wait, but terrifying as fuck.

He wanted to tuck her into his chest and keep her safe from...well, fucking everything. However, there was only one thing that was going to terrify her right now.

Him.

"Come on, smelly, let's get you into the shower," he joked, wanting to delay the inevitable for a few more minutes.

"Hey, you said I smelled delicious!"

She did, but he knew she'd be more comfortable dressed when he told her.

As it turned out, he waited until they'd eaten dinner. And watched a show. Then he ran out of excuses.

He glanced at the clock.

Is it too late now?

What time was the right time to announce to the female he loved that he was the world's most dangerous predator? Literally.

Craig.

Boss man.

Just call me prince if you want to be all official and shit.

Nah.

He smirked inwardly.

I think I might be here a while. Everything okay over there?

Yeah, Regan's talking up a storm. I've briefed the SLCs, and one of the LCs is now his personal guard.

Okay. Select three of our best LCs and advise them they're off to Italy tomorrow. Top secret level. Book them on commercial; they go undercover and bring home his family.

Roger that. There was a moment of silence before he continued. *Kurt is going to watch things for a few hours. I'm heading out.*

Brayden fell silent. It had to be important for Craig to leave his station at a time like this. Then again, here he was, sitting in his female's living room watching *Supernatural* or some shit. He watched the screen and tilted his head. The car and music were awesome, he'd give them that. But this was different; he was the prince and Willow was his mate. This was important for the royal family and the vampire race.

He frowned to himself. He knew where Craig was going. And it was very fucking interesting that he was choosing to go amidst the chaos.

I'll be back in a few hours.

Go. Just...fuck me, Craig.

I'm not going to hurt her, Brayden, hell.

He sighed. He needed to let the two of them do what they wanted. Craig wasn't a male who would take a female without permission. Brayden trusted the guy with his life; surely he could trust him with Willow's best friend.

He liked Brianna, and for that reason, he didn't want

to see her heart broken. Especially after he'd just freed her from that bondage.

Do me one favor. Flash through her memories. I did a thing. You'll find them behind my energy signature. Then decide how you want to proceed.

Yeah, okay.

He looked down to find two beautiful eyes staring back at him. Leaning down, he kissed her lips.

"Are you going to tell me how you got to the park so quickly tonight?" she asked once again. "Were you following me?"

He let out a deep sigh and stretched.

"No, baby. But you're going to wish I was."

As she frowned at him, he sat her up and turned them so they were facing each other on the sofa. He felt a chill run over his body and shivered.

Willow tensed and her forehead furrowed. "Brayden, what's going on? You promised me you weren't married. Tell me you are not fucking married? Was that man dangerous? Are you part of some gang? What is it?"

He reached and rubbed her arms. "No, calm down, please. My heart belongs to you, Willow. One million percent. There's no other female—woman, fuck. Just no. I'm not in the mafia or a gang."

I'm a vampire. Say it.

She nodded, taking a deep breath. "Then what's going on here?"

V A M P I R E. Say it, for God's sake.

"I really fucking love you."

"Okay, now you're freaking me out. What is going on?"

"I want you to know that under no circumstances would I hurt you. Ever. Nor will I let anyone else hurt you. Not a hair. Ever. Not now, not ever."

Brayden watched her face begin to pale.

"You'll be under my protection forever. All our protection. This isn't a movie or a book, Willow. We're a family, a community, just as humans are."

Eyes full of confusion and disappointment at her world falling apart in front of her filled his chest with a pain he never knew was possible. He had failed her. She had seen him as the perfect man and fallen in love with that dream.

He wasn't a man. He was a vampire.

"I'm a prince," he said, nodding though he had no idea why he was doing it. "My brother, Vincent—he's the king."

The pain in her eyes shifted as she blinked. They narrowed a little as she peered at him. A slow swallow and a little nod.

"I see." The pity in her voice nearly made him smile, but he didn't.

"His mate—wife...well, mate. Kate. She's our queen."

More of that nodding, the kind you did when you met a mental patient and felt it best to just agree with them. Her body shifted away from him a few inches, likely an unconscious move.

"The family business," she finally said, humoring him.

He nodded.

"You are a prince of a royal family." It wasn't a question, but he nodded again.

He took her hand, and she looked down at the spot their bodies joined. She was dead still but for the moisture beading on her palm.

"Prince of...?"

Her heart began beating faster. Some primal part of her was beginning to understand.

They stared at each other. She swallowed. He

counted the seconds before he said the words that would change her life and his forever.

God, I love her.

His heart was physically aching.

"The vampire race."

Willow's eyes widened and her eyebrows shot to the top of her brow. Then they narrowed, and she slightly turned her head while her eyes remained affixed to his.

All righty then. He hadn't factored in the possibility of her not believing him.

"I see." She nodded over and over. "So you're a vampire. A vampire prince?"

He nodded.

"I see," she repeated.

More nodding.

"Willow..."

She stood and took a few steps away, then turned. "Is this what you do during the day? Hang out with your vampire people?"

He nearly—*nearly*—let out a little laugh. Willow thought he was playing vampire dress-up with a group of people. He cringed. He could only imagine what she was thinking right now. He wanted to chuckle in that laugh-during-a-funeral kind of way, but Brayden saw it for what it was. Willow was looking for some rational explanation to make sense of this all. While she enjoyed watching paranormal entertainment, having it show up in her reality was a whole different thing altogether. It would be unkind to let her stay in denial for long.

"We're not people. We're not human, Willow. We're vampires."

"Hmm, yes. Right. Of course." She gazed around the room, chewing her lip. He could feel her pain and confusion.

"Willow, listen. I know this sounds crazy," he

started, walking over to her and wincing at the disgust on her face. "Let me prove it to you."

"How? Do you have fangs?"

He nodded.

"Jesus, Brayden, I heard you could get them done at the dentist. Christ, is this why you were at that clinic?"

He frowned, confused. Then it clicked. "Oh, that clinic? No, we were there for Vincent's...argh, never mind. No, we are born with them. All vampires are."

Willow shook her head and screwed her nose. "Jesus fucking Christ. I can't believe this. I thought I'd finally met the perfect man. I'll be honest; I've been waiting for the other shoe to drop, but this"—she waved her hand at him—"I never saw this coming!"

Brayden hated that she was looking at him like a crazy lunatic, but soon, the real fear would set in.

And that would be far, far worse.

He had two days. Two fucking days to help her adjust to this new reality before taking her back home with him. If she chose to go. It wasn't a lot of time and dragging it out wasn't helping either of them.

"Let me show you." He began to open his mouth, and her eyes flew open. "Damn it, Willow, I'm terrified of scaring you. Fuck!" It went against every cell of his being.

"You're my mate, for God's sake, this is—"

Willow's eyebrows shot through the ceiling as he realized what he'd just said. Nothing like putting all your cards on the table.

"A what, now?" she yelled, her heart rate pounding in his ears. "Oh my God, are you going to put me in a pod or something?"

"A what? Why would I put you in a pod?"

"You need to leave." Willow began pushing him toward the front door while grabbing his jacket off the arm of the sofa. He grabbed her wrist in one hand, her arm in another, then gently stopped her. Fear lined her face as she felt his strength, and the truth began to sink in.

"Please."

"Willow, sweetheart, I'm not going to hurt you. Ever."

"Please just go."

Tears formed in her eyes as she pleaded. Brayden shook his head and led her to the sofa. He sat opposite her on the coffee table, his legs surrounding her shaking body.

"I'm not crazy, Willow. Please look at me right now, and I'll tell you everything."

She lifted her head.

"You love me. I love you. Remember that. Remember all the time we've spent together. How we've made love. Remember how protective I've been of you."

She nodded while her shaking increased, shock beginning to take hold.

"I'm going to show you my fangs. The ones I was born with. Do you want to hold my hand?"

Willow shook her head, then nodded.

Brayden held her hand gently in his as he slowly peeled his lip back and extended his large, sharp incisors. As he did, the veins in his eyes began to fill with blood, an automatic response that meant nothing but looked menacing.

"Oh God!" she gasped and pulled away. He understood it was fear, but it irrationally burned a scar on his heart. "How?"

"We're a different race. We've always lived among you and other animals on planet earth."

Willow simply stared, so he continued.

"When humans first appeared, we existed in relative

peace, as we did with all other creatures. We were predators, they were hunters. At one point, there was even a collaboration type of coexistence. As they continued to evolve and their brains developed, the ego appeared, and the desire for dominance ruled. Humans saw everything as a threat that needed destroying."

He noted her breathing beginning to calm as he spoke in even tones.

"It will be your eventual downfall, but that is neither here nor there today."

She blinked at that, and he imagined her asking more later.

"Eventually, humans were able to grow more dominant due to their fast reproduction rates, and we chose to hide in remote areas. As civilization's matured, we adapted to blend into the human way of life. It was difficult in those days, as we're nocturnal beings. Not just nocturnal—the sunlight kills us."

"I never see you during the day," she said slowly, her eyes drifting left to reflect on her memories.

"No."

Willow chewed her lip and he continued.

"So, with the slow growth in our population and the wisdom of longevity, we have lived among you, gaining wealth and staying an unknown entity." He took her hand. "We are no threat to the human race, despite our speed and power, and before you ask, no, we do not run around draining the blood of humans."

Well, some vampires thought they could and tried, but the royal family had decreed it against their laws, and those who were caught were punished. They survived on wild animal blood just as well. Plasma was the most nutritious source, no matter the animal it came from. Rich with proteins, the royal family had a regular supply of the yellow juice from local medical facilities.

Willow began to shake as the adrenaline overtook her body. Okay, fuck, he could have worded that better.

"Shit. Breathe. Please remember I love you and you are safe."

Her wide eyes held his. "Am I?"

"Yes, God, yes." He scrunched his eyes. "Look, I'm going to return your memories, the ones I've taken from you since we met. You will know absolutely everything. I want there to be no lies between us."

Willow squinted in confusion. "You took my memories?"

Instead of explaining, Brayden held her eyes with his and spoke. *Remember, Willow.*

A few seconds later, her hand flashed to her mouth. It was a lot. The teleporting, the robbery at the ice cream parlor, socializing and having sex with vampires. Once or twice when his fangs had escaped, he'd done a quick wipe.

"OhGodohGodohGodohGodohGod."

He sat still, holding his place, giving her time.

"You-You...how did we get to those places?" Her hand covered her mouth.

"Teleportation. Humans will be able to do it eventually. It's just an evolutionary thing. Manipulating matter. Energy. Nothing magical."

Her eyes flew around the room. "You protected me. The gunman. Craig was there...oh, he's a vampire?"

"You're my mate, Willow. I will always protect you," he answered, ignoring the last question.

More flying eyes.

"Brianna, you—oh my God! Craig! Fuck." She stood up. "We have to warn her. He's a vampire!"

He pulled her back down. "He won't hurt her."

"You don't know that," she yelled, trying to rip her hand out of his.

"Yes, I do. Craig reports to me. Remember I told you I'm the prince, so I'm kind of a big deal."

Narrowed eyes filled with fury stared at him.

"Let me clarify. If he hurts her, I will kill him. So he won't."

She gasped, hand flying to her chest.

God, he was absolutely shit at this. He ran a hand through his hair and sighed.

"So you won't eat or kill me?'

"What? No!" he yelled, exasperated.

Willow jumped.

Shit, fuck, hell.

"Willow, baby"—he took her hands—"I genuinely love you. All of this is real. You are my girl, my mate."

She shook her head, tears threatening again as the emotions ravaged her nervous system. He could see the exhaustion begin to take place.

"I don't understand any of this. Make it all go away, please."

"I am sorry."

She blinked at him. "How can I be your mate if we are different species?"

Brayden chose his words carefully. He'd told her he would always protect her, never hurt her, and that was true. From anyone but himself.

He would, in fact, be killing her.

He counted his breaths for a few moments before continuing. "It doesn't matter. My feelings are real. No one can fake the mating bond. Willow, I have fought this. I didn't want this for you."

She burst into tears all of a sudden, her face falling into her hands. Brayden pulled her into his arms. Incredibly, she melted into him. He allowed himself a moment to soak up her warm, soft, feminine body.

"I'm so terrified," she sobbed as he rubbed her back.

"My mom was human," he said unexpectedly. She mumbled against his chest, indicating she had heard and wanted to hear more. "She loved my father more than all the stars in the sky. Her words, not mine. I'm not a poet."

He felt a grunt against his chest that felt like a little laugh. Then she added, "I'm still scared."

"I know. If it helps, I've been terrified of telling you."

She raised her bloodshot eyes to him. "Why?"

"Because, my beautiful human, I love you so fucking much my chest hurts every day worrying I'm going to lose you. I've lost count of the hundreds of ways I've imagined that happening. Telling you who I am was right at the top of the list. Being rejected even though I know it's from fear."

About seven different emotions crossed her face over the next thirty seconds. He patiently let his words sink in, desperately hoping they made an impact. They weren't rehearsed. He'd never spoken truer words in his long existence.

He ran his thumb over her cheekbone. "However, I will walk out of here tonight and never return if it is what you want. It will kill me, but I'll do it."

Willow's eyes bulged wider, and he shook his head. "Not literally, baby."

Mostly.

"Oh."

"You've had a huge shock. Lie back on me and we can figure out what to do when you are ready." Brayden reached up and dimmed the lights.

She tensed. He murmured for her to relax and shifted them so she was lying against him. She stayed, and he prayed to a handful of gods in thanks.

They lay staring at each other in a way he never

thought he'd do with another living being. Especially not a human who'd just learned that he was a vampire.

Eventually Willow let out a big sigh. "I am safe with you."

It was both a statement and a question.

"Yes."

"You are not going to drink my blood?"

He shook his head. Not tonight, at least. He'd tell her that part another day.

"Don't touch my memories again."

"Never."

"Promise me."

"I swear."

"Can I meet your family?"

"Yes." He nodded.

"Which I guess will be tomorrow because you're leaving."

And you're coming with me, Willow.

He wouldn't be leaving without her. Not only because she was his mate but because her life was now at risk thanks to him.

He touched her mind, something he had meant to do earlier, and found the memories of her time in the park. A face he didn't recognize, but an accent he did. Italian. One of Russo's men. He'd approached her, asked her how her vampire lover was, and had fortunately been interrupted by his phone call.

Thank fuck he'd rung when he did. The vamp must have wiped her memories then and there, and ran away.

"Yes, I'll take you to meet them after we've had some sleep."

"Because you can't go out in daylight?"

"Correct. We sleep for a few hours during the day."

When she opened her mouth to ask the inevitable, Brayden couldn't resist a grin. "No coffin. I sleep in a regular bed."

Cue the adorable blushing.

"It was dusk when we were at the park."

"The cloud cover was sufficient. It's the direct, hot sun which can kill us."

"So no tropical beach holidays for you."

He shook his head. It was these conversations which reminded him of his mom. Willow didn't know it yet, but it was soon to become her reality.

Brayden had promised his future mate one thousand years ago that if she was human, he'd let her choose her future. She could become a vampire or walk away and remain mortal and live out her human life.

Now, with Willow in his arms, he wondered if he could, in fact, let her walk away.

They sat up on the edge of the sofa and their shoulders bumped.

"What do you want Willow? For me to go or to stay?" He would stay outside the house keeping watch if she asked him to leave.

"Both. I'm scared, even though I know you would never hurt me."

"I've just burst your whole sense of reality to pieces, so it's natural to feel this way."

She looked around her house while nodding. "What will happen when I meet your family?"

He drew in a long breath. "I'll introduce you to my brother, the king, and his mate, the queen. I won't lie; the compound is full of vampires." Her eyes widened at that. "There's nothing to fear. No one will dare look at you, let alone touch you."

"Because you're the prince."

"Yes. Among other things."

Like the fact that he'd rip their fucking heads off.

Willow slumped back on the sofa. "Here's the thing.

If you leave, I'll end up freaking the hell out and running away to Switzerland to hide from you, or something."

He narrowed his eyes. "Don't do that." He cursed himself for not trading blood with her yet so he could track her.

"Then you better stay."

She hadn't yet realized that the mating bond was creating her need to stay with him. As he'd demonstrated to her the other evening, there was a physical pain when they weren't together.

Willow likely thought he was being romantic, but teddy bears and rose petals aside, it was a physiological truth for the mate of a vampire. She might not be a vampire yet, but it still impacted her.

Brayden pulled her into his arms. "I'm not going anywhere. We'll need to leave early."

She mumbled against him.

"Okay, let's get you into bed and see if you can get some sleep."

He carried her into bed, grateful for whatever was allowing her to be with him. It could be shock or it could be the mating bond.

But why look a gift horse in the mouth.

CHAPTER TWENTY-NINE

Craig stood outside Brianna's place and stared.

Then stared a bit more.

He gave pacing a go until he realized he didn't have time to fuck around, so he needed to grow a pair and knock. Or go home.

Brianna opened the door as she wrapped a short white silky gown around her.

"Jesus, woman, you're just asking to be attacked!"

"What are you doing here?" Brianna asked, startled, before she crossed her arms defiantly.

"Clearly protecting you from being molested."

"I was in bed safe and sound before you woke me up with your loud banging," she countered, hands on her hips.

His cock twitched. "God, don't tell me that."

"What are you doing here, Craig?" she repeated.

Good question.

He plunged his hands into his pockets and upped his shoulders, all tough guy, which he was not. Okay, he totally was when not around this redheaded beauty. As soon as he was in her presence, he felt like a young vampire tripping over his tongue before racing home to jerk off.

Last time he'd been here, it had been a disaster. He'd squeezed himself into the taxi, leaving Brayden and the others outside the bar after insisting he'd see Bri home safely.

The ride had been tense, with short glances at each other as their bodies touched and bumped with the movement of the vehicle.

He'd paid the driver and gotten out with her.

Truthfully, he'd had no expectations nor any plans of what was going to happen next. He'd simply not been able to walk away from her.

Brianna had turned and held out her hand to stop him from following her up to her house. There had been little honesty in her body language, in the scent of desire that was rolling off her, so he'd taken a step forward.

Her slow blink had been the beginning of him losing all control. He'd gripped her hand and pulled her up against him, kissing her harshly. The universe had responded by letting off a gazillion fireworks in their honor, and it was all going fucking fabulously until she had suddenly ripped herself out of his arms.

Okay, so he had let her. There was no way she had the strength to budge him even if she had wanted to, but he never forced a woman.

Standing there panting, they had stared at each other for a long moment. No words. Brianna had then turned and run up the stairs. One final glance, and she had closed the door. Stunned, Craig had stared at his big black Nikes for a long moment before he kicked the concrete step and ported back home.

Now he stood at the top of the steps. "I wanted to apologize."

"You came all this way to apologize for a kiss which meant nothing?" Her eyes narrowed in disbelief at him while his chest tightened.

Ouch.

"It's not too far. Anyway, you don't know where I live, so how..." Craig frowned and shook his head. "That's not what I'm apologizing for. In the bathroom, at the bar. That."

"When you were going to fuck me and didn't."

He cringed. "Look, can I come in?"

She tugged her silk robe closer. "So you can reject me again? No, thanks."

What?

He stepped closer, close enough to feel the warmth of her body and for his hands to twitch at the need to touch her. Her breathing sped up and she swallowed deeply. He took another step.

"Stop," she said quietly with absolutely no truth in her voice.

"Are you angry with me?"

Her mouth slightly opened, breathing shallowly, but she did not answer.

"Why?"

"It doesn't matter. You should leave."

He couldn't. Craig knew he should be elsewhere right now, focused on the shitstorm happening with the royal family. Yet here he was, standing outside this female's house trying to understand her. Trying to understand why he hadn't just unzipped and plunged into her a few nights ago in that disgusting bathroom.

"Tell me." He leaned closer, breathing in her fruity scent.

Brianna let out a long, exasperated breath. "Fine. You rejected me. All right? It hurt. Now you can go."

He blanched, pulling back at the thought of her feeling rejected by him. Hell no. He hadn't. "Are you kidding me, woman? My cock has been hard since we met and won't go down."

She rolled her eyes. "Charming."

He spun around and took a few steps away, throwing up his hands. "Fuck, what do you want?"

"Nothing! I want nothing from you. I want you to go

away so I can forget you and everything that happened between us."

Fury poured through his veins. He marched back to her and gripped her arm.

"Bullshit. You want me as much as I want you."

"I most certainly—"

Craig smashed his lips down on hers, surprising them both. Then her body responded, melting against his.

Her mouth opened, giving him full access as her nipples hardened against his chest. A guttural groan escaped him as her nails dug into his arms. He wanted those nails in his back, in his hair, as he took her to paradise.

She tasted like strawberries—sweet and juicy—a contrast to his masculine sweat. He cupped her small bottom and pulled her into his hard erection, hoping to God she could feel how much he wanted her.

A quick look inside her house, and he calculated how long it would take to get into her bedroom and rip the white robe off. He'd have to use human speed, but if he flipped her over and lifted the silk, he figured it would be forty-five seconds at most. He could wait. His cock couldn't.

All of a sudden, she released his mouth and began pushing against his chest. Craig relaxed his hold slightly and stared down at her, frowning. She wouldn't look at him.

"I'm leaving in a couple of days," he said with his arms on her hips. She nodded. "Brianna, look at me."

She chewed her lip then finally looked up.

"I want you, Bri. Invite me in."

She gave a small shake of her head. "I can't. I just can't do this."

"I never rejected you, beautiful. I simply didn't want to fuck you in the shitty bathroom. You deserve better."

She stepped away further. He let her. Reluctantly. She tugged the silk around her and redid the tie.

"And fucking me in my bedroom and then leaving is better, is it?"

What could he say? The answer was fundamentally yes, yet he suspected it wasn't the answer she wanted.

"Better than never having you, yes."

She began to shake her head. "You need to go. I get it. There's some incredibly strong chemistry between us, but I'm not like the girls you normally hook up with. Yes, I know it nearly happened the other night, and I can't explain why." She shook her head. "I'm ashamed of myself. I'm angry with your rejection, but it was probably for the best."

His head spun as he tried to figure out all that human emotion.

"The truth is I feel out of control when you're around, Craig. It's good you're leaving."

God yes, be out of control. Please.

"You really need to go," she finished before he could get the words out, the look in her eye indicating she knew what he was going to say.

Craig ran a hand through his hair. He should leave. This all felt too heavy. He was used to sex being fun, easy, and playful. With her, it felt like fire and lightning. Like fireworks sparkling in the air between them. They both felt it.

"I'd really like to see you out of control under me, Bri."

She swallowed loudly, her nipples turning to pebbles and her pulse increasing its pitter-patter. His cock incredibly got even harder. Bri peered down at it as he stepped closer, touching her hip, and then suddenly she slipped away.

She stepped back and closed the door.

In his fucking face.

CHAPTER THIRTY

Willow awoke feeling like she was trapped underground. Gasping for breath, she suddenly found herself flipped onto her back.

"Willow! You okay?"

Gasp, gasp.

She sat up and pushed him slightly away from her. "Jesus, Brayden, give me some space. You nearly suffocated me holding me so tight."

He lay back down and let out a groan. "God, I'm sorry."

She sucked in a few deep breaths, enjoying the cool, fresh air. She lay her head on his chest and ran her thumb over his skin.

It seemed strange to be comforting him. Surely any sane woman would have caught the first flight to New Zealand or some far flung country after her boyfriend had told her he was a vampire. Strangely, once the initial shock had begun to subside—because God knew it hadn't disappeared—she had begun to look at the situation from Brayden's perspective. Not completely, but she could understand his fear that she would walk away. It was her own fear of never seeing him again that allowed her to understand.

Despite everything, the thought of not lying in his arms, of not being held in those ethereal silver eyes, of never feeling the magic they created sexually felt...wrong. It was the only word she could find that described it.

Not like when you broke up with a boyfriend and felt the sadness of never seeing him again. This was different.

Her mind flashed to the day Brianna had found out about her husband. They had just finished lunch and were loading the dishwasher and wiping down the benches when the knock at the door came. Her friend had glanced at her and then dried her hands.

Something had made Willow follow her. Some deep instinct. As the door opened and the man in uniform came into focus, her stomach had sunk. There were usually very few reasons for a visit like this.

Brianna wobbled then sunk to the ground as the man continued to deliver his message, regret lacing his face. Willow fell to the floor, pulling her friend into her arms. As Brianna howled, Willow rocked her friend, aware she'd never heard a more guttural sound.

A tear slipped from her eye at the memory.

"Hey." Brayden tipped her face to his.

"I'm okay. It's all just a lot." He nodded, leaned forward to kiss her nose, and lay back down.

While it seemed entirely disrespectful to compare her situation to losing a military husband in such a devastating way, Willow only knew that if Brayden walked out the door, she wouldn't be able to breathe. Despite him not being human. Despite the fact he had fangs. Despite the fact she had no fucking clue how they could ever be together.

She only knew she had to stay with him. At least for now. "What time is it?"

"Around four. We'll need to leave within the hour."

After a shower and seven outfit changes, she was ready to go. Turns out that jeans, a white knit sweater, and a pair of sneakers was what one wore to meet your vampire boyfriend's family. Who knew?

It was all so surreal she felt she was just walking in a daze.

"I'll drive," Brayden said, studying her as he took the keys.

They drove along the freeway, and Willow used the time to ask as many questions as she could to feel prepared. None of it felt real.

Outside the vehicle, life continued around her as normal. Traffic lights changed from red to green to amber. Early morning joggers danced on the spot at crossings. Some buildings around them had lights left on, while others were completely dark. Courier vans speed to deliver online shopping.

All normal. While she sat in her car with a vampire. One she had been having sex with for the past several days. One she felt she could barely breathe without.

She glanced over at him as he began answering her next question. His shoulders were big and round, leading to even bigger biceps and thick forearms. He was tall with a broad chest and strong jaw. She'd never questioned the layers of muscle on his abdomen, but she assumed it had to do with him being a different species. He also had thick thighs and solid lower legs. Hell, even his hands were large and powerful.

There was no inch on his body that wasn't muscular, but not in a bodybuilding way. His olive-toned skin was smooth and soft. While he had a strong jaw, he didn't look hard. Brayden was beautiful, a strange word to use for a man, but he was. Every time she looked at him, she found herself transfixed by those silver eyes that seemed to swirl like liquid metal.

Yet despite her feelings, a voice in her head screamed *Run!* constantly. Her feelings and memories were what kept her where she was; however, the fear fought for dominance in her mind.

Brayden had been more sexual, kind, funny, supportive, and protective than any other man she'd ever met. He'd also been caring, loving, and tender—okay, perhaps not always tender, but she liked it that way just fine.

Vampires existed. Brayden was a vampire.

Run!

No. He wouldn't hurt her. She peered down at his hand holding hers as he drove one armed.

Run.

Some of the answers she received made her cringe, and she noticed how uncomfortable it made him. He'd told her about their predominant food source—blood and plasma—and she'd nearly vomited her stomach bile. Still, she needed to know more, and so had pushed him.

"It depends on where the vampires are located. Medical centers or legal hunting provide for most of our needs. Stretching our predatory legs in the wild, as nature intends, is important from time to time." He looked at her, then back at the road. "It's why we own so much land on the planet. That and you humans simply fuck it up. On offense."

"Well, it's true."

"I can assure you we don't play with our food. We simply kill and drain their blood."

She nearly threw up in her mouth.

"It's a few times a year, Willow, not every day or week," he said defensively.

"Right."

It was hard for him also, she tried to remember that.

"Do you desire to drink from humans while near them?"

"Yes, though the older we get, the more able we are to curb our appetite."

She covered her neck irrationally. He'd never hurt her, and yet she had been unable to stop the reaction. "Do you want to drink my blood?"

Both his hands gripped the steering wheel tight and he nodded.

Run!

Run!

Her heart thumped, echoing in her ears, as panic set in. She grabbed the door.

"Hey." He whipped his head around. "I do, but I won't. Do you understand?"

Run!

"I'm an incredibly old vampire, and my desire to protect you, as my mate, is *far* stronger."

What did one even say to that? Oh, cool, thanks, I'm sure it'll be fine.

She hadn't asked about mates. For one thing, if she quoted some vampire movie or book and looked like an idiot, it would be embarrassing. Secondly, if any of them were even remotely close to the truth then she knew there was no getting out of this, and right now, she wanted to take Brayden at his word that she was safe.

First things first, she had to meet a vampire king.

What did one call a group of vampires, she wondered? A nest? Christ, she had to stop thinking. Looking at Brayden to remind herself she wasn't going into some bat-infested cave, she asked, "What do I call your brother?"

"Your majesty, until he invites you to do differently. The same goes for Kate, the queen."

Boy, they really took this royal thing seriously.

"You're doing really well, *mi amore*," Brayden said, squeezing her hand.

The damn broke and she needed to know.

"What does it mean to be your mate? What if we

break up and I know all this stuff about vampires?"

Brayden looked away. "We won't ever break up, Willow." His voice was strained as he continued destroying the steering wheel with his grip. "Let's talk about it later, okay?"

It didn't take a genius to figure out he would take her memories. She could no sooner control it than change it. She sighed as they turned down a long driveway and continued to the end until they reached a security booth beside two huge gates. A man—correction, a vampire stepped out.

"My lord," he said surprised. "I didn't recognize the car." The man bowed as the gates opened.

"People bow to you?"

"Yes. You should too." She began coughing in disbelief. She slapped his arm when she saw his smirk. "Relax, I prefer you on your knees in front of my cock."

"Brayden, stop it." He winked as he turned off the car.

She looked around. It was like a village, not unlike a secure housing complex. The security looked high level, and the buildings all interconnected. There were very few people around. Vampires. Not people. The sun was about to rise, and she suspected that was why it was so quiet.

"Come."

Taking her hand, Brayden led her into one of the largest buildings. They walked down a maze of corridors before coming to a door. They walked through and into a large entrance that immediately had a luxurious vibe. A large chandelier hung in the middle of the ceiling, while thick rugs lined the floors. They took two flights of stairs and then turned down another hallway. Large framed paintings hung on the walls, but she was unable to take in any detail.

It felt royal, it really did, which was amusing, given she was in California.

The space was moody rather than dark, with little lights along the baseboard. At the end they came to a set of large double doors. Placing his thumb on a panel, the doors clicked open.

Hand on her lower back, Brayden led her inside. She recognized the room immediately from their calls. "This is your home."

He nodded and dropped his phone and her car keys on a side table near the entrance. "Yes."

She wandered around the large space, acknowledging the beautiful interior design. A living area, bedroom, bathroom, and kitchen were all visible. Leaning her head into the bedroom, she noticed the king-size bed with a duvet and pillows. Not a coffin in sight. A large dresser with a large mirror above it busted yet another myth.

She turned back to the living area. One wall was covered with six screens.

"On top of being the prince, I am captain of the Royal Army," he said.

"Oh. An army?" she asked and he shrugged.

"We're no different in that regard."

She walked over to a pair of heavy drapes and nudged them aside, discovering a large private courtyard with elegant outdoor furniture and a water feature. There were fairy lights draped around the garden, giving it a soft, romantic feel.

"That's nice," she said. He nodded, stuffing his hands in his pockets, and shrugged as if embarrassed. "So, no coffins."

"Nope."

"Looks pretty normal."

"Except for the coating on the glass which protects us from the sunlight, yeah, we live just like humans. Diet aside."

"Except you're not. Human."

"No."

There was a strong need to keep reminding herself of that fact. She didn't want to fall into the trap of thinking things were normal when they weren't. She might have fallen in love with Brayden, but it didn't mean she was okay with any of this.

She wasn't.

She was trying to understand and trying not to freak out. Could she fall out of love with him and walk away? Because what was the alternative? Live with a vampire?

Panic set in again. What the hell was she doing here? How could she stop loving him and live without him?

She felt his breath on her neck. "Hey." Strong hands rubbed up and down her arms. As her breathing returned to normal, Brayden leaned down and kissed her jawline. "I've wanted you in my bedroom since the day we met."

"Hey, I have a vampire king to meet, remember?"

Ignoring her, he tugged her into the room and she found herself lying underneath the large, sexy male. She couldn't deny how damn hot he was. Locks of his dark curls fell onto his forehead and along his neck as those piercing eyes burned into hers. She reached up and ran a finger over the tattoo curled along the edge of his shirt.

"He's busy for another hour, so we have some time."

Willow swallowed. "I know I probably look okay with all of this, Brayden, but I'm really not."

He stared at her for a moment before pulling them both up. Understanding and patience lined his face as he mindlessly rubbed his thumb over her thigh. "What can I do?"

"Be human." As the words fell out of her mouth, she suddenly wished she could take them back. Hurt flashed across his eyes. "God, Brayden..."

He nodded. "No, I get it." He went to stand but she grabbed his arm. "I understand Willow, I really do." He rubbed his hand over his face and through his hair. "Look, my mom was human, and she resented falling in love with my father. I always hoped my mate would be a vampire. I'm so damn sorry."

Dread ran through her body. "Wait. Sorry for what?"

Brayden stood up and paced. "Fuck. Let's just take it one step at a time. After you meet Vincent, I'll tell you everything."

She stood up too. "No. This is my life, Brayden. I want answers."

He stared desperately at her.

"Don't you dare touch my memories," she demanded. "You promised."

If he took away the memories of this conversation right now, she'd be pissed. Eventually. Just as soon as she remembered.

He nodded and pressed his lips together.

She watched his anguish and took a guess. "You wish I was a vampire?"

"No. Yes. No, Willow, I love you exactly the way you are."

She bit the side of her mouth as tears pooled in her eyes. She hadn't meant to react, but as he spoke and she imagined him rejecting her for a female vampire, the emotions had flooded her.

Immediately he reacted and came to her, pulling her into his arms. God, he was so perfect—vampire stuff aside. With those big arms wrapped around her, she felt safe and protected. More than that, she felt loved. Closing her eyes, she soaked up his warmth and strength. "What's going to happen?"

She felt him shake his head. "Nothing you don't want. I promise you. On my life."

Willow let out a long, deep breath. She hadn't realized how much energy she was using. He wasn't going to hurt her. Brayden tightened his arms around her and kissed her head. "I'm so fucking sorry, Willow."

She tensed. Pulling away, she looked up at his gorgeous face. She was done with wondering. She was done with ignoring the situation.

"Would you let me walk out of your life?"

The sound of her heart beating pounded in her ear drums. The longer he stared at her, not answering, the louder and faster it became. Soon her throat dried, and the long swallow she eventually took was rough and painful.

Brayden, on the other hand, was as still as death as he stared down at her. The only movement that came from him was the swirling in his eyes which gave away a dozen emotions, all of which terrified her besides one.

Love.

Every woman knew that look. Love was unique. It was powerful, possessive, and protective. She watched his love fight for dominance as his eyes bored down into hers.

"I do not know," he finally said darkly, sending shivers down her spine. A knock at the door interrupted them, jolting her out of the trance. "Stay here."

She didn't. She followed him into the living area and ignored the frown he threw back at her as he opened the door.

"I thought we were coming to you?" Brayden said to the man who was slightly less broad and an inch or two shorter than him.

Despite the size difference, power and authority radiated off him.

"I thought your mate might feel more comfortable meeting me here."

CHAPTER THIRTY-ONE

Brayden stepped aside and let Vincent inside as he glanced at Willow, who looked like a deer in the headlights.

He quickly shut the door and went to her, pulling her to his side, and sat them on the sofa.

"Brother, sit."

Vince sat in the armchair, all kingly and shit, and smiled at Willow. Then in a quiet voice so as not to break her, he said, "Welcome."

Brayden rolled his eyes and held out his hand. "Willow, this is Vincent, my brother. Our king."

Beside him, she trembled ever so slightly, and he suddenly had the urge to kill every vampire on the planet until she felt safe. Then kill himself. Which was fucking ridiculous and yet, it was how he felt.

"I'm going to make this really brief, because as a mated male, I know how dangerous my brother is right now. You're scared, and Brayden is one dangerous vampire."

Brayden's eyes shot to his hairline and his mouth dropped open. "Are you fucking serious right now?"

Vincent held up a hand. "Sorry, um, fuck. I should have brought Kate. She said I would mess this up."

"You think?!" Brayden shot back.

Laughter. The two Moretti brothers stared at each other a moment in confusion before turning to Willow, who continued to laugh.

"Are you okay?"

Tears ran down her face. "You guys are really terrible at this."

He glanced at Vincent.

"I think she's delirious." Brayden nodded in agreement. "Should I get Kate?"

"No!" Willow blurted out. "No. Just one vampire at a time, please. Jesus, I think I'm losing it."

Ah, yeah, she fucking was. Yelling at the vampire king was not a good start.

"I think you might be doing better than you think," Vincent said. Willow stared at him for a moment and then nodded. Brayden felt her grip his hand and he returned a squeeze.

"Maybe." She took a deep breath. "It's nice to meet you, King Vincent."

Brayden smiled. Close enough.

"You are safe here. No one will harm you. You are my guest, and as Prince Brayden's mate, you...oh God, what now?!" The king's voice raised. "Have I said something else wrong?"

Brayden shook his head, exasperated. "No, but stop talking because you are about to," he informed him. "We haven't discussed the mating bond in detail yet."

Willow groaned beside him.

"She deserves to know, Bray."

"I know!" he yelled, causing Willow to jump. "Sorry, babe."

She stood up, pushing him. "Stop. Both of you. Someone had better start talking. I want to know what this mate business is all about. Whatever it is, you need to remember I'm a human with constitutional rights. I'm a US citizen!"

Despite the situation, both the Moretti brothers'

eyebrows shot up and they stared until finally a smirk hit their lips. Brayden tried to hide it by chewing his lips, but he was too late. Willow had seen him.

"You think that's funny?"

Holding out a hand, he replied, "No, I... well, a little bit."

"Willow." The king stood. "My brother has a lot to share with you. I came to welcome you to my court and our family." He walked to the door. "Show her around, do what you need to do, Bray, but you know the delicacy of our situation. Don't dally with this."

"I'll *dally* as long as I want to!" *I will not do what our father did to mother.*

Vincent looked at Willow.

She cannot remain among us as a human, you know this.

I will not force her.

Then she must choose you, and fast. We leave tomorrow evening.

The transition would take longer than that, and you know it.

You endanger her, brother. Turn her. Imagine what would happen if the Russos got their hands on her.

He growled at the thought of that happening.

Give me two weeks. She needs time. I will not have her hate me as mother did our father.

You forget how much she also loved him.

I remember how much she resented him. I do not want to see the same look in my mate's eyes.

"Hello?" Willow asked, not aware of the conversation taking place. He turned to look at the woman he loved. No. He would never force her. He'd wait until she agreed and accepted his offer of immortality.

And if she didn't?

His stomach turned.

Two weeks. I need two weeks.

You will bring her home with us.

A demand or a question, brother?

Both, if it makes you feel better.

He growled deep in the back of his throat. Vincent never directed him. Brayden knew the rules, and as king, it was Vincent's right to enforce them. Willow was Brayden's mate, which meant she was now an unofficial member of the Moretti royal family; a potential mother to future princes. The king was also responsible for her safety.

If the rebellion got their hands on her, they would use her against him. Painfully. There wasn't anything he wouldn't do to keep her safe. Anything, except force her to turn into a vampire.

Okay. I will bring her home.

You have one week.

Two!

It's too dangerous, Brayden. Don't be a fool.

I'll protect her.

Vincent shook his head. "Willow, I look forward to seeing you again soon."

"Nice to meet you," she politely replied as the king opened the door.

I've never had to say this before, Brayden—

Don't.

*—I am the fucking king. You have **one** week.*

Fury ran through his veins, causing his muscles to tense.

"Bray?" He felt Willow grasp one of his arms.

Don't challenge me on this, Brayden! You may be the only one able to produce an heir for this family. If you lose your mate and something happens to me, that's the Moretti line gone. You would never mate again. It is my duty to protect our family.

He glared at his brother.

This is your duty as prince and protector of your mate.

"Leave. Now!" he yelled at the king.

"Brayden!" Willow gasped, unaware of the conversation. Vincent frowned and shook his head.

"You are not our father, and you never will be. Have more faith in yourself, brother." Vincent closed the door behind him.

Brayden stared at the closed door for a long moment, then turned and pulled Willow into his arms.

For the first time in his life, he felt torn between his obligations as prince, as a Moretti, and something else. Never had he entertained thoughts such as those running through his mind right now, visions of overpowering his brother. But then what? The king was right. They both knew it.

If it weren't for his stubborn refusal to turn Willow, there would be no issue. But he wouldn't. Vincent hadn't spent the same intimate amount of time with their mother as he had. While Vincent was training to become king, Brayden had spent years with her listening to her stories, watching her eyes fill with emotions from her human years and lost possibilities.

Yet both brothers had been given the life-altering task of fulfilling the promise his father had made to his mother on their one thousandth anniversary. Standing side by side, Vincent and Brayden had taken a sword and beheaded their parents. It had been a promise their father had made to his mate, the queen, after turning her a vampire without her permission. She had hated him for it.

Eventually the senior royals had made peace with one another, and their love had flared to life again. Guiliana had given birth to Vincent and then Brayden, neither of whom suspected anything until 1891, exactly one thousand years later. Desperate to gain her trust and love back, their father had offered to give Guiliana back her mortality after a lifetime together, which together they agreed would be one thousand years.

The memory of seeing their heads rolling on the ground after both princes had been tasked with decapitating the royals was forever seared in his eyes. The consequence for his father's actions. Willow would have her choice, and that was final.

It was true that just by being his mate, he had fated her life.

He squeezed her tighter until he heard her moan.

"Hello! Human under here."

Releasing her, he held her face. "Willow, I'm so fucking sorry."

She paled. He watched as the truth they both knew she'd been ignoring came flooding to the forefront of her mind. Her face elongated and mouth fell open.

"Jesus, you're going to kill me, aren't you?" Tears poured down her face as she began to shake uncontrollably.

CHAPTER THIRTY-TWO

"Willow, breathe, you're hyperventilating." She tried to pull in gulps of air, but her throat began constricting. "Dammit."

Brayden picked her up and took her into the bedroom, setting her on the end of the bed.

He's going to kill me.
He's going to turn me into a vampire.
I've got to get out of here.
Run!

She tried to stand up, but he held her in place, which just made things worse.

"Baby, please. It's not like—I'm not going to—fuck! I can't even say it."

"Uck...ya...lut...me...goooo."

He pushed her head down between her legs and told her to breathe over and over again. She struggled and pushed against him until he let her go. She ran out into the living room until she realized she had nowhere to go. Turning, she saw him standing in the doorway to his bedroom looking nearly as hopeless as she felt.

"Fuck. Willow. Please." He held out his hands.

Focusing on her breathing, she waved her own hands out at him. "Stay there. Are you fucking mad? You want to kill me?"

He shook his head. "No. It's the last thing in the world I want to do."

Breathe in. Breathe out.

"Then take me home!"

He shook his head. "You know I can't. It's daylight."

"Can I leave?"

Brayden's eyes dropped and he shook his head. "It's too dangerous, sweetheart."

Breathe in. Breathe out.

"Why, because I might die?! You're planning to kill me anyway!"

His eyes flicked up at her in surprise, a dose of anger in them. "I am not going to kill you, Willow, let's get that straight. You will be alive and thriving after the transition. IF you choose it."

Her stomach turned, and she placed a hand over her abdomen.

"Out there," he said, pointing toward the window, "are my enemies. They would torture you. Slowly. You are safer with me. I am not letting you out of my sight."

She blinked.

He wiped a hand over his face. "There's a lot going on. Some vampires have been poisoning the king, and last night, one of them approached you at the park. If I hadn't shown up..."

Her eyes widened.

Her life was in danger. Being with Brayden had brought danger and death to her door. All strength left her body, and she collapsed on the floor.

Except she didn't because Brayden was a vampire, so as he'd done the first day they had met, he caught her. He then lifted her into his strong arms while she shook uncontrollably. He cooed at her like she was a baby. She was powerless to do anything.

For what felt like hours, he wrapped her in his arms as they lay on his bed. She felt his kisses, felt the way his hand ran over her arms and back, down her legs. When she relaxed into the strength of his comfort, reality came flooding back, and she began to shake all over again.

Over and over.

Finally, she twisted and looked up at him.

"Why don't you just do it and get it over with then?" She burst into uncontrollable tears and began punching his arms.

"Because, my love, I really fucking don't want to."

She watched as a tear ran down his face. Then another. She froze as she took in the raw emotion of the man she loved. The face of her killer.

He blinked them away and rolled onto his back, sighing.

"I guess there's no instruction manual for this," Brayden said, his voice full of gravel. "My mother was human when my father met her. The impatient bastard took her virginity and then her humanity minutes after she discovered he was a vampire."

Willow's eyes widened. He glanced over at her.

"I won't do that to you, Willow. She loved my father, yet deep down, she resented him, and I never want to see you look at me with that bitterness."

Those same conflicting feelings tore through her. If he gave her the opportunity to walk out right now, she'd likely run for her life while hoping he'd follow.

"I never, ever, want you to feel the same way." His eyes were wet, his mouth downturned. A little mark on the top of his cheek was the only evidence of the fallen tear.

How could someone who wanted to take her life look so torn? How could someone who loved her want to take her life?

"Perhaps," she said quietly, "you should take my memories, and I'll move to another state."

Brayden stared at the ceiling then closed his eyes. After a few moments, he rolled over. "Is this what you want?"

No. What she wanted to do was turn back time to when she was falling in love with him. She wanted to be eating ice cream with him, making love to him, telling him about her stupid day.

Not negotiating for her life.

He was a vampire with a dangerous life. If she had to choose between relocating and losing her memories or dying, then she had to choose life.

She had to.

So she gave him a little nod and rolled away.

CHAPTER THIRTY-THREE

Brayden wanted to vomit.

At least, he guessed he did. It wasn't something he'd ever done before; however, his stomach felt like it was making its way out his throat. At the same time, his heart felt like someone had reached into his chest and was attempting to squeeze it dry.

Watching Willow roll away from him after deciding to let him go was the most painful moment of his life.

His mate didn't want him.

He'd been infamous for his orgies and sexual appetite. He'd given little thought to meeting his mate back then. More recently, he'd been distracted with Vincent's illness until the day he had met Willow. She'd taken him by surprise and satisfied his every desire. He had never wanted anything in his life like he wanted this female.

His brother was right. If he lost his mate, he would never find another. There was only ever one mate for a vampire.

Brayden could take her memories from her, and she'd go on to live a life where she'd never find complete fulfillment. She would never love again. If she married, it would be for convenience with, at best, someone she cared for. It was a cruel punishment.

Brayden would simply die inside. He could never forget, nor would he choose to.

He felt the beginnings of anger stirring within him.

Fear, anger, anguish. Swallowing it down, he took a deep breath. He had to be strong for Willow.

Sitting up, he pulled her around and back into his arms. Every part of him wanted to howl, scream, and punch a wall, despite the gentle way he handled her. Surprisingly, she came to him without resistance.

"If this is what you want, sweetheart, I will do it."

Willow nodded and went into the bathroom. He left to give her some privacy and went out into the living room, turning on the screens to distract himself.

Craig was meeting with the rest of the senior team. On another screen, he watched as Regan, the POS, walked down the hallway with security on his tail. The rest of the facility was quiet as they slept the day off.

Brayden ran his hand through his hair as fatigue finally caught up with him. He could go without sleep for days if necessary, but all the emotions had drained him. This was a defining moment in his life. One that would head him down a dark, cold path, and he knew it.

"Screens off," he said, resting his ass on the edge of the sofa.

His vampire hearing heard Willow's soft steps. She stopped at the doorway and watched him. He let her think he hadn't heard her. Brayden closed his eyes and listened to her heart beating.

Bump. Bump. Bump, bump. Bump.

He squeezed his eyes, feeling himself wobble on the precipice of darkness. Losing her was going to change him in ways not even he could fathom.

At least he had a Russo or two to take it out on right now.

He wanted to bare his fangs at her and tell her to hurry up. He also wanted to get on his knees and beg her to want him. It was the latter which was tearing him apart.

"I, umm..."

"What?" he snapped before he could stop himself. She jumped.

This time he didn't feel the need to go to her, to comfort her. Instead, he just stared at her.

"Are you ready?" he asked when she didn't answer.

"Yes. Are you okay?"

He nodded and walked to the door, collecting his things. "Let's go."

"Wait." He slowly turned and looked at her. She didn't say anything.

"Willow, let's go. It's going to take a lot of work and resources to do this, so we need to get going now."

They walked to the security office in silence. As he reached to scan his finger, he felt a hand on his arm.

"Brayden," her small voice whispered. "I know you're mad, but can you please not be so cold? I'm scared."

He turned, towering over her with his height. He wanted to both shake her and kiss her. He did neither.

"You don't get it, do you? I fucking love you," he said. "And you've just told me you want to forget everything about me. How would you feel if I said I didn't want to remember you?"

Her mouth dropped open. "It's different. I don't want to kill you."

"And yet, you are," he replied, pushing through the door. His voice echoed around the room. "Craig! Drop everything and follow me."

The vampires all turned and stared. There was no doubt he was a powerful alpha; however, his current agitated behavior was unprecedented, and he knew it was causing them alarm.

Nothing he could do about it.

Nothing he wanted to do about it.

What he wanted to do was fucking kill something.

Craig stood up and marched across the room. "Lance, take over."

Yeah, his commander knew there was something very fucking serious going on. The door banged closed behind him, and his eyes shot between the two of them.

"Willow," he greeted, nodding.

"Hi, Craig."

What's going on?

I need you to relocate Willow. Urgently.

Brayden began walking, and the two of them followed him into another room with a boardroom table, chairs, and a computer.

What? What the fuck?

Yeah.

Craig shot a look at Willow and shook his head. Brayden's hackles raised. It was okay for him to be angry, but he didn't want anyone else upsetting her.

She's terrified, Craig.

Sure but...no, fuck this!

"Willow, what the fuck?" Craig asked.

She looked up at the vampire, confused, before understanding dawned and she exclaimed, "He wants to take my life! And you better stay away from Brianna."

A sudden snarl came from Craig's throat, and Brayden turned to see the man's fangs exposed. Willow took a step back and a little cry escaped her.

Instinct made him protect her. He pulled her into his arms and shot out a fist, pushing Craig up the wall.

"Stop!"

"Sorry. Fuck."

Brayden released him and the guy turned and slapped the wall behind him with his open palm, frustrated. Then he swung around.

"I'm sorry. Look, I can't imagine how terrifying this

is or how hard it is on both of you, but Bray, have you explained what will happen once her memories are removed?"

Craig and Willow stared at him as he shook his head. At Willow's raised eyebrow, he released her and told them to sit down.

They ignored him.

"It doesn't matter—"

"The fuck it doesn't. Willow, you're his mate. It may be a vampire thing, but it impacts you too. Sure, you'll have no memories, but you'll never love again. You'll be left with a broken heart and never understand why."

Brayden watched her face as she took in the new information, her eyes darting around the room and back at him.

"But I'll be alive," she said quietly.

"Forget it," he growled. She was never going to choose him, and he just needed to get this over and done with. "Where do you want to relocate?"

She shrugged. "Hawaii, whatever, I don't care."

"Is anyone going to listen to me?" Craig asked frustrated.

"House or condo?"

"Condo."

"Oahu?"

"Maui."

"Fine." He turned to Craig. "I want the property purchased and movers packing up her house by tonight. Book flights for the morning."

Craig shook his head at them both. "Yeah, fine."

"I can't buy a house on Maui; do you have any idea how much—"

He turned and placed his hands on his hips. "You are my mate. It's my job to look after you whether you remember or not. I'm buying you the fucking house, and it will go into your name."

He left her fish mouthing the air.

"Alert me when it's done," he ordered Craig, then took Willow's arm and led her out of the room.

"Just fucking talk to each other, would you!" He heard Craig call out as the door shut behind them.

They walked silently back to his room. Willow sat down on the sofa and he handed her a glass of water. She sipped at it while he chucked back his. Everything about this felt like shit.

"I need to get some sleep," he said, wiping a hand over his face. "You can...I don't know, watch TV or sleep or whatever."

Willow looked at him as if he'd told her to go play on the yellow dotted lines. She flicked her eyes at the door then back at him.

He let out a bitter laugh. "Aside from the fact it's locked, I can't imagine you would risk walking out into a compound full of vampires."

"Then you don't understand how terrified I am of dying."

Brayden shook his head. "If I were going to kill you, I would have done it already. God, Willow, I've been completely honest and given you the choice. You've made it, no matter the cost to me."

Willow jumped to her feet. "Honest?! Don't talk to me about honesty. I've been sleeping with a fucking vampire for days!"

"And when would have been the right moment to tell you? While I was fucking you over the sofa?"

Her face flushed. "Don't say stuff..." Her eyes dilated. His eyes dropped to her lips. She licked them. "What cost to you? You're not dying."

Her question snapped him out of it. For a moment, he had imagined his lips meeting hers for one last time. Just for a second, he had wanted to feel her warm, soft flesh against his as he showed her how much he cared.

His eyes flashed to hers.

"Forget it." He stepped away.

She grabbed his forearm. "Tell me."

"No." He was barely holding himself together as it was. "I'm going to sleep."

She dropped her hand and nodded.

Brayden went into the bathroom and took a quick shower. The warm water flowed over his large naked body as he tipped his head back. Every inch of him felt hard and cold against the world now.

Sure, he could turn her, and like his mother, she'd eventually accept it. His father wasn't the first or last to do such a thing. All the humans, men and women, soon came to enjoy their life as a vampire.

To be the mate of the royal prince was a highly desired position, but Willow had never given him a chance to teach her about his life. She had asked to leave, and he had agreed. He was dreading the darkness which would overcome him the moment she left. Brayden slipped
between the sheets and stared at the ceiling.

CHAPTER THIRTY-FOUR

Willow heard the shower turn off and the rustle of the sheets as Brayden climbed into bed.

She had so many questions.

What would she tell her friends? Moving to Hawaii overnight was hardly something she would do without a lot of planning and consultation with at least Brianna.

She pulled out her phone and stretched out on the couch. There was no way she was going to tell a soul about the vampires and put them in the same position as her, but she could warn Bri off Craig, whatever was going on between them.

Hey Bri, how's your day?

Hey girl. Good. What are you up to?

Oh, not much, just fighting for my life in a vampire compound, lost the love of my life, and moving to Hawaii. Apparently.

Been thinking. You're not into Craig, are you?

No. What? No.

Okay. Good. He's bad news. Stay away from him, okay.

Totally. His ego can't fit through my door anyway.

Oh God, she did like him.

I mean it, Bri. He's not what he seems.

If only she could expand on it without endangering her friend's life. The thought of anyone else going through what she was right now, even her worst enemies, was incomprehensible. She would never do anything to put someone else in her shoes.

Gotcha. Running into a meeting. I'll call you tonight x

Love ya x

Who knew if she'd have any recollection of this conversation, or what would happen, but she wanted her friend to know she was loved.

Aww you too xx

She looked around the apartment, taking in all of Brayden's decor. On the coffee table in front of her, she noticed a coaster from the bar they'd visited last week. Willow picked it up and realized it was the one she'd drawn little hearts on the back of. She smiled sadly. Beside it was a little blue box.

She glanced at the doorway before reaching for it. Its little hinges creaked as it opened. Her mouth opened as she touched the little silver heart locket hanging from the matching chain. She pulled it from the box and let it fall into her palm. As it did, the heart flipped over to expose the engraving.

My Willow. Yours forever. Love, B.

Tears sprung to her eyes and began falling down her face. Before she could stop herself, the tears had turned to hiccups. She hugged the piece of jewelry to her chest.

Wiping her eyes with the back of her arm, she looked up and found Brayden standing in the doorway. Naked.

She stared.

He stared.

"I..." she started to say, but he was in front of her before she could finish, taking it out of her hands.

"I'm sorry. I shouldn't have opened it."

"Shh," he said, and undid the clasp, placing it around her neck. "It belongs here, even if you never remember where you got it."

Willow hiccupped. "I hate this."

His eyes were soft with pain as he nodded. They sat in silence as he rubbed his thumb over her hand, the ache to be with him so powerful it began to override her fear.

She blinked.

Willow saw the moment he recognized the shift. His pupil slowly decreased and the silver eyes she loved, now with a dark line surrounding it, looked back at her. Determined.

"Come," he said softly, no room for disobedience, and stood.

She let him lead her into the bedroom, undress her, and put her in his bed. They fell asleep wrapped in each other's arms.

CHAPTER THIRTY-FIVE

"He's doing what?!" Vincent boomed.

Christ in a handbasket, could the guy stop yelling? Since Craig had shown up unannounced, the king had yelled every damn sentence.

"Maui. Brayden has purchased a house there and is relocating Willow."

"You said that."

Craig had, in fact, repeated it three times now.

The king stood with his hands firmly on his hips, looking between him and the queen. She shrugged.

Brayden would be furious with him for coming to the king and queen with this, but it was his only option. He was concerned. He'd seen how males who lost their mate fell into the darkness. He wasn't going to sit back passively and let his best friend make a life-changing decision he couldn't reverse.

Craig had done what had been asked of him. The flights were booked, the property purchased, and movers were currently packing up Willow's home. Then he'd hot-tailed it to the royal chambers.

"If this is Willow's decision, Brayden will honor it. You know how he feels," the queen said, her jaw clenched.

"Ah, if I may, your majesties..."

"Speak freely, Craig."

He usually did, but Vincent appreciated formalities on occasion, and he respected the male greatly.

"Neither of them is thinking clearly," he said, crossing his bulky arms. "She's clearly scared out of her brain..."

"She is, but she has moxy." They nodded.

"You're right, your majesty. Willow has some sass about her; however, Brayden has reacted to her rejection and withdrawn emotionally. She's genuinely scared."

"Humans naturally are," Kate added, and they all nodded in agreement once again.

"Yes, but she also loves the prince a whole fucking lot." Craig looked between the king and queen. "I can't believe I'm about to say this, but here it goes. I think Brayden is scared."

Two blank faces stared back at him.

"No way."

"Nope."

"Hear me out. Our boy is trapped in his head between the fear of losing Willow and fear of her resentment should he turn her without her agreement like your father did."

Vincent waved him off. "That's no secret. He's always felt this way about our mother's situation repeating. In any case, I gave him a week to integrate Willow into our world, so why the sudden turnaround?"

"She's rejected him."

"In less than a day?"

"What happened?" She turned to the king in question.

Vincent held out his hands in defense. "I didn't say anything. Okay, I said a lot of things, but they seemed fine when I left."

Craig and the queen glanced at each other. Neither believed his last statement. The king had likely had his foot in his mouth right from the get-go. The guy was useless in front of humans; nobody ever left him alone with one.

"Oh, darling, what did you say? I told you I should have gone with you."

The king raised his shoulders and began to explain the conversation.

"...in any case," Craig continued. "What I'm trying to point out here is that Brayden is in a position he's never been in: rejected by his mate. And I saw a change in him that has me concerned."

Now he had their attention.

"He's trapped in this belief he'll destroy her life just like your father, our Great King, did to your mother. But as we all know, they enjoyed a great love for many years."

A thousand years to be exact.

"And could have had many more if not for their ridiculous promise," Vincent added.

Craig had borne witness to the terrible day both princes had beheaded the king and queen. It had changed them both forever; in fact, it had changed the entire vampire race. Shock and surprise had rippled through the vampire kingdom. Vincent had made many changes since his coronation.

"He knows what life without his mate means. I saw the darkness in his eyes. Frankly, it terrified me, and truly little does."

"Hmm," the king hummed, now with his full attention. "We need to show Willow our world and eliminate her fear. Get them talking."

Kate stood. "A small gathering. We'll invite some former humans, and they can share their stories."

Craig nodded. Something had to work, or Brayden would be one dangerous motherfucker to himself, and potentially, the race.

"I'll extend the invite."

"Best I go with you this time, darling," Kate said

sweetly and gave Craig a wink.

CHAPTER THIRTY-SIX

Brayden woke up to find Willow draped over him. One of his arms was tightly wrapped around her, the other flung out across the bed. Her head on his broad chest, one hand wrapped around his bicep, was how they slept most nights. Except this would be the last time. His chest tightened while he stared coldly at the ceiling.

He'd heard Willow opening the jewelry box and had squeezed his eyes shut. He'd waited for her to throw it across the room in yet another act of rejection. Instead, he'd heard her tears, and they had clawed at his heart. Without thinking, his body had climbed out of bed and gone to her. She hadn't turned him away.

For a moment, he thought he'd seen a shift in her beautiful eyes, one that looked like acceptance and love, but he was in too much pain to trust blindly. He would continue with her plans. Any moment now, Craig would alert them, and he would remove her memories.

His chest heaved, and his little human stirred, eyelids fluttering open while she shifted to look at him. Tears formed and began flowing down her cheeks onto his chest. He ran a hand over her hair and kissed her head. Despite the growing pain and darkness that threatened to overtake him, he still felt the need to comfort her. Even in the face of her painful rejection.

"I love you." Her words startled him.

"Willow."

"It's okay. I understand if you don't feel the same

way after I chose to leave."

He sat up, clutching her arms. Did he dare believe?

"Willow. I love you. Now and always." His lips pressed against hers. As her hands squeezed his arms in response, he took a risk and plunged his tongue desperately into hers. She opened and welcomed him inside.

He hardened.

"I need you," he said against her lips, and nearly cried when she nodded.

Reaching down, he placed her legs on either side of his large hips then found her core. His fingers pushed through her delicate flesh, groaning when he felt her wet. Gripping his cock, he wasted no time. He pushed as Willow pressed, and together, they moaned into each other's mouths.

"Fuck, Willow, you are mine."

Soon they found a smooth rhythm, and Willow began to ride him. She half sat up, giving him access to her breasts. He sucked one nipple and she threw her head back.

"Bray, fuck me, Bray, please."

Hell yes, he would. Flipping them, he placed her under him and pushed her legs up to her shoulders.

"Take all of me, Willow." He pressed in balls deep, thrusting again and again while his mate cried out.

He slid a hand in between them and rubbed her clit, taking her cry to a scream. Her pussy tightened around his cock, and his seed released in a powerful explosion that ran through his entire body.

Brayden released her legs but stayed inside her while she panted. He took her face in one of his hands and kissed her lips. "Forever, Willow. Even when you no longer remember me, you will always be my only love."

She burst into tears.

He slipped out of her and pulled her into his arms, his cum spilling between them but he couldn't give a shit.

"Hey. It's okay." It really fucking wasn't. He shouldn't have said that, but goddamn, he needed to have his moment to love her one last time and say how he felt. Then, when he knew she was okay, he could let go and slip into the darkness.

If only he could keep her here in his arms forever. Yes, he could, but he loved her too much to take away her choice. He would never do what his father had done. He would never watch his mate stare upon him with disgust. He'd seen enough of it today. It was as bad as he'd imagined.

"I don't think I can do it," Willow said.

"You don't have to do anything, sweetheart. You'll be home soon, in your new home in Hawaii, and remember nothing."

She pulled away from him. "No. I mean I don't think I can leave you!"

Oh.

What the fuck.

"Please don't play with me, Willow. This is killing me."

She gripped his face in her hands. "Brayden, I'm not playing games. I love you. I want you in my life, but I'm so fucking terrified."

He could hear her heart thumping loudly inside her chest while his own head was trying to make sense of her words.

What was she saying?

The only way he could take the fear away from her was to remove her memories. Or she had to face it.

He wanted to ask her to stay, but if she said no, his heart would tear in half. Again.

The darkness within him was sitting in his mental

waiting room just tapping its feet, grinning sadistically at him. Brayden wasn't a pussy; he would hold back that motherfucker until he'd gotten his brother and the queen home safely. Then with his newfound fury, he'd take his vengeance out on the Russos, who had infiltrated his family and poisoned his brother.

He stared at the glistening green eyes waiting for him to respond.

Fuck, Brayden, get your shit together.

He needed to man up. He was a goddam alpha vampire. Was he not capable of growing a bigger pair of balls and risk breaking the rest of his shattered heart? Was she not worth it? The fuck she wasn't! If he lost this female because he didn't have the resilience or strength to ask her one more goddamn time, then he'd regret it for the rest of his life.

And it would be a long fucking life.

"Come home with me, Willow. Give me a week, another damn week, to show you who I truly am. To show you my life, what an immortal world could mean for you, and then you can decide."

She stared at him, eyes still dripping tears, fear pouring from them.

"I promise you, on my life, you will be safe. Nothing will happen to you, and if you still want to return to your human life, I will take you home."

"All right. I'll go. I'm so scared, Brayden." She gulped through the tears.

His eyes burst open in surprise, then pulled her into his arms and squeezed his eyes shut.

"Thank you, sweetheart. My God, thank you. I know you are and I'm going to do everything in my power to support you through this."

Now he had the biggest job of his life: convincing her to accept his world and become a vampire.

Shit.

He released her, kissed her nose, and stared into those beautiful green eyes. "Get dressed. We're going to have company in thirty seconds."

CHAPTER THIRTY-SEVEN

"That was barely a knock," Kate admonished as Vincent let himself into Brayden's apartment after he half-heartedly rapped on the double doors.

He shrugged. Brayden would have heard them approaching. "Tough."

Vincent was running out of patience. To be fair, he wasn't a patient male by nature, and if you added the fact he'd been being poisoned for the past few months, yeah, he was out of patience.

"Bray!"

"Yeah, I heard you."

His brother walked out of the bedroom knotting the strings on a pair of sweatpants. He ran a hand through his dark hair. The leaning against the doorjamb coupled with a calmness which hadn't been there before was interesting.

"Brayden, I've come to speak with Willow," his queen said. "An invite."

"There's no need," Brayden replied, lifting his arm to accommodate his mate as she appeared beside him in the doorway.

Had Craig been mistaken? They looked almost happy, though the lines of their faces showed it had been a long day.

"Kate, meet Willow," Brayden introduced. "Baby, this is our queen. Vincent's mate."

The human smiled kindly, though her widened eyes

were alert, proving she was still not comfortable. "Nice to meet you. Um, your majesty."

"Kate will do fine when we're in private. After all we are—will...er...hopefully will be family. Oh damn. Darling, I'm sorry. I'm as useless as you."

Vincent frowned at his mate and shook his head. "If we could all stop calling the king useless, it would be super great," he said, ignoring Brayden's smirk.

"Willow has agreed to return to Maine with me and spend a week learning our ways. Afterward, she'll make her decision."

Vincent could see the strain in the prince's face. His half smile showed relief but didn't reach his eyes. He could only imagine the pain his brother was going through.

Well, he had some experience with that. Mating was not always straightforward and without its challenges. He turned to his queen and they shared a knowing look.

"It will be wonderful having you at Castle Moretti, Willow. I can introduce you to many of our former humans who can answer any questions you have," Kate said gently. "I was going to host a cocktail party this evening to get started."

Willow peered up at the prince, who shook his head. "Let's wait until we get back east. Willow needs to pack, and we want some time together as she adjusts."

"Thank you for the nice offer, though."

The king smiled at the polite human who was nervously wringing her hands and giving his queen another kind smile.

The poor girl was terrified; Craig was right. This was why, in his opinion, it was better to simply enforce the change and deal with the aftermath. The mating bond was strong enough to overcome the breach in trust. Too much time, and worry created unreasonable fear and suffering.

He turned to Brayden and gave him a little frown.

"This is our decision. I will see you at the airfield tomorrow night." The prince's eyes bore into his, challenging him.

"A great decision it is," Kate said, smiling. "Hopefully, you will be with us for the ball. It's a Victorian theme, so we'll have beautiful gowns and jewels to wear. Oh, how I miss the fashion of that era."

Brayden let out a little cough. "Yes, well, we were all a little different back then."

"What's it in celebration of?" Willow asked boldly despite her fear.

A smile crept to Vincent's lips. Of course his brother would choose a mate with spirit. He bet once her fear faded, she would be quite the dynamite.

"It's the annual royal ball held each year on the anniversary of my coronation," Vincent answered.

Kate laid a hand on his arm. "We host over three hundred guests. Some years it's held on the great lawn, but this year, the grand ballroom will be decorated in all its glamour. We're even having a jazz band."

"For a Victorian-era theme?"

"Oh yes. Jazz began near the end of the Victorian era. We loved it, didn't we, Brayden?" Kate grinned. "The king isn't much of a dancer, but he was forced to step up in order to get my attention."

Vincent shook his head, kissing his mate's head. "These two will never let me forget it either. I hope you can dance, Willow; your mate is quite famous on the dance floor."

He watched as Brayden pulled the human closer against his side and glanced down at her possessively. A warmth spread through Vincent as he watched his brother with his mate. The love was front and center, leaving no question as to whether she was the one. That and Brayden now had the solid ring around his iris that confirmed he was mated.

If the human accepted him, she would be loved by that brother of his beyond anything she could ever dream. He would be loyal, strong, passionate, and protective unlike anything she'd seen. The private smile they shared gave him hope.

Kate leaned into him with a sigh. She'd seen it too. He wrapped an arm around her, and they shared a smile. He remembered the moment he realized he loved Kate. He had been such an idiot. When they had finally gotten together, the fireworks had lit up the skies. He felt his pants tighten.

The poison was leaving his system and his strength was returning. While he wasn't fully recovered, he certainly had enough energy to pleasure his queen. His hand slid down onto her hip, and she laid a hand on his abdomen and let her nails dig into him.

A silent groan rumbled in his chest.

"Let's just take it one step at a time." Brayden smirked. "No pun intended."

Willow grinned, shaking her head, and Vincent hoped, for the sake of their bloodline, it was a positive sign.

"We will see you both on the jet."

While they could teleport back home, Vincent had decreed they should act as humans when appropriate to fit into the world around them. Appearing in different parts of the country or world without a travel footprint was something they did only when it was an emergency.

Vincent held the door open for Kate and let it close behind them. She began to walk off, but he grabbed her hand and pulled her up against his chest. "Where do you think you're going?"

"My lord?" She gasped playfully.

Pushing her up against the wall, he nudged his knee between her legs. "We have some lost time to make up for. I want these panties off, and your legs open for me."

Dude, take your smooth moves elsewhere. I can hear you in here!

He groaned, shook his head, lifted his mate into his arms, and flashed into their rooms.

You might have learned something, brother. He quipped back.

Pfft.

Yeah, he had a point.

CHAPTER THIRTY-EIGHT

"Leaving in five, Willow."

It was the second time he'd called out. He understood the enormity of the situation, but did she really need two suitcases of belongings for one week?

"What if I never come back?" she had asked.

"Of course we can come back. We can teleport or bring the jet. If you choose to become a vampire, you can port back with me. If you choose."

He'd answered many questions over the past twenty-four hours while trying to be patient, but with so much on the line and his own fears in the mix, it was exhausting. Though an exhaustion he was happy to have the opportunity to have.

In the back of his mind was the king's safety, and he was eager to get back to the airfield and be near his family. Craig was on the ground there already with many of the king's senior team, including Regan, preparing to depart on the second jet.

She stepped out of her room dressed in a pair of tight blue jeans, white heels, and a flowing white top. Her brown curly hair flowed around her shoulders, dominating her small frame. His heart stuttered as it did every time he saw her.

Nowadays she had a vulnerability to her that hadn't been there before. He hoped it would pass as she became used to his kind, and their world. As she learned about his life and their role in the royal family, it would become evident to her, as his mate, that she would become a Moretti princess.

He hadn't yet imagined what their ceremony would be like or how she'd look like standing beside him as they said their vows. Or how their little vamp babies would look with her beautiful hair and his dark features.

Okay, so perhaps he had, but he couldn't get excited. Not yet.

"Hey, beautiful."

She walked into his arms and tiptoed to reach his lips. He lifted her, hands on her hips, and felt his chest swell when she giggled. "Vampire strength has some great benefits."

"Oh, baby, you don't know the half of it." He slid her down his body, keeping his lips on hers until she reached the floor. "But you will, and I'll show you it's worth it."

Willow tipped her head to the side. "Where were those moves last night?"

He stood to his full height, towering over her as he held her eyes. "One thing at a time, Willow." He ran his thumb over her lips. "I won't do anything to risk losing you." Brayden felt her shudder beneath his hands as she gave him a little nod of understanding.

"Let's get your bags before I use my superpowers to throw you on the bed."

That smile. He wanted to see more of it. Brayden planted another kiss on her rosy red lips and stepped away.

An hour later, they were pulling up in front of a private jet with *Moretti Enterprises* painted on the tail.

"Whoa," Willow said in awe.

If this impressed her, she was going to lose her shit when they arrived at the castle. The Moretti assets were vast and matched those of the wealthiest families on the planet. In all honesty, they probably exceeded them.

Very few knew the exact figure, likely the king, Regan, and their accountant. If Brayden cared, he would be given the number, but he didn't.

With thousands of years of investment and income behind them, the Moretti family had amassed a fortune in properties on every continent, art, precious jewelry, shares, and other collections.

Not all vampires were wealthy. Many had chosen to work night jobs so they could live in the human world. Where necessary, the Moretti Foundation had contributed by setting up their houses with the appropriate protection on windows so they could function without turning to ash from the sunlight.

Modern technology allowed them to fit into life on the planet with more ease. Shops were open longer, delivery services, computers—they all contributed to an easier life for the ten million vampires currently on earth.

It was a small number and spoke to the low fertility rate of their females. While the gestation period was the same—nine months—female vampires ovulated only a few times a year. Like all animals, the only sign was an increase in desire, which given the healthy sexual life of a vampire, could easily go undetected. Hence, very few vamp babies.

Brayden helped Willow out of the vehicle, shaking his head. It was the second time he'd thought about damn babies today. Some alpha he was.

"What?"

"What?" he asked, confused.

"You look annoyed."

Oh. "I'm not." He pressed his lips to her forehead. "I'm just nervous. I'm scared of fucking this up, Willow."

It was a clear night with a crisp breeze. He pulled her

into the warmth of his arms.

"I want you to promise that if anything scares you, you'll tell me. Immediately."

Willow surveyed the airfield and the steps to the entrance of the plane where two vampires stood waiting.

"Everything scares me, Bray. Everything."

He took a deep breath. "Yeah."

"I will, though. I'll tell you." She gripped his forearm. "I want this as much as you do, honestly. Stay by my side and I'll do my best, okay."

He nodded. It was all he could ask of her, and damn, he was proud of her courage.

"I'm not going anywhere, baby. You're safe and so fucking loved."

She leaned into his chest and he wrapped his arms around her. As he held her, he glanced around, wishing he could teleport them somewhere the two of them could just exist without any of their challenges. In their own bubble. He'd never wished to be human. Never. Not even now.

Okay, maybe just a little.

"Your highness," Margaret, their private flight attendant, greeted them as they boarded. He gave her a small smile. With a hand in the small of Willow's back, she stepped into the aircraft.

"Oh my goodness."

He smiled at her reaction. The interior was very luxurious. The entire space was white with a rich blue and black accent colors. Seats in rows of two, a dining area, curved sofas, and two private rooms made up most of the aircraft.

"I feel like a movie star," Willow said as she strapped in.

"Would you like a drink, your highness?"

He glanced at Willow in question and she ordered a

vodka, dry. "I'll have a whisky. Neat."

Willow's eyes followed Margaret as she left to get their drinks, then looked around the cabin before finally returning her eyes to him.

"Does everyone call you that?" He nodded. "Is it weird?"

Brayden smiled. He'd been called *your highness* for thousand years. It was inappropriate for most of the race to refer to him otherwise. She had much to learn, and it would take time, which he respected. Not only was she entering a new race she hadn't known existed until recently, but Willow was also joining a royal family with traditions and rules.

"No, I'm the prince."

She chewed the corner of her lip, nodding. "I guess I keep forgetting. By the time I get to Maine, it should be etched in my brain with all the branding around me."

He peered at their family crest on the seat across from them and laughed. "That's our Moretti family crest, not a logo." When he saw her face, his laugh faded. "Sorry, just sounded funny. It's not like we're Coca-Cola."

"What do you call the thing on the outside of the plane then?"

He shrugged. "I call it fitting in with humans. We have to have a business and pay some taxes."

Willow threw out a hand, all *told ya so,* and said, "Ergo, a logo, smarty-pants."

"Okay, fine, but it's still a family crest."

"Noted," she relented with an eyeroll.

Clomp. Clomp. Clomp. Brayden reached over and took Willow's hand. She'd paled. They could both hear Vincent's voice as he ascended into the aircraft. As could the people in Africa, the guy was so loud.

"No, I need both bags. Kate, ask him to bring it on

board! Oh hey, Brayden! Willow! You're here."

Brayden pinched the bridge of his nose.

Pipe down, brother. Can you please not scare my mate.

CHAPTER THIRTY-NINE

The king suddenly slowed his walk down the aisle and looked back and forth between her and Brayden.

She lifted her hand in a small greeting.

He was an intimidating man. He seemed to always wear black leather pants and a matching black shirt. On his arm was an enormous watch. Like Brayden, he had dark hair, except his was shorter and appeared to have no curl. His eyes were dark brown. Their face shape, solid jaw, and big eyes made it obvious they were brothers.

Both gave off powerful vibes, yet with Vincent, there was something different. He was the king. It was in the way he stood tall with his legs wide, his shoulders back, and complete authority in his face.

He'd shown her kindness whenever they had met, but Willow couldn't help feeling that if she met him alone in a dark alley, she would be fearing for her life.

It was different with Brayden. She'd been overwhelmed with attraction and sensed his protectiveness right from the start. Yet his power was his own.

"Your majesty, welcome on board."

"Thank you, Margaret. I'll have an ale for takeoff. Kate?"

The queen stepped into the cabin, looking as beautiful and graceful as she had the first time Willow had met her. How she got her blonde hair so shiny was a mystery. Likely some vampire magical power.

"Just a small glass of plasma, Margaret."

Brayden squeezed her hand.

"Oh God, I'm sorry, Willow," the queen said. "I hope it didn't freak you out."

"I guess that's what I'm here to learn." Her voice came out all squeaky, which was completely embarrassing.

The couple took a seat on the opposite side of the plane as their drinks were served.

"Can I get another one of these now, please," Willow asked Margaret pointing to her own drink, knowing she was going to need it.

Another woman stepped on board, followed closely by a tall man in what looked like a black military outfit. "Sorry, sorry we're late."

"Hey," Brayden said sounding surprised. "What are you doing here?"

The man lowered his head. "Captain. Your majesty."

"Welcome. Sit!" Vincent bellowed then shot an apologetic look at her. "The queen and I invited Sera and Carlos to join us on the flight home."

"Please find a seat," Kate said.

Willow glanced at Brayden, whose narrowed eyes suddenly softened before he nodded.

"What's going on?" she asked quietly.

"It's okay. Seraphina is the king's secretary and Carlos is her mate. He's also a lieutenant in our army."

Which did nothing to explain why he had tensed when they arrived. "And?"

He shook his head. "No one usually flies on the royal jet except family—"

He was interrupted by the queen. "Sera was a human before she met Carlos." Willow glanced at the female and nodded in greeting. "I thought you could ask her questions. Learn about her experience. If you wanted.

There is no pressure."

Willow turned to Brayden.

"Kate, I know you're trying to help, but I haven't had a chance to talk to Willow about anything. At all."

He looked down at her. "I'm sorry. This is all too much, too fast."

Her palms began to sweat as the aircraft lifted into the air, and not from fear of turbulence.

"Your highness, if I may."

"Speak freely, Seraphina," Vincent prompted, though her question had been directed at Brayden.

The brothers glared at each other.

"Keeping the information from Willow will only increase her fear as her imagination runs wild." Willow nodded slowly, giving the female a little smile.

"That may be true, but I will be the one to tell my mate what to expect."

Vincent waved his hand. "The floor is yours."

"Stop, brother! I will not do it while we are thirty thousand feet in the air with nowhere for her to run."

The king shrugged and mumbled, "Seems like the safest place to me. She can't run."

The queen told him off, and beside her, she heard a groan.

"I'm not going to run." Maybe. Probably. "Seraphina is right. I need to know."

"Christ, this is an absolute ambush," Brayden growled, mad. "She's my fucking mate! Do not"—he pointed to the king and queen—"try another stunt like this without my knowledge. You hear me?"

His voice was low and dark, but the message was clear.

"Be careful with your tone, prince," the king warned, glancing at his queen.

The air was thick with testosterone, sending panic

through her body. Her heart began thumping wildly in her chest as she prepared for violence to erupt. These people were predators—who knew what they were capable of. Instead, she noticed they were all staring at her.

Brayden wrapped an arm around her shoulders. "I'm sorry."

"Okay, look, I'm sorry too. I just wanted to help," the queen apologized.

"I want to hurry things up!"

Brayden growled again. To break up the two alpha males, Willow squeezed Brayden's leg.

"Fine. So tell me. How does it happen. Becoming a vampire."

Well, that shut everyone up. There was a whole bunch of silence all of a sudden.

More silence.

"I'll tell her if you—"

"You will not!" Brayden snapped at his brother. "Come with me." He led her down to the rear of the aircraft, into a bedroom. Inside was a large bed, a bathroom, and some furniture affixed to the walls.

"We do this alone. Well, as alone as one can get with vampire hearing."

They climbed onto the bed and she sat facing him, cross-legged. Brayden leaned against the headboard, one knee up with his arm flopped over it. With his other, he took her hand.

"I've never turned a human," he started. "There is a reason, one which I am blood bound not to share with you. Until, or unless, you become my mate."

She nodded, not understanding.

"Even telling you this is crossing the fine line. Right now, Vincent will be wiping the minds of Carlos and Seraphina. As I will have to do with yours, should you choose to leave."

"Yes." Her mind whirled. There was so much to learn and understand, most of all the decisions she had to make at the end. To become a vampire or lose Brayden.

"If you decide to change—"

"To become your mate."

"No, you are already my mate. We are bonded in ways you do not understand yet."

She narrowed her eyes in confusion.

"One thing at a time," he placated, rubbing his thumb over her fingers. "If you choose to spend your life with me, you must become a vampire. For your safety and because it is our way. The hours I have been keeping are not sustainable long-term, nor could you function in our world."

Brayden's eyes ran over her face, watching her reaction. Her chest barely moved; her breathing was shallow from the trepidation of hearing his next words.

"If you do..."

"God, Brayden, spit it out."

"Then I will bite you." His eyes looked apologetic yet full of determination. "I will drink your blood to connect us. Blood has power, even yours as a human. Then you will drink some of mine."

His fingers tightened around her as she sat frozen, listening. "It will trigger a genetic change in your body. Over the next few days, I will continue to feed you until the transition is complete."

She attempted to swallow what felt like sand. "Is it painful?"

He nodded.

"Could I die?"

He held her stare for a long time. "No."

She looked at him in disbelief.

"No, Willow, you will not die. Some have, but I

swear on my life you will not die."

She choked and started coughing. "What, because you decree it, or some other reason?"

Cough, cough.

Brayden looked around the room, his jaw set in frustration.

"Both," he said firmly. "For the reason I mentioned earlier which I cannot divulge more on. You will be an immortal once the transition is complete. After that, the only ways to end your life is a knife in the heart or decapitation."

Her mouth gaped at his words.

"To be fair, you can die those ways right now." He shrugged.

She couldn't argue with that. He was right.

"So I'd live forever?"

He nodded.

"What do you do all day?"

Brayden let out a little laugh and pulled her into his arms. "Prince stuff. I'm also the Captain of the Royal Vampire Army, so I keep busy when I'm not wooing my mate."

She snorted. "What would I do?"

He brushed hair off her face and kissed her lips gently. "Anything you wanted. The world will be your oyster. There will be royal duties as my mate; however, if you want a job, we could create one or find something you want to do. Or you can keep running your business for a while."

She realized what he meant. Eventually, she would draw attention when she didn't age.

"What about my friends?"

He frowned. "It's tricky. Most of the turned vamps seem to leave their human lives behind. Those are the things you could ask Seraphina. There can be no risk to the race, for our survival and safety."

She snuggled into him, her mind ablaze with information and thoughts which were both terrifying and confusing. The idea of losing her friends, of never seeing Brianna again, was heartbreaking. Yet for reasons she couldn't explain, the idea of losing Brayden made her body shake and her stomach nauseous.

"Tell me about being a mate."

He pulled back from her and tipped her chin up. "For a vampire, there is only one mate. When he mates with a female, the other is impacted whether they are human or vampire."

Oh.

"We don't understand why it's possible to cross-mate, we just know it does happen. It's a chemical reaction chosen by both parties, so I want to be clear this isn't something I have forced upon you or vice versa."

The desire to kiss him came over her. She knew she should be paying closer attention, but she suddenly couldn't keep her lips to herself. He moaned, and with surprising speed, bit her lip gently in response, then pulled away and smirked at her. She giggled.

"Mates are, for the most part, inseparable. Being apart is painful. An ache in your chest you can't relieve. A need which can't be fulfilled any other way."

"Do humans experience these feelings as well?" she asked, curiously.

"Yes, but it may be more visceral for vampires. Have you ever felt the same way with a man as you do with me?"

She shook her head. It was true; she hadn't. However, she'd assumed it was because she'd fallen in love with Brayden. Their sex life was incredible, and she never felt happier than when he was around. The pull to be near him was palpable for sure.

"Once we are officially mated and you've become a vampire, those feelings will intensify."

"If."

He nodded sadly. "Yes. *If.*"

"I can't imagine wanting you more than I already do, Bray." Willow nudged up against his erection, which had appeared not long ago.

"You will."

He cupped her bottom and pulled her into his body, plunging his tongue into her mouth. Melting in his arms, she let herself forget for a moment what they were talking about.

"If we didn't have an audience, I would fuck you right now," he said against her lips.

Wet pooled between her legs.

"Do it," she whispered.

Brayden shook his head.

"I share you with no one."

He rubbed a thumb over her nipple, and it hardened. Lifting her top, he took it in his mouth and flicked it with his tongue. "As much as I want to."

Willow gripped his cock.

"God..."

She unzipped his jeans, and knowing he would be commando, reached in.

"Fuck."

Taking advantage of his surprise, she slipped out of his arm and climbed down his body to take his hard shaft in her mouth.

Holding the base of it, she opened his top button to gain better access.

"Willow, fuck, baby."

Taking him into her mouth, she slowly eased him to the back of her throat. In and out. In and out. Teasing his cock with her tongue.

He threw his head back and clenched the sheets. She let him fall out of her mouth, and she slapped him on her lips. Back in he went, and this time, she sucked harder, wishing he were inside her.

A hand grabbed her hair and tugged.

"Deeper, baby," he said quietly, but they both knew it was useless. Everyone could hear them. Gliding him in and out of her wet mouth, Willow felt him grow bigger, getting close. "Put your fingers in your pussy for me, baby."

Heat flushed through her veins, roaring her body to life. She reached down, slipping her hand under her panties and feeling her wetness. Further she went until two fingers were inserted. She groaned.

"Yes. Yes, God, that," he cried as quietly as he could. "Now, let me taste you."

Brayden all but ripped her arm up to his mouth and sucked her fingers hard. "Fuck, yes, fuck." One hand in her hair, he pushed his cock into her mouth, forcing her to take him deeper as he sucked on her fingers coated in her wetness.

He came hard and fast while she swallowed deep. When he was spent, he pulled her up his body, swiftly ripping off her panties and spreading her over his open jeans.

"Sit down on my cock, Willow." He was hard again. It no longer surprised her. He lifted her and placed her on his cock.

"Mphhm," she let out, trying to muffle her cries into his chest.

"That's it, oh God." He groaned. "Ride me."

Again doing all the work, he gripped her hips and moved her up and down his cock. The denim from his jeans rubbed harshly on her bottom, but she didn't care.

"Come. Now," he instructed, and her body obeyed.

"FuckfuckBraydenohfuck."

"Yeah, baby, milk my cock dry, that's it. Oh God." He came again, grabbing her head and slamming his lips against hers.

Together, they collapsed and lay panting. She could feel his heart under her chest and enjoyed just listening to it beat.

Finally, she raised her head and said, "Good talk."

He smirked.

CHAPTER FORTY

Brayden was aware Willow had used sex as a distraction from the heavy conversation. And hell, he wasn't complaining. He would give her whatever she wanted in whatever order and time she required.

Goddamn his fucking brother and Kate for ambushing them. Sure, he realized they were trying to help, but Brayden was trying to manage her exposure to information—shocking information—in a way that stopped her from wanting to bolt.

They had no idea how delicate this situation was. Perhaps if they'd seen her meltdown the day before they would understand. He didn't know whether she was now in total denial, the beginnings of acceptance, or overwhelmed.

As he watched her re-dress and give him a sexy smile, he really hoped it was acceptance. "Do you want to talk some more before we go back out?"

She shook her head and sat down on the edge of the bed to put her shoes on.

"Wil." He sat up and kissed her neck. She immediately leaned into him. So reactive and sexy.

"Yeah?" She turned and her lips found his again, soft, moist, and welcoming.

"We go at your pace, okay? I'll manage my family."

She nodded.

He put his cock back into his pants, splashed water on his face, then opened the door, Willow ducking under his arm. Three, two, one...

"Nice chat?"

Seriously, was I this cruel to you when you mated Kate?

You have got to be joking, right?

Yeah, he probably was.

Okay, but she wasn't human, so ease up.

Suck it up, buttercup.

He coughed, surprised by the enjoyment Vincent was getting from his angst.

By the way, I wiped Sera's and Carlos's memories of your conversation. You went too far with information about our blood.

Yeah, I know, but I had to give Willow some reassurance. Hopefully, she'll be a Moretti soon and it won't be a problem.

I hope so too.

"So, tell me about your transition. Was it painful?" Willow asked Seraphina, who nodded.

"I won't lie; it was long and painful. I didn't know what was happening, so I felt like I was fighting for my life."

He watched Willow frown. "You didn't tell her?" she asked Carlos, who shook his head.

"Not many vampires do. The common perception is, it's easier to convert and then apologize." The vampire gazed at his mate. "It took a while for her to forgive me, and I'll never know whether it was the wrong or right thing to do, but I couldn't live without her."

"And you forgave him?"

"Eventually. There is a lot of grief in leaving behind your humanity, your human life, and your friends," she said. "However, it becomes hard to fake it after a short time. All the lies you have to make up when you can only see people at night are a really small example."

She reached over and took Carlos's hand, then looked back at Willow.

"Your mate is your life. Brayden wasn't joking when he said you can't live without them. I know now I would never have loved again."

"Is it true? Could I never love another man? Ever?"

The growl came out of nowhere, along with the fangs. Then all hell broke loose.

"Ah, shit. Willow," the king said, standing up and reaching for her.

"Step away from my mate!" he growled, fangs on full display.

Kate stood up and collected her jacket. "Okay, folks, to the back of the plane. NOW!"

Brayden watched the four of them retreat, shepherded by the queen, while Willow moved as far away from him as she could in her seat, looking terrified.

He wasn't surprised they'd all gotten the fuck out of there. There was nothing more dangerous than a mated male triggered.

"Brayden," Willow said, fear thick in her voice.

Fuck.

He needed to get a handle on things.

Hearing Willow ask if she could love another man had tripped him up. That she could want it ripped at his heart and made him furious. Not at her. At the imaginary man.

God, he was so on edge. Was she in danger around him?

No. Fuck that. He forced his fangs to retract and stood to get some space. He began to pace. "I'll never hurt you, Willow. Fuck me. I'm sorry!"

She tucked her legs up and wrapped her arms around them. If she began to rock, he was going to punch himself in the face.

"You looked like you were."

He dropped to his knees, taking hers in his hands. "Just don't fucking talk about being with another man."

Willow dropped her face to her knees.

"Baby. Listen. What if I told you I had a girlfriend back home?"

He was playing with fire here. There was a whole raft of females who would be upset back home, and vampire females were not shy or bashful; they'd make their disappointment known loudly, so planting this seed could backfire on him. Yet, he needed to make his point so she understood his reaction.

It occurred to him her possessiveness had yet to be tested. Her head whipped up and she glared at him.

"Do you?"

"How would you feel if I did?"

"*DO* you?"

He shook his head. "Answer the question."

"I'd be furious. DO. YOU?"

He sat back on his heels and took a breath. "Yes. And no. I've had many women in my bed over the years. Some recently. None since the moment I met you."

Anger pooled in Willow's eyes as her mouth became taut. "When were you going to tell me, Brayden? Or were you going to invite them into our bed?" she seethed.

"In the past, I would have done so. I held many orgies."

Her feet dropped to the floor. "Are you fucking kidding me right now?" She pushed against his shoulder. He smiled. "You think this is funny?"

He grinned.

"What is so fucking funny? You fucking other women?"

Brayden stood and sat back in his seat. He turned and

pulled an angry Willow into his arms. "No, baby, I will never, ever, ever touch another female again in my life. Nor do I want you to be with another man. But please, do me a favor and don't ask if you can love another man. Fuck, Willow, I nearly punched a hole in the side of this goddamn plane."

She began to relax slowly, then eventually melted into his arms. "This is so friggin' hard."

She wasn't wrong.

A few hours later, they landed. Sera and Willow had sat talking while he and Vincent caught up on royal business. They had promised to catch up while she was staying at the castle.

"We'll leave you to settle in and see you for breakfast tomorrow eve." Kate gave Willow a peck on the cheek, and Brayden watched carefully as his mate allowed it, comfortable.

They were making progress.

He led her to his vehicle. The black Lexus LS 500 had been parked at the airfield for months while they were on the West Coast.

"Nice wheels."

He opened the door and she climbed in. It was so good having her in his life. They drove the forty minutes to the property, and as they neared, he felt it was time to prepare her.

"Willow, like any royal family, I've told you we live in a castle."

"Sure, that makes sense."

"Have you ever seen a castle?"

She shook her head. "I didn't know we had them in the United States."

He pulled up to a set of big gates, the system recognizing his vehicle and scanning his face. They began to open.

"No. Officially, we don't. Although"—he glanced at her—"you probably know there's one in Hawaii."

She grinned. "Yes, I've been. It's a palace, not a castle, but details, details."

Brayden wound down the long and winding driveway. "Well, unofficially, we do, and you are about to see it. Prepare yourself."

Willow laughed. "I think I will be fine—whoa. Holy mother...Jesus, what on...you live here?"

Yeah, that. Brayden listened to an abundance of expletives and shock pour out as he drove past the enormous gray castle set on seven acres of land. He followed the road through another set of gates, past the west wing, and then parked in his private garage. He currently had six vehicles and one motorcycle—a Ducati Testa Stretta.

Brayden turned to face the only human to ever set foot on their property. "Welcome to Moretti Castle."

She gulped slowly.

They entered the castle through an internal lift which took them directly to his wing. The west wing belonged to him. Kate and Vincent were in the south of the castle.

The doors opened into a huge alcove filled with luxurious rugs and furniture. Above them, a balustrade formed a semicircle accessible from the sweeping staircase nearby. The walls were white stone, with glass doors and windows treated with a protective surface. Outside, it was still dark, the lawn lit up with little lights, and thick trees beyond for as far as you could see.

Downstairs, there was a large sitting room, a kitchen—even though there was a main kitchen with chefs in the castle who created meals for them—a dining room, library, and bar.

Willow silently took it all in as she followed him

upstairs. There were four bedrooms, each with its own bathroom, to the right, but Brayden took her hand and led her to the left.

He opened the door to the master suite.

"Oh!"

The room was enormous. The size of half a normal house. In the middle was an enormous four-poster bed with white draped fabric. He'd had his staff change it from the red when he knew Willow was coming home with him.

"This is gorgeous."

Classic antique furniture in rich woods were scattered around, and paintings hung on the walls. A set of beige sofas sat off in one corner with a small table. On one wall was a large fireplace with a plush wool mat in front just waiting for him to make love to Willow on.

Two double French doors opened out to a balcony where fairy lights blinked and sparkled. In the master bathroom, there was a large hot tub, an enormous open shower with over ten different jets, and a double vanity. One wall was completely made of mirrors.

He opened a door.

"Are those my bags?"

"Yes. I asked them not to unpack."

The wardrobe was spacious, allowing for three walls of racks which were half filled with his clothing and shoes. In the middle of the room was a velvet-lined antique seat with enough space to fit four people.

"Well, I could do with a sweater. It's much cooler here."

Brayden lifted her suitcase onto the seat and opened it for her.

"Brayden, this is...I mean, I knew you were a royal family, but I'll be honest, I thought it was more of a token gesture. This place rivals the English royals."

He laughed.

"Actually, Windsor Castle is the largest in the world. Our Moretti castle in England is larger and much older than this one."

"You have two castles?" she asked, her mouth gaping.

They had more than two.

"We have property all around the world. I was telling the truth when I said it was our business. Or at least, we own a lot of property."

She nodded slowly then stepped into the bedroom.

"It's incredible. Can we do a tour?"

Excitement shimmered in her eyes. Despite the fact that she was shacked up with vampires, her cheeks had a pinch of pink.

He nodded. "Tomorrow. The sun is rising, and we should sleep."

As if on cue, the sun popped its nose above the horizon, adding an orange glow across the sky. "Close blinds," he instructed, and the automatic blinds obeyed.

"Fancy," she said and sighed. "I cannot imagine life without the sunshine."

He pulled off his jacket and joined her on the end of the bed. "I know there will be sacrifices, Willow. These are the decisions you'll need to make." He shifted her up the bed and placed his forearms on either side of her head. "For now, let me show you one of the benefits."

Her pretty eyes dilated as she stared up at him. "I think I'm familiar with this one."

He made fast work of removing her clothing, lifting her arms to the bed frame and tying them with a silk scarf.

"Bray?"

He hadn't tied her up before. She knew he was a dominant lover, and God, he needed this with her right now. "Spread your legs, Willow."

Undressing, he ran his eyes over her gorgeous body now spread out before him. Her brown locks flowed over his white linen while her body began to wriggle with need.

He stroked his erection eagerly. It had been too long since he'd felt the control over her body he desired. With all that had happened, the need was powerful. An addiction.

While she may never admit it, he felt her need for his dominance in return.

"I'm not sure..."

"Wider, Willow. Let me see the pink of your core."

Coyly she spread her legs a little. He took another silk tie and wrapped it around one of her ankles.

"Oh, God," she whimpered, making him even harder.

After tying the second leg, she was fully open. The view of his mate so vulnerable and ready for him to do as he pleased, hell, it made his cock so hard he was dripping in precum. He ran a hand over his mouth. God. He could plunge into her right now.

"Touch me, please." Willow moaned, her need growing, her pupils flaring with desire.

Brayden ran his fingers across her soft abdomen and down through her freshly waxed pink pussy. He flicked her clit, and passion roared within him as her body responded. Moaning, Willow twisted within the restraints of the silk.

Kneeling on the bed, Brayden took a pink nipple in his mouth and sucked—hard—creating just the right amount of pain. The little cry that escaped her lips had his erection twitching.

Lifting her head, he directed his cock toward her mouth. "Just the end, Willow, no more."

She opened her red lips and he pushed in. Obeying

him, she took the tip of his cock, licking and sucking him. Soon she was stretching for more, and he tsked at her.

"Be a good girl. If you take it all, you'll be punished." God, he wanted her to take it all. He was punishing them both.

She muttered something incoherent, then thrust forward. He hit the back of her throat, and as she gagged, he groaned loudly. Working him skillfully with her mouth, Brayden fought for control. It would be so easy to cum.

He took two clips from the bedside cabinet and placed them on her nipples. She arched, opening her mouth with him still inside, and let out a delicious cry. Pulling out, he stroked himself, up and down, then slapped her lips with his cock.

"My bad girl, you are oh so fucking good."

Making his way down her body, he flicked the nipple clips and enjoyed the way her body arched some more. He had to remember to be careful with his mortal. She knew he was a vampire, but he still couldn't bite her. Doing so would trigger her change, and she had yet to decide. He couldn't let his need to dominate and please her take the choice away. No matter how much he wanted to dig his fangs and cock into her simultaneously.

He ran his fingers through her drenched pussy, spreading her wide and licking every inch of her as if he were starving. Colorful groans drove him further, his tongue pushing in. He pressed two fingers inside, salivating at the way her body gripped him.

"More, more...I need...!" she cried out.

He retrieved a dildo from under a pillow and turning it on, he ran it over her pelvic bone and thighs, teasing.

Yeah, he had all the toys; he had the whole setup.

He'd never claimed to be a virgin, and Willow would learn he'd had a lot of lovers over the many years of his life. She wouldn't like it, he knew. She would, however, learn to love his skills.

"I'm going to fuck you with this toy, baby. Then watch you come. Relax for me now."

He needed full and total control. He needed to possess her. Completely. Releasing the silk ties with speed, he flipped her over, her soft, round bottom now in the air. With his thigh, he pushed her legs wide apart. Moisture glistened, inviting him to take what was his.

Face buried in the pillows, she mumbled and pushed out her ass. Wet, swollen, and ready, he ran the fat round tip over her folds and began to push in. He was torturing himself as he filled her with the sexual device.

Reaching, he rubbed her clit, salivating as she panted and groaned. He pushed in further. "Take it all, Willow. That's it, oh shit, good girl."

He began to stroke himself again. Up and down, up and down, watching the toy go deeper and deeper into his mate. His erection was begging to be inside her. Deep now, he increased the vibration and fucked her gently, then faster, faster, changing angles to increase her pleasure.

His cock took over. Burning with desire, he could wait no longer. Would she allow him complete control of her body as she had before she knew what he was? Before she knew he was a vampire? Spreading her juices across her rear with his head, he nudged her puck. Willow let out a gasp.

"You'll let me in," he instructed. "That's a girl. Oh God, fuck, yes."

He pushed in gently, the dildo continuing to fuck her pussy. Holding her around the waist, he lifted her upper body against his chest.

"Bray, oh fuck," she cried.

He wasn't going to last. The glorious and addictive dominance sent pleasure roaring through his body.

Plunge, plunge.

"Willow, tug on your nipple clips."

"I...I'm going to—"

"Do as I tell you. Now," he growled into her hair.

She gripped her breasts and twisted the little clips, howling as the desire took her over the edge. Her muscles clenched tightly around his cock.

Yes! Ecstasy overtook him. He had to be inside her core. He pulled out, removed the vibrator, and tossed it onto the bed. Then finally, he was inside her.

"Bray, shit."

"Keep coming, Willow. Come on my cock."

As her muscle contractions continued to milk his cock, he pumped in hard and deep, roaring as his orgasm joined hers. Pleasure flashed through every inch of his body, and they collapsed on the bed.

He wasn't done.

CHAPTER FORTY-ONE

Stars filled Willow's eyes as she lay panting. Brayden was draped over her back, his strong, talented hand running across her thigh. He pulled it back and draped it over his own large leg.

"I need more of you, baby."

She could barely talk, so instead, she let out a muffled moan and arched her back, giving him her answer.

Things were so confusing in her world right now. But this, right here, with Brayden—the way he dominated her—she felt safe, loved, and protected.

She needed it.

He shifted, propping himself against the pillows, and lifted her onto him. Lying along his body, he whispered into her hair with that husky, sexy voice of his.

"Relax, I'm going to pleasure you some more."

He nudged her legs to fall apart at his waist and guided his erection inside. Together they sighed.

"You feel so amazing."

"Do I fill you up?"

Did he ever. "Yes, so perfect."

He moved rhythmically, kissing her neck, his hands gripping her breasts, needing them. One hand reached down to rub her clit, and immediately, she was on the edge.

"OhGodohGod."

She tried to arch but his thick arms were holding her

body as he pleasured her. Beneath her, she felt the solid strength of him, and her pants turned ragged.

"Your body fits with mine so perfect, *mi amore.*"

"More, Bray, harder."

He raised his hips and sped up. Thrust, thrust.

She fought for control, but was completely at his mercy in this position. Just as he liked it. Just as she liked it.

"Patience, my little sex kitten."

She had none; she needed release. Her muscles clenched around his cock and he hissed.

"Willow, fuck."

He sat, pulling her legs into a sitting position, and thrust deeper. His strong arms wrapped around her, and he pumped. Again and again.

"Yes!"

"Gods." The deep growl in her hair.

Their orgasms struck together as he controlled the movement of both their bodies. Clutching his thighs, stars filled her eyes as her cries joined his.

After they'd cleaned up, she lay in Brayden's arms feeling surprisingly content, given she was inside a vampire castle. She knew he would never hurt her. The more information she gathered, the more empowered she was to decide.

Did she want to become a vampire? No.

Living forever had never been a desire of hers, so the opportunity to become immortal wasn't as appealing for her as it might be for others. She knew some people hunted for the fountain of life. Not her. She didn't *want* to lose her humanity. She loved being human. Still, she couldn't remain human and be with Brayden.

Life without Brayden?

That was a strong *no* also. Sure, she'd only known him for just a over a week, but this was how deep her feelings went. A glimpse at his life over the past few days, and it was clear there would be a huge adjustment to her life. He was a freaking prince! And a vampire. She sure knew how to pick 'em.

And he wasn't a prince just in name; he lived in a ginormous castle with hundreds of staff who bowed. Jesus.

"Your mind is making whirring sounds." He ran a lazy hand down her back and across her bottom.

"Just processing. Everything."

A kiss landed on her forehead. "Sleep, Willow. Tomorrow I'll show you around the castle where you'll learn more about my life. What could be our life."

She sat up and stared down at him.

"I thought I was ready for all of this, but I'm not sure."

He drew her face to his lips and gently kissed her. "It's not going to be easy, sweetheart. Just take it minute by minute." He narrowed his eyes, a slight tilt to his lips. "Did I not tire my female enough?"

She flopped her head back on his chest. "No. I'm so unsatisfied. Poor me."

She felt his chest shake in silent laughter, and a grin hit her lips.

They woke up many hours later, the sun dipping low in the sky.

Willow stood by the large window staring out across the castle grounds. While it was vast and she could see from her view all the people bustling around, there was a peaceful feel about Castle Moretti.

Despite being full of vampires who would probably love to bite her. She shivered.

"You ready?"

She turned and her heart missed a beat.

"Willow?" He stood in the doorway, hand frozen in the act of doing up his watch, a look of concern on his face. She knew now he could hear her heart rate, so any time it beat faster, he became a mother hen. Or rather, her protective rooster.

"What's wrong?"

She grinned and shook her head. Some days he was so naive. Today, he had on tight black jeans which hugged his thick thighs and long legs. He'd chosen a navy-blue, long-sleeved cotton top which clung to his six pack. Hair, still a little wet from their shower, curled around his ears.

He was freshly shaven, and had grinned when she had insisted she put moisturizer on him. Afterward, he had suddenly lifted her off her feet and kissed her forcefully.

"Just reminding you I'm a powerful vampire despite letting you do that," he had said in a deep, exaggerated voice.

She had been breathless as he grinned, placed her back on the floor, and walked away looking incredibly pleased with himself. He had no need to prove anything. Brayden was all alpha. Dominant, tall, broad, and gorgeous. Every woman's desire.

And he was hers. He was also a vampire. So not exactly perfect.

"Nothing's wrong," she said, coming back to the present moment. "Just...I'm just admiring the scenery."

He smirked. "Let us go on our tour."

They walked around the castle for what felt like hours, where she was introduced to dozens of castle citizens and staff. They treated her like royalty, which had been the greatest surprise. Many of them curtsied, and when she had glanced at Brayden, he'd simply given a little nod indicating it was right and proper.

She'd rather they curtsy than bite her, so she let it go.

"This is the center of our security," Brayden said, swiping his finger across a security panel. He glanced at her before pushing inside.

"Lance"—he placed a hand on Willow's hip—"set Willow up with access."

All four of his team were seated around the room at various desks.

"Yes, sir. Welcome home, my lord." He then smiled at her. "And welcome, pr—ah, Willow."

What was he going to say? "Hi, Lance."

She recalled the night out in Los Angeles where Lance had left with two of Brianna's friends. He was a good-looking guy and seemed to have charmed the pants off them.

Probably literally.

"Come around here." He indicated to a device on the desk. Brayden then introduced her to Tom, Kurt, and Marcus.

"So, you're the one distracting our prince, huh," Marcus teased. Brayden stood protectively close, as he had from the moment they'd met. Right now, she appreciated it more than ever. These men were large, dangerous looking, and downright gorgeous. All of them were over six foot three with wide shoulders.

"These are my senior lieutenants. If you ever need to, you can trust them with your life. They report to Craig—"

"Did I hear my name?" The powerful vampire barged into the room and gave her a wink.

"Hey, Craig." She'd met him enough times now to feel some semblance of comfort, though she doubted she ever would feel completely comfortable. He had a powerful and dangerous vibe like the rest of them, but there was something else too. A darkness. An edge.

Think bad boy on steroids. His good looks likely melted panties, and she really hoped a pair of them hadn't been Brianna's.

Unless it had been really damn good, and just the one time. Heck, everyone deserved a good old-fashioned one-night stand at least once in their life.

"Welcome to the castle." Craig sat at his desk and leaned back. "Regan is secured; I've got two discrete guards on the job. Now we wait."

Kurt crossed his arms. "I don't think we should just wait."

Lance directed Willow's finger across the scanner while she listened to the conversation around her.

"We need to keep this contained. We've sent a crew to Italy, but it could be a long game. Let's see what happens at the ball," Craig said firmly.

Willow glanced at Brayden, who appeared to be more interested in her finger than the discussion. She wasn't fooled, though.

"He's received no more correspondence, which raises some questions," Marcus continued.

Bray looked up. "None?"

Marcus shook his head. Craig shrugged. "He said communication was sporadic. I don't think it means anything."

Back to watching the scanning of her finger. When they were done, he pulled her into his side.

"Next forty-eight hours, my priority is getting Willow settled into the castle," he said. "Brief the LCs. They need to know what's going on. It goes no further than that tier."

Craig frowned. "We're not telling them about Regan."

"No." He shook his head in agreement. "They just need to know there's a potential coup at play here. I want the hall and the grounds prepared for it. Our guests arrive in a week." Brayden gazed down at her, looking serious. "Let's not make the mistake of assuming it won't happen until then."

Tom coughed. "What do we tell the officers?"

Craig answered, "Increased rebel activity and the prince's mate is in residence."

"That'll do it," Tom agreed.

"He's right," Brayden said, directing Willow to the door. "Use Willow's presence here as the reason. Tell them the new princess is here."

What?

Wait, what?

The door closed on Craig's muttered, *"Fuck me."*

Brayden gently pushed her frozen-in-place body along the corridor. "Keep walking, beautiful. I'll explain. Close your mouth; you'll catch flies."

She looked at his grinning face and nearly tripped over her feet.

"Do I need to carry you?"

She straightened and stuck out her chin. "I don't know, do princesses normally get carried around by princes?"

He let out a laugh. "Probably. Let's do it and see if anyone says anything."

Next minute, she was scooped up in his arms and squealing. By the look of the mile-wide smile plastered on his face, he was having far too much fun to let her down, so she didn't bother asking. She knew he was too stubborn anyway. Fortunately, there was no one in sight, so she just laughed at him.

They pushed through a pair of double doors which led into an open courtyard with a glass dome overhead. Stars sprinkled across the sky beside a stunning full moon. Around them were dozens of trees and stretches of bright green grass. Bench seats were placed at random spots along a cobbled path.

The inside park was filled with dozens of vampires. It looked like an everyday scene, except for one thing: they were all exceedingly beautiful and healthy looking.

In hindsight, she hadn't yet met an average-looking vampire.

"Put me down, silly."

He did. "We can use this area day and night. Like all the glass in the castle, the dome is coated in our protective treatment."

So she could live here as a human and just change her body clock. As usual, he read her mind.

"No, Willow. To protect the existence of our race, and for your safety, you need to turn."

She pouted. "You'll protect me."

He shook his head, dragging her along the path. "I can't be with you always. You'll be a member of the royal family, exposed to dangerous vampires."

"A real princess?"

He smiled. "Yes. *My* princess."

Shit. So. It was really a thing. No wonder people were curtsying.

"Vincent was telling the truth when he said the longer we wait, the more dangerous it is. But I'm not leaving your side for now, so don't worry. No one will harm you."

She stepped a little closer to him, and he squeezed her hand. How many people would want to harm her? Exactly how serious was this threat? As a vampire, how would she be expected to protect herself? She had so many questions.

"What if someone tries and you can't protect me?" A reasonable question.

Apparently not. Brayden nearly broke her hand with

his squeeze. "Let's talk in here."

Through two huge floor-to-ceiling length doors they went, and into what was very obviously the throne room. It was empty of people but not of decor. Two beautiful thrones made of wood and covered in black, white, and red material sat at the end of the room on a raised dais, with the Moretti crest on top of each and in multiple spots around the room.

Rows of chairs lined the side of the room on top of dark red carpet. In the middle was a large table which appeared to break down into smaller sections.

Brayden closed the doors and turned. He looked around the room and stood listening.

"This room is soundproofed. We can speak in private." He led her over to a big window where they looked out toward the water in the far distance.

"I didn't mean to offend you," she offered.

Turning, he took her face in his hand. "I meant it when I said no one could hurt you. One day I will explain in detail if you choose to become a vampire, but I need you to feel safe."

"I do. I just need to understand the dangers. I know you want to protect me, but if someone—"

"Willow, please. Listen," he said, gripping her chin a little tighter. "Vincent and I are two of the strongest vampires in existence."

Oh.

"Craig is a close third."

She believed him. Nodding, she said, "Okay."

"There is much for you to learn. The dangers, the relationship between the king and I, our history." He looked over to the thrones.

Oh. Did he want to be king?

"We were in LA because the king was being poisoned."

What?

"Oh my God—wait, I thought you couldn't die like a mortal?"

"We can't. His illness was extremely confusing for the small group who knew. A few days ago, we found the traitor; however, it's part of a larger coup."

Great, so she was in a castle full of vampires who were at risk of a coup taking place. One with other dangerous vampires.

Things were just getting better.

"This is why you must decide soon, and if the answer is no, I will take you to the new house in Hawaii. With your memories wiped."

Willow imagined her life in Hawaii. Sun, sand, and aloha vibes. The tropical lifestyle was one she had dreamed of. Yet, she wouldn't have Brayden.

"I think it's dangerous being here."

He nodded. "It is."

"I know you think you're powerful, Bray."

He smiled. A dark, dangerous smile. "I don't think anything, sweetheart. I am *THE* most powerful vampire."

She sucked in a small gasp. Brayden wasn't a show-off. For him to say something like that, she knew it had to be fact. Or at least, for him to strongly believe it.

"Willow. Never repeat those words, do you understand? Especially not to or in front of the king. He must appear as the most dominant alpha of our race," he warned.

She nodded.

"Your safety and protection are, and will forever be, my priority." He turned to look out the window. "So you needed to know."

Willow leaned her head on his arm. "Thank you for trusting me with the knowledge."

Brayden would still wipe her memory if she left, but she liked that he had shared such an important piece of information with her.

His arm went around her.

"I will do anything for you, Willow. Anything. Which makes me vulnerable, especially while you're human. I know you need this time, but please know that every day you wait increases the risk."

During this dangerous time, Brayden was putting the royal family in a tenuous position by being so vulnerable and distracted.

"I'm surprised Vincent is okay with this."

"He's not," he replied, giving her a small laugh. "You've seen his mood."

Oh.

"Still. Why take the risk?"

"Because you're my mate. You're the mate of a prince. Should you choose me, you and I will continue the Moretti line." He wrapped his arms around her and planted a kiss on the forehead.

"But the king..."

"So far they haven't produced an heir; we don't really speak of it. It's complicated for vampires, and a lot for you to take in on day one. Let's get something to eat. A meal has been prepared for us."

Willow followed her vampire prince, and mentally made a note to continue asking about that important topic.

If she were to become a vampire, she needed to know if she could become a mother. That seemed important.

So many questions remained unanswered. So many questions she had yet to learn that needed answering.

CHAPTER FORTY-TWO

The next evening, Craig stood in front of his pinboard full of Post-it notes, photos, and string with his arms crossed, one hand tapping his chin. Contemplating.

When would the fuckers strike?

The prince was right. It could happen at any time. He'd kicked himself for assuming it would be at the royal ball.

Or had Regan purposely given them that impression? He still didn't trust the guy, no matter his story. Sure, yeah, they had his mate and daughter, which sucked, but it didn't mean the old vampire was telling the entire truth. Craig may not be a mated vamp, but he'd seen enough to know loyalty always sat with the one you loved. Even the royal family, he suspected, would choose their mate if pushed. Though that was not something he would say out loud—he wasn't fucking stupid.

It was why he'd gone to the king and spoken to him about Brayden. The prince had looked out of his mind that day. He still looked on edge, leaving him worried that his long-time friend was going to make a particularly bad decision.

He had never questioned Brayden's loyalty to the race or to his family. But the day the prince had asked him to purchase the house in Hawaii, the powerful vampire's eyes had been drunk with pain. It still gave him chills. Brayden would be an extremely dangerous vampire if allowed to go rogue. He knew from experience. Craig had once been on the edge—very fucking close—something only the prince knew.

He sat down at his desk and sighed. They were living in dangerous times, more dangerous than they realized. It's not like anyone could have guessed the king was being poisoned. Goddamn! No one even knew it was possible.

It was clear they were on the brink of a coup by their greatest enemy. An enemy who now likely had a lot more knowledge of the royal family than ever before.

Regan was a piece of shit. He'd never trusted him, something that hadn't sat well with Vincent and Brayden over the years. He didn't give a fuck. He was the commander, not the diplomatic relations fucking officer. Regan should have fronted from the beginning. They could have found and evac'd his females; the old vampire knew the superior skills held by Brayden and Craig.

Love. It fucked with males' brains. He was better off without it in his life.

And now they were in a damn mess. At least the king appeared to be recovering quickly and they were back inside the castle. Yet with Brayden—the most powerful vampire on the goddamn planet—distracted by his mate and standing on the edge of darkness, Craig was more nervous than he'd ever felt. If Brayden lost Willow, they would have a much greater threat to deal with.

He heard footsteps. Psychic motherfucker.

"Craig."

"What's up?"

The barely muttered greetings were one of familiarity. Both warriors, they didn't bother with fake smiles and bullshit. He tapped the marker pen on the pad in front of him as Brayden leaned against the windowsill, crossing his arms. He stared at the floor for a long while.

"I want you to stop."

Watching me was what he didn't say. Of course Craig was watching him. His every fucking move. He didn't want to lose the male, and he'd save him if it started happening, just as the prince had done for him.

"No."

"I'm not going to snap."

He dropped the pen on the desk. "Bullshit."

Brayden looked up and shoved his hands in his jeans pockets. There was nothing passive about his movements. They were lethal and threatening.

To anyone other than him.

Probably.

"Brayden, if she chooses Hawaii—"

"She won't!" His fangs extended, face darkening.

Craig shook his head, stood, and turned to face the board on his left again. "Whatever. I'm preparing for the possibility," he said. "You have to know if you go over the edge, I'll have to kill you."

Brayden smirked, but there was no joy in it. "You could try, my friend."

"Then don't fucking make me." He glared at the male who had saved him from the brink once upon a time.

"It's not me you have to convince. My fate lies in the hands of one spectacularly gorgeous would-be princess," Brayden pointed angrily.

"That's bullshit and you know it. You're the strongest vampire alive—in mind and body!"

Brayden snarled at him. "So you think she *will* leave?"

"I don't know. My job is to protect this kingdom. The king. You."

"I don't need saving." Brayden pointed at the board. "Keep your mind on the job and off me."

Craig shook his head. "You are the job, my prince. Whether you can see it or not, right now, you're a very real and potential threat."

Brayden stared at him with darkness swirling in his eyes. "It won't come to that."

He hoped not. If it happened, it would be up to Craig, and Craig alone, to track and destroy the prince. In the process, it might just destroy them both.

Running footsteps. They both turned to the door as it flew open.

"Regan has received a call," Marcus said, panting. "They want to meet in two hours."

Brayden planted his hands low on his hips. "Where?"

"The bar at the Dunegrass Golf Club."

"Get a team. I want every word and visual streamed to me in real time," Brayden instructed.

Craig nodded. "Roger that. Meeting in five. Go round up the others. Bring two of your best LCs."

"Yes, sir." Marcus disappeared.

Brayden began walking toward the door.

"Focus on your mate. I'll alert you immediately if there is an issue." He looked his friend dead in the eye. "You saved me once. Let me have your back now."

Brayden frowned, then nodded and left.

CHAPTER FORTY-THREE

Willow glanced around the enormous, opulent room and took another sip of her iced tea.

Tea with the queen. Not a place she'd ever expected to find herself in. Certainly not in America, and not with a queen this exquisitely beautiful. No offense to the other more widely known human queens, but Kate simply radiated elegance.

Brayden had left her with the three vampire ladies— *females?*— to take care of something, and she was doing her best to relax. How was a human to do so surrounded by vampires, no matter how friendly and beautiful they were, Willow wasn't sure. Right now, her *relaxed* anxiety levels were about a ten.

Ten hundred.

"Before your dashing male returns, do you have any other questions?" Seraphina asked.

She had a lot, none of which she really wanted answers to. Not really. Willow just wanted this to all go away.

While keeping Brayden.

"How strong are you?" she suddenly spat out as Kate choked on her tea and attempted to wipe her mouth with a napkin, covering it up.

"Oh." Seraphina laughed. "I wasn't expecting that, but it's a good question. One that if I'd been given the opportunity may have asked myself."

She hadn't been. Like many vampires, her mate had

forced the change upon her, and asked for forgiveness later. She was grateful to Brayden for this time to decide for herself. Mostly. In some ways, it would be easier to be angry at him then find forgiveness. She knew why he hadn't. Watching his mother harbor resentment and regret for so many years, he'd promised he would never do it to his own mate if she was human. Unfortunately for him, it turned out she was.

"Yes, I have so many questions it's driving me a little bit crazy, I'm afraid."

"Would...no, never mind," the queen began.

She knew what her question was. Willow shook her head. "No. He's done the right thing. It would have damaged our relationship if he'd taken the choice from me." She glanced at Seraphina, who had been turned a few hundred years ago. "No offense meant. Modern women are far more independent. I would be far less inclined to forgive something like that."

Seraphina tipped her head. "I do believe you are right."

The queen added her nod to show agreement.

"Well, the answer is that we're extraordinarily strong. Let me see. I could lift a vehicle, should I wish to. Not that I can think of any reason to do that, mind you."

Willow's eyes widened. "That strong?"

They both nodded.

"And males are by far stronger than females, but even then, it varies from vampire to vampire."

"Katrina was also human. She helped me through my transition. I'm not sure I could have done it without her."

The other female smiled. "Not true. After the shock subsided, you adjusted quickly. Half the battle is saying goodbye to your humanity." She glanced at Willow. "My mate allowed me the choice, so I understand what you are going through."

Oh. "He did?" She nodded and Willow got excited. "What did...well, obviously you chose him." Her brain scrambled with questions.

"Ask anything you like, Willow. I truly feel for you, and am honored to be able to help our future princess."

She glanced at Kate, who returned a kind smile. "It's all so much. Vampires, my God. No offense." They all shrugged. "A royal family. I could be a princess!"

She put her tea down.

"But first I must let him kill me. I mean, I don't know where to start!" It all came flooding out of her. "How did you decide to go through with it?"

They all looked at her with such pity she wanted to scream and cry at the same time.

"I didn't."

Willow halted. *What?* "But you just said...?"

Katrina shook her head. "I was terrified, just as you are now," she started. "It's hard to remember exactly, it was a long time ago, but I do remember the fear. It's not natural to choose to end your life, Willow. Please don't make yourself wrong for feeling the way you do."

She swallowed deeply, grateful this woman understood. "So, you left him?"

Katrina nodded. "I did. I packed a bag, stole a horse, and rode for days without stopping." She gazed out the window. "I was both fearing he would find me and hoping he would."

Willow felt the woman's words deep inside her. Every moment of every day, she felt this way. She wanted to be safely wrapped in Brayden's arms while fighting her instincts to run.

"Eventually I had to stop and replenish my food and water, and sleep." The faraway look in her eyes vanished as she turned to Willow. "There was something else I had been ignoring. A pain inside which grew and grew like someone had reached into my heart and was clawing and squeezing it."

Willow leaned back, aghast. "From the mating bond?"

When the woman nodded, she turned to Kate. "Would that happen to me? Even with my memories gone?"

The queen put her glass on the table and tucked her legs under her on the sofa. She looked thoughtful before giving an answer. "Yes, except you won't know why. You'll feel a loss and emptiness which won't make sense."

The queen brushed invisible lint off her dress. "Willow, you need to understand one more thing. Sera, Trina, can you leave us, please."

The two females stood and nodded, unfazed at the dismissal. Seraphina looked at her, then quickly leaned down to give her a hug.

"I hope you decide to remain with us."

"I have a feeling you'll choose your man. After all, the prince is the most desirable bachelor in all of the race." Katrina winked.

Yes, she'd noticed during the day all the shy glances, flirtatious flicks of hair, and how some of the females had tripped over themselves to speak to the prince—to Brayden. Shit, now she was calling him a prince. Too weird. She smiled at the retreating ladies.

"Brayden is on his way back, Willow. Before he does, I need to speak with you. This must remain between the two of us."

Willow swallowed and nodded.

"He is immensely powerful. Each of the brothers has their own strengths. Vincent is a leader, an alpha in his own right. He has a sharp mind with a natural ability to gain a following."

"A king he may be, but his vampires follow him out of choice. For the most part."

Kate waved her hand out in front of her all *that's by the by.*

"The prince, though, was born with a strength and dominance unmatched. He is the true alpha in the Moretti family. It's not discussed, nor is it an issue. Brayden is smart enough to know Vincent must appear to be the most powerful."

Brayden had shared as much with her, and she wondered if it was difficult for him.

"I can't see Brayden wanting the throne."

Kate smiled. "No, he definitely does not. Brayden has nearly as much power as the prince, and he is captain of the Royal Army. The brothers are remarkably close—despite their bickering."

Willow smiled. "I've noticed."

"The prince loves his family, and he loves me, his queen."

Willow had a sudden desire to punch the queen in the face. Brayden would not love another female.

Oh. Where had that come from?

The queen smiled. "Good. I am pleased I pushed your buttons."

Willow looked away, embarrassed.

"You need to understand that he is a loyal and dedicated brother and member of the royal family. And yet, Willow, should you walk away and choose your humanity over the prince, there is great risk for him and our race."

"What do you mean?" She frowned. They'd both be heartbroken for sure. She'd have no memories and a lifetime of emptiness, while Brayden would be left with his. It would be hard for him, she realized. He was a deeply loving and passionate male. But over time, he would heal, his memories would fade, and he'd take another lover.

She looked down and found her fists clenched. Her stomach turned at the thought of him with any of the females she'd met today.

"Do you think he would survive being left by the female he loves?"

She fish mouthed for a moment before nodding. "Yes, I do. Eventually."

Kate shook her head. "No. A predator such as Brayden with so much power loves just as intensely. I watched him deny you were his mate and then fight his love for you. He's known all along just how dangerous this is, and yet he remains committed to give you this time to make your decision."

"What are you saying?"

"There is every chance we could lose him should you leave. I'm not telling you this to manipulate your decision, simply to provide you with all the information."

"I don't agree. He's strong."

"His love for you is stronger."

"Which is why he's given me the choice."

"Yes, but he won't survive one of your choices. I have known the prince for over one hundred and thirty years. I've seen his light and dark side. He's balancing on the edge, awaiting your decision, Willow."

She stood and paced. "Giving up my life is a huge choice. I cannot feel responsible for any of this." Willow threw out her arms wide.

"Would you let the male you love slip into madness and destroy himself and potentially all of us?"

Willow stared at her horrified. "No! Of course not."

"Well," the queen said calmly, leaning back into her chair, "now you have all the information. I appreciate the complexity of the situation you find yourself in, but it's my role to protect this kingdom and family."

Willow glared at her.

"You will make a fine princess, and I also hope you'll choose Brayden and join us."

Willow returned to her chair and let out a big, frustrated sigh.

"Your mate is close. He'll pick up on your distress, so let's talk of something more cheerful," Kate indicated.

Willow sat up and chugged the rest of her tea down.

"Shall we have a dress made for you for the ball? You are far too petite to fit into mine. I think a pale blue or silver would be gorgeous on you."

The queen tapped on a device, and the screen on the wall displayed several gorgeous dresses. Heck, Willow wasn't dead yet. Who didn't love a beautiful ball gown?

"And a tiara! Oh yes, let's dig into the royal jewels. How fun."

She raised both eyebrows. "Really?"

"Yes! Oh, I hope you choose to remain, Willow. I would so love a princess to play with."

She couldn't help herself; she burst out laughing. Right on cue, Brayden stepped into the room, darkness swirling in his eyes.

The queen was right. She looked at her, and they shared a knowing look.

CHAPTER FORTY-FOUR

"The queen is lovely," Willow said as they walked back to his wing of the castle.

He nodded. "She is."

"Do you have much to do with her?"

Part of him cringed at the near miss with Kate when they were back in LA. He had to forget; they both did. He had greater concerns right now. Instead, he smiled down at his mate and took her hand.

"Yes, I've known her for a long time. She's my brother's mate; my queen."

Willow shrugged. "Sure, but it doesn't mean you know her well. You might not spend much leisure time with her."

He laughed. "I spend quite enough time with my family, trust me."

He held the door open for her and grinned when she placed her hands on his chest and snuck a kiss before she proceeded inside. The world was a brighter, lighter place with Willow Thompson-Davies in it. Soon, he hoped, she would become Willow Moretti.

Yes, he planned to put a damn ring on it. If she would let him. The thought of a big diamond sitting on her ring finger made his heart roar joyfully. God, he was up and down. One minute he was flying high in love with the female, the other he was dreading her decision.

Craig was right to be concerned. He'd been trying too hard to keep his head above the water to acknowledge it.

"Screens on. Mute."

Willow watched as the far wall came to life with images from the castle and a bar venue.

"My team is running interference on the traitor you heard us speak of earlier. It shouldn't take long, but I want to monitor it."

He sat down on the sofa, pulling her down onto his lap. The softness of her skin and dress was a contrast to the taut muscles in his arms and legs. She was the opposite of him in every way.

Running his hands over her hips and down her thighs, he began to feel the rightness returning; the one he only felt when he was touching her. She sighed into him, feeling it too. Her head turned and their lips met.

"My Willow."

"What is it like being a vampire?'

He wanted to smile at her naive question, but the love he felt for her right now was blowing up his chest. "What's it like being human?"

Honestly, he was expecting her to laugh and say touché or some such thing. She didn't. She tipped her head and said, "Precious."

He ran his fingers over her soft, full pink lips, contemplating her response. He'd never understand how it felt to be mortal, but he could appreciate the perspective.

"For most it is. For you, sweetheart, no."

She remained in his arms, completely vulnerable and trusting. He knew she wasn't aware of how much she was adjusting to her new situation, and he wasn't about to alert her to it either. "Because I get to choose immortality?"

He nodded once, letting it sink in.

"Being a vampire is a gift. We get to experience and live life to its fullest while being witness to the evolution of the planet and the species we cohabitate with."

He ran his fingers over her delicate collarbone.

"We're the most powerful predators on the planet, yet we have less violence among us than any other inhabitants on Earth, while at the same time, causing it less harm."

When her mouth opened, he closed her lips with his fingers, smiling.

"This planet would thrive without humans. Like the animals, we would hunt and survive on their blood. We've had to adapt to luxury and technology to blend in with the *Homo sapiens*. Not that we don't enjoy them, but they're not as necessary to our survival as they are to human's."

Willow shook her head.

"I don't believe you. Look at all this opulence. You're just as reliant as we are."

"Our strength and diet deem luxury unnecessary for our survival. Sure, there would be those among us who grieved the loss, but unlike the humans who've forgotten the simple tasks of hunting for food, we would quickly thrive."

She humphed.

"I think you underestimate the basic survival instincts of humanity. And our ability to adapt. Not all of us, but many of us."

He laughed.

"You forget I've lived over a thousand years and witnessed much stupidity," he replied cynically. "You're killing the planet with your greed and ego. In time, if you don't change, the planet will be inhabitable."

She frowned. "Perhaps you're right."

Willow began running her hand under his T-shirt—a habit he was beginning to love.

"Maybe I should become a vampire."

"I think so." He smiled and smacked a kiss on her lips, looking all cool and collected while his heart thumped loudly in his chest. Had she decided? Was this where the conversation was headed?

"What if I said yes?"

Now he felt like throwing up. Slowly, he drew in a breath, calming his heart which had nearly broken through his skin.

Breathe. Breathe. Breathe.

"Are you?"

She chewed her lip.

"Willow."

She climbed off his lap and walked around the living area, glancing at him from time to time. He watched as she frowned, then narrowed her eyes, then chewed her lip. He couldn't read her.

"I don't want to die, Bray, but I don't want you to die either!"

Whoa. What? He sat on the edge of the sofa and held out his hands.

"Hey, I'm not going to die." She stared at him in disbelief. "Talk to me. Where has this come from?"

Willow shrugged. "Are you telling me you won't suffer if I leave? That you won't be impacted by this?"

Who had she been talking to? Not Craig; they hadn't been alone.

"Yes. I would. Very much. There would be no worse moment in my life than if you left me." A big statement for someone who'd beheaded one of his parents. She didn't know about that yet.

"So, you wouldn't...I don't know, do something stupid?"

He narrowed his eyes. "Like what? Commit suicide? You know I'm immortal, right?"

She turned, hands on her hips, and growled at him.

Literally growled. His eyebrows raised and he bit his lip to stifle the smile attempting to break through. It wasn't really funny, but it was a little bit. He couldn't understand where this was coming from.

"You know what I'm talking about. You'll go over the edge."

"Willow, I cannot off myself. Tell me what this is all about."

When she simply stood there, he began to stand.

"My answer is no."

He froze. Sat back down.

"My answer is no, Brayden. I choose to remain a human."

His heart stopped momentarily, then began to beat rapidly. His breathing became nearly nonexistent. She took a step toward him, but his eyes were beginning to blur, a ringing in his ear. "Okay."

Who had spoken? It had sounded like his voice, but they weren't his thoughts. Brayden swallowed back the nausea rising from his gut. He stared as his future without her flashed before his eyes. Darkness. Emptiness. He felt himself go cold.

"Brayden." He heard a voice, a beautiful voice. "Brayden, please, look at me!"

He looked up. His mate. Willow.

"I'll take you home." He stood, his legs stronger than he expected, though he felt robotic. She tried to grab his arm, but he pushed her off and walked across the room.

"Brayden, STOP!" Willow screamed.

He turned. Stared at her with dead, dark eyes.

"I lied."

The earth below him tilted. He felt as if his mind were filled with cotton wool, his thoughts unable to flow. Willow walked toward him as he stared mindlessly at her.

She tentatively laid her hands on his chest, big eyes gazing up at him with regret.

"Lied?"

"I love you, Brayden. I'm not leaving you."

What?

For a long moment he just stared at her, until finally, his brain was able to comprehend her words. He wrapped his arms around her, then pulled back, grabbing her shoulders instead.

"Stop. No. Why? Why would you do this?"

"I'm sorry, but I had to see for myself," Willow said, shaking her head. "I can't do that to you. I can't allow you to shut down your heart and destroy yourself."

He growled, dropped his hold on her, and turned away. What was she saying? Was she only choosing him because she couldn't stand to be the cause of his destruction?

That wasn't love. It was manipulation. Who the fuck had gotten into her mind?

"No, Willow. I want you to choose this because you want this lifestyle, because you want me, because you love me. Not because you fear what it will do to me if you don't."

"I do!" she cried. "I just saw the darkness in your eyes. I love you! Just as you could never hurt me, I could never walk away knowing I had killed you."

"I would not die, Willow," he countered sadly, looking down and shaking his head.

"Perhaps. But you could hurt a lot of people."

He looked up.

"Don't lie to me, Brayden. I know I don't fully understand your strength or capability yet, but I sense your power. I saw a moment of your darkness."

He drew in a breath.

"You must choose this for you."

She stepped forward. "There is no more me, only us. I am your mate," she said, placing her hands on his chest again. "I'm beginning to feel it."

He took another breath, taking her hands in his. "Willow."

She closed her eyes. "I am sorry I did that to you, but I had to see for myself. I will never lie to you again."

It *had* nearly killed him, but he couldn't help being mildly impressed by her courage. While he would never harm her, she wouldn't have known. Not truly.

"Fuck, Willow." He pulled her into his arms and used as much care as he could not to crush her. She nudged him and reached for his lips. Gripping her head, he ground his mouth to hers, painfully. Necessarily. Gasping, they came up for air. He held her face.

"You are sure?"

She nodded. Or as much as she could in his viselike grip. "Yes. Well, I'm still terrified, but yes."

Another harsh kiss.

"Bray, I don't want to kill the moment, but you're really hurting me."

He released her and stepped away, dropping his hands to his sides. Then he grabbed her again, more gently. "It's fine. You'll heal when I turn you." He smirked. "I'm joking."

She shook her head, giving him a cute smile. He whipped her up into his arms, heading for the stairs to his bedroom, when he glimpsed the screens.

"Ah, fuck." He peered down at her. "We will celebrate after this meeting, I promise."

He carried her to the sofa.

"Dying isn't exactly a celebratory moment, you know." Willow frowned.

He looked down at her, taking her chin in his hand. "No. I'm sorry."

"I get it. You're happy."

"Ecstatic," he said honestly. "Yet I promise never to overlook your feelings as I just did ever again."

Her courage never failed to surprise him. Brayden loved this female. She was his everything. From this point on, he swore to put her first, second, and third. Hell, he already did.

She sniffed. "It's fine. I'm just an emotional basket case."

You catching this?

Craig.

"Unmute," he commanded the screen, squeezing Willow's knee affectionately.

I am now.

Brayden turned up the sound and listened in.

"Where's Luca? I usually deal with him directly," Regan was asking the tall, lean vampire sitting beside him at the bar. Lean, but Brayden bet he was fast and strong.

"I'm here to ask the questions, *Advisor*, now answer the question."

Regan took a long drink of his beer. "I told you, nobody knows a thing."

The guy leaned closer and sneered. "Then why do my males on the inside tell me the king is looking healthy and well."

So they had more people on the inside.

Catch that?

Sure did. Just as we suspected.

Regan shrugged. For a traitor, he looked remarkedly calm.

"Before you answer with another lie, vampire, remember this"—he lifted his phone—"one call and the heads of your wife and daughter will be sent to you in a box."

If he starts dialing—

We've got vamps on the ground. No call will take place, Captain.

Regan shook his head. "I don't know what to tell you. I've been giving him the herbs. Perhaps they're not as potent."

Brayden expected the rebel vampire to explode. Instead, he leaned back and nodded, glancing around the bar.

"Something's not right," Brayden said out loud.

Brayden! Shit. Motherfucker! Craig's voice exploded in his mind.

"Who is that man?" Willow asked at the same time.

Fuck. They're in the castle!

Brayden stood up, his mind working in military mode and speed as he turned to look down at Willow. He pulled her to her feet. "I need you to stay in the bedroom. Do NOT come out until I am back. Do you understand?"

Her eyes widened. "What's going on?"

I'll be there in a minute. Send three lieutenants to guard Willow immediately.

Done.

One look at Willow and he saw she was frozen. "Come. Guards are now outside our doors, so you will be safe."

He didn't fucking know if they had arrived yet, but she would not be safe with him. Brayden had to find the king and the rebels.

It's still an assumption, Craig said.

You know as well as I do they're inside.

Yeah, fuck.

Without asking, he lifted her into his arms, ported them up to the bedroom, and placed her on the foot of the bed. He then strapped on weapons, put on steel-capped boots, and a leather jacket.

"Bray," she said, hand over her mouth.

He lifted her hand and pressed a hard kiss to her lips. "I'm sorry, Willow, I love you."

"Brayden, what is going on?"

He stared at her for a moment and realized he had to respect she was his life partner. She deserved to know. "The rebels are in the castle. It's vital you stay here and extremely quiet. Do you understand? I will be back as soon as I can. Fuck, baby, I love you."

She nodded and mouthed *I love you.*

He teleported out of the room.

CHAPTER FORTY-FIVE

Vincent!

"I can't believe we didn't fucking see this," Craig said, running a hand through his hair.

He was standing in front of the security cameras as they flicked through them one after the other looking for issues.

On the screens, Brayden saw pairs of vamps in their military uniforms discretely moving along corridors to get into position. Craig had moved them up a security level.

"We could be wrong."

They weren't. He could feel it in his bones.

"They're either in here or on their way," Lance added.

Vince!

Marcus, Kurt, and Tom were strapping on swords and knives over their black one-piece Moretti royal uniforms, sleeves rolled up their forearms.

Lance leaned over an officer who wore the same black uniform with the Moretti logo, except—like all soldiers who held positions lower than the Senior Lieutenants—he had red piping along his shirt.

Brayden watched them flick through the past few hours of footage.

"Where's the king?" he asked Craig, a chill running through his body as his attempts to reach his brother remained unanswered.

"They were in the throne room, but now it's empty," Lance replied. "Wait."

Craig glanced at Brayden at the same time he did.

"That's not right," Lance continued.

Brayden's chest tightened.

Simultaneously all of them, except Lance, ran out of the room and toward the throne room.

BRAYDEN!

Well, at least he's fucking alive, he thought.

Vincent, where are you?

They have Kate. They have THE QUEEN!

Fuck, fuck, fuck.

"They've got the queen." He ground to a halt, holding out a hand to stop his team from rushing in. There was no running into this anymore. It was now a hostage situation.

Are you in the throne room?

No! She's in there with them. Those fuckers are going to die!

Port to the security room right now.

"Tom, Marcus, get your men surrounding the throne room, but nobody goes in," Craig instructed.

"Go to high alert," Brayden told Lance when they arrived back to the security office. "I want as many of our citizens in their rooms and out of conflict areas as soon as possible. This could get ugly, and who knows how long it will last."

The officer pushed some buttons and lights began flashing throughout the castle. Everyone knew what they meant. They'd run drills.

Brayden looked over at the king. He was standing right in front of the cameras waiting for the feed to refresh, legs wide, fists on his hips, ready to kill.

"Get these fucking cameras fixed!" he suddenly roared.

"Doing what we can as fast as we can, my lord," Lance said, frantically tapping on the screen while telepathically talking to his crew.

Craig and Brayden shared a look. Unsaid words, nothing to do with the current conversations happening around them, were exchanged between them. This was how the two of them worked. An unspoken ability to strategize with a look. After all these years, they knew each other's thoughts. A glance, a scowl, a flare of the nostrils.

"I go in," Craig finally said.

Vincent marched up to them. "If anyone is going in, it's me."

"Don't be fucking crazy, Vince; it's you they want. They want the throne!"

"You think I give a fuck about the throne?! That's my mate!"

Brayden got it on a level he never would have a few weeks ago. However, as king, it wasn't an option. As captain of the Royal Army for the royal family, as prince, it was his job to keep the king safe. And fucked if he was going to take the damn throne if this all ended up a shit show.

More of a shit show.

"You are *not* going in."

Vincent stepped up to his face.

"Clear the room!" Craig boomed and everyone ported out. The guy knew that no one could bear witness to the two royals challenging each other, no matter the situation.

"We don't have time to fight about this, Vince! Craig and I will get Kate out of there. You're buying into their fucking ploy. Let us do the thinking and do our jobs."

The king clenched the edges of Brayden's leather jacket. "One chance could be all they need to take her head."

He understood the madness. Shit, he'd been there barely minutes ago himself with Willow.

"It's yours they want, for God's sake. Stop wasting time."

He was running out of patience. He gripped the king's hands and removed them from his jacket, the guy's eyes widening.

The screen to the throne room suddenly flashed to life. Inside there were a handful of vampires—some he recognized, some he didn't. And Kate.

"Hello, Morettis," Stefano sneered.

Get the others back in here.

As Kurt, Lance, and the officer ported back in, Brayden stepped to the center of the room.

"Turn on the microphone," he instructed, then said, "Let the queen go and I'll spare your brothers' heads."

Stefano let out a dirty laugh. He was standing in front of the queen, who had a knife held to her throat by his brother, Luca Russo. She looked angry and shaken.

"You. Will. Fucking. Die!" the king boomed from behind him.

He didn't blame him.

"No, Vincent Moretti, it is *you* who will die this night. You and your brother the prince." He laughed.

Brayden shot a quick look over at Craig, who was doing what he did best; find a way out of a damn dangerous situation. The vampire's eyes darted around the screen, assessing and looking for opportunities and risks.

"No more Morettis. Oh, boo-hoo," Marco Russo mocked.

There's at least seven of them in there from what I can see.

Could be more in the castle.

"You have five minutes to get your asses in here or the queen's head will be the first to roll," Stefano said, waving his sword around recklessly.

Go! Brayden told Craig. The guy disappeared.

This was their playground, and the Russos' first mistake. Never attempt to take down your opponent in their own backyard. They had spent years setting up the castle in the event of a coup or human invasion.

He nodded to Lance, who muted the feed and shut down the two-way video feed, allowing them to see inside the room while the Russos were now blind. Brayden ran his hand down his face.

A glance at the other monitors showed the castle halls were quiet now that everyone was safely in their rooms. The drills ran over the years were paying dividends today.

He had to get the queen out of there. Sending the king in would only make matters worse; however, stopping him would be impossible.

Four minutes.

Vincent began marching to the door.

"Fuck, Vince. Give me a second."

He whipped around. "Tell me what you would do if it were Willow in there?"

Brayden hissed. "Lance, get some more backup in here. Kurt, you're with us."

"Yes, sir."

And Lance. The guy stared at him. *If anything should go wrong tonight, I want you to get Willow out of here immediately. Wipe her memory and take her home.*

He couldn't watch the guy's reaction.

We're in place, Craig reported.

Vincent and I are going in.

Are you mad?

You think you can stop him? Be my guest.

Yeah, fuck. Okay, Plan B.

He nodded briefly to Tom and Marcus as he gripped Vincent's arm to halt the guy from barging in.

We're here, he told Craig. *Going in on five.*

Vincent was a powerful vampire when at full capacity. In a sword fight, he'd win with that Moretti blood pumping through his veins. In a hostage situation, with his mate's head up against a sword, he would be no help. In fact, he'd be a volatile and irrational hindrance.

Four.

"Take my lead," he muttered quietly.

Three.

Two.

One.

All five of them stepped into the room, silent, dangerous, and with fury rolling off them.

Kate's skin was pale, her eyes filled with fear and apology for allowing herself to be caught in this position. No one blamed her. She was a brave and strong female, but not a match for the Russo males.

The king stiffened next to him, ready to bolt.

Don't fucking move.

I'm powerful enough.

Are you fast enough? You've been ill. You would risk your mate's life? Our queen?

Luca held the razor-sharp sword at her throat with his strong, muscular arm. Brayden knew the guy had the will and speed to do it. He wasn't faster or stronger than the Morettis, but he had the advantage of being already in position and stupid enough to do it.

What they needed was a distraction.

The one thing Brayden knew about power-hungry assholes was that they got high on this stuff. Drunk with ego and with the right trigger, they'd mess up. Hopefully before they hurt the queen.

"Let's talk, Stefano. Tell us what you want for once in your goddam life. What is it you want?"

The tall vampire grinned and spun a knife around his fingers threateningly. Brayden couldn't wait to stick the thing in the guy's anus. That would be a fun ending to this circus.

"Brayden Moretti, how nice of you to finally ask. I'm sick of you sending your little soldiers to spy and infiltrate my homes."

He didn't respond. The guy ignored his ignore. So, this was fun.

Stefano loved the sound of his own voice, so he gave in first. "I want the fucking throne. It's no damn secret. This whole damn royal family is outdated." He waved his hands around. "Plus, you took my father's head, so I will have my revenge."

Vincent took a step forward, but Brayden tugged on his jacket. *Be careful, brother.*

"Your father challenged the king, and he lost," Vincent said, voice laced with hate. "But at least he did so with an official challenge and his honor."

Stefano grabbed Kate's hair and dragged the knife down her cheek. She squeezed her eyes shut and cursed at him.

"That is exactly why it's time we have a democracy. The old ways are done."

Brayden let out a little laugh. "So you want the throne, but you also want a democracy? Which is it, Russo? And where do your brothers fit into this little plan of yours?"

A few eyes darted around at each other.

"Who becomes king?" He pushed further. "Are you all kings, making decisions together?"

There would be no democracy. All the reports he'd received back from their spies said that Stefano was a narcissistic dictator. Forget a royal structure; the guy would turn the vampire race into a controlled state of fear.

Brayden was proud of the way Vincent had evolved the royal ways, inserting compassion and modern thinking into his reign. He'd included Brayden and Kate in many of his decisions, along with his heads of states where appropriate. He was a strong, collaborative leader who influenced people to follow him without the use of a strong arm or sword, though at times that was needed with a predatory race.

"Enough with your questions," Stefano sneered. "My brothers follow me."

Marco coughed. "No. We're equal partners."

Stefano's expression hardened as his jaw twitched. Without looking at his brother, he said half-heartedly, "Sure."

"Three kings?" Vincent asked beside him, cottoning on to his ploy. "Who is the final decision-maker?"

"Hold on, I thought they wanted a democracy?" Brayden asked, not looking away from the sword at Kate's throat.

Get ready.

Roger.

"Enough of this questioning!" Stefano yelled, stepping forward, threatening them with the knife.

"Don't come any closer." Brayden stepped in front of the king, his voice low and threatening.

"You don't hold the cards here, Moretti. Look around you!" He laughed like a madman. "We have your queen. Oh, and..."

Brayden froze.

"Bring in our new guest," Stefano called, his eyes glistening with excitement. He didn't turn as the side door opened; instead, he held Brayden's eyes and beamed in delight. A male vampire came into view, pulling a female with him.

Brayden knew who it was immediately. They ripped a cloth bag off her head, and he felt every muscle and bone in his body expand.

"I'm so sorry," she said, her eyes swimming with tears and fear.

He felt powerless for the first time in his entire life. Cold ran through his veins. Time stopped. His life would be meaningless if the woman before him died. Brayden couldn't take his eyes off her.

Fuck, if he'd turned her, she would have been stronger and able to communicate telepathically with him. But it was too late for *what ifs*.

With too many moving pieces—meaning vampires—Brayden couldn't calculate a safe way to ensure Willow wouldn't die.

Craig. Stand down. They have Willow.
Brayden, don't do this.
She'll die. I've done the math.
Let me do this.
No. Stand the fuck down.

"I see we have your attention now, little prince," Stefano said as he stepped toward Willow.

Brayden clenched his fists. "Touch her and I'll rip your head off with my bare hands."

He circled Willow, smelled her hair, and ran a finger down her arm. All the while, Willow squeezed her eyes shut as she stood shivering. It was taking everything in him not to flash to her side and pull her into his arms.

Wait, weren't there seven of them?
Craig! Whatever you are doing, fucking stop it.
Fuck you.
The fuck! This is the queen and princess!
Yeah, and you mush heads can't think straight. I'm

taking over.

Beside him Kurt, Tom, and Marcus shifted. Brayden glanced at Vincent, then back to his mate.

"I'm warning you, Russo, take your hands off my mate. She is human. Let her go."

It was worth a shot.

"Surrender the throne, Vincent. Both of you. On your knees, Morettis, and I will let both females live." Stefano pointed the knife to the floor in front of him. Brayden didn't believe a word of it. He gripped Vincent's wrist.

"You will never have the throne, you piece of shit," Vincent snarled. "Hand the females over and we will let you return to Italy."

"No, they won't. Don't listen to them, brother," Luca said.

Stefano squeezed his eyes shut. "Luca, shut the fuck up. I'm not stupid."

"Don't call me stupid, *stronzo!*"

Stefano shook his head, patience wearing thin with his fellow kidnappers. "Oh, we will be returning to Italy," he said before pointing at the thrones. "With those!"

Then he expanded his fangs and leaned into Willow. "And perhaps one of these." Stefano placed a hand over one of her breasts and she jumped.

Brayden's blood boiled. Without a thought for anything else, he leapt toward his mate.

CHAPTER FORTY-SIX

Now! Craig roared inside all their heads.

Vincent leapt for Kate as Craig took out Luca, the sword clanging to the ground. He now lay with a Moretti engraved knife sticking out of his chest.

"Go! Get the queen out of here now. Go to the bunker!" Craig yelled. It didn't matter if anyone had heard. No one could get in. Only the king, queen, and the prince had access to the solid iron room protected by the most high-tech security available.

Around him, Marcus, Kurt, and Tom fought with the remaining vampires. Craig had dealt with one earlier, which of course the beady-eyed Brayden had noticed.

"Put them in the dungeon!" he instructed them.

Willow cried as Brayden lifted her into the air. Craig flashed to his side.

"Let me take her."

"No!"

"Fuck, Brayden."

Stefano lunged at them as Willow continued screaming. Her arm had blood pouring down it, the scent filling the air with her human delicacy.

"Oh crap." Brayden halted, his eyes dilating.

"Oh God, must have her," Stefano cried, reaching for her like a drug addict.

"Brayden!" she cried, terror in her voice.

One glance behind Craig confirmed Marco was down; he also sported the new Moretti-branded accessory inside his chest. He'd let the royals decide if they let them live or not. His money was on the latter.

The other vampires were headless corpses.

"Stefano, the game is over," Brayden growled as the rebel vampire swung his sword at Craig.

"You killed my father and now my brothers!" he roared, swinging widely, his skill better than Craig would have expected as the two of them leapt from over the tables and chairs dueling.

Willow was wrapped in Brayden's arms, his fangs close to her neck. The blood call of a mate was so enormous, Craig wasn't sure his friend could fight it.

"Bray!"

Bang. Clash. Leap.

"Fuck you, Russo!" Craig pushed with his sword and knocked the guy back enough steps to buy himself a few seconds. Racing over to Brayden, he pulled the two of them apart.

"Don't, Bray, you'll regret it. Let me take her to get cleaned up." Brayden stared at him, confused. "You take Stefano."

The last thing he wanted was his friend biting his mate and regretting his actions after the promise he'd made to himself all those centuries ago. He'd waited this long for Willow to choose him; he could wait a bit longer. Craig knew how important this was to the prince. Heck, he'd stood by Brayden's side as he swung his sword and took his father's head.

"What?" Brayden's eyes cleared and his forehead creased.

"Luca and Marco are down. Take Stefano. I'll take Willow."

Brayden stood up and tucked his mate under his arm. "Where the fuck is he, Craig?"

What?

Craig whipped around and began running around the room, looking under the table and out the side door.

"Stay here." He heard Brayden say to Willow.

"Are you kidding me? No!" Willow cried, her voice giving away she was following them.

"Jesus Christ. I can't wait for you to be a vampire, woman."

Wait what?

An hour later, with the whole team searching, they returned to the security room. Brayden threw a blanket around Willow and seated her at his desk. The human was wiped out.

Craig's mind flashed to Brianna and what she might be doing.

Shut it down right now. Fuck, man.

"He must have flashed out," Lance said. "He went out the side door, but there's a blind spot."

Brayden cursed. "The fact he knows that kind of detail...Jesus, we have some work to do."

"What do you want us to do with Marco and Luca?" Tom asked.

Yeah, technically they were the male's brothers-in-law. Brayden glanced at him briefly.

"That's the king's decision. Put the other bodies out in the daylight to ash them. Go speak to Lucinda, Tom," the prince said.

"Thanks, man." Brayden simply nodded.

"Okay, let's clean up," Craig instructed the team. "I want the LCs to do another sweep, then lower the alert and let everyone out of their rooms. Go shower, the rest of you." He sighed and sat down, removing his weapons.

Clunk. Bang. Thump.

When it was just the three of them, he looked up. Brayden was staring out the window, a mere inch from his mate, his hand running over her hair.

"I'll clean up here," he said.

Brayden turned, his eyes blazing with emotion. "You didn't know, Craig."

He scowled. "I fucked up. We both know that."

Brayden pulled Willow to her feet. "No. Fuck. Maybe. But you couldn't have known."

"No, but I should have put the safety of everyone and everything first. I didn't, and that's an enormous fuck up you can't ignore, Brayden."

He wasn't the commander of the Royal Vampire Army because he made excuses for his actions. He took full responsibility for his complete lack of judgment. He had let his feelings—or the feelings of the prince—distract him, and now their number one enemy was out there somewhere.

"So you're sticking around?" he asked Willow.

"Yes. If people stop trying to kill me."

He was happy for the prince. Willow would be a stark reminder of that sexy redhead every day, but then again, she had never left his mind.

"You should probably let the king and queen know they can come out."

"I don't know. It's nice and peaceful for a change."

The edges of their mouths lifted.

"I'll let them out. Double their security. I doubt Stefano will be in any position to act again quickly, but I've been wrong about him before. He's a fucking psychopath."

Craig kicked the foot of his desk. "We have a lot of work ahead of us."

"That we do, my friend, that we do." Brayden began walking out but stopped and turned around. "Oh, and by the way, don't even fucking think about quitting, and you're not fired. Get back to work."

Craig grinned. It was more than he deserved, and as always, he'd give his prince one hundred percent.

CHAPTER FORTY-SEVEN

Willow sat cross-legged on the bed which was covered in plastic. She had a towel wrapped around her.

"This is all kinds of fucked up."

Brayden stared at her nervously. "Do you want to do it somewhere else? Another room?"

She dropped her head in her hands. "Can't I get a sedative or something?"

Brayden crouched; his brows knitted. There was really no way of doing this without inciting fear. He could barely imagine how she must feel. "Willow, do you trust me?"

"Yes. No. I mean, for God's sake, you're about to kill me! How am I supposed to feel?" She jumped off the bed. "I need to ring Bri. I know you said I shouldn't, but I haven't spoken to her since the day we left LA...and can I go to the beach just one more time?"

Brayden ripped the plastic off the bed and folded it up. He had let her drive to the beach twice already over the past five days, each time during the day when he couldn't go out. With Stefano on the loose, it had nearly killed him. He'd paced the castle and punched walls the entire time she was gone.

"No," he said as calmly as he could.

He realized then, finally, he had been too accommodating, and it was to her detriment. It was one thing to give one's mate the choice, but to ask them to lie down and have their life drained was pure torture. He saw it now. And it was time to be cruel to be kind. This was what unconditional love was about. A gift, and a curse.

"What are you doing? Are we stopping?"

He didn't answer. There had been enough talking. Dropping the plastic into the cupboard, he took off his shoes and pants, then his shirt.

"While I appreciate this strip show, what are you doing?" He stalked to her, tugged on the towel, and as he knew she would, she let it fall to the floor.

"Oh, this is much more fun." She grinned. "I like the way you think."

He gripped a breast and tugged her to his lips. "I love you, you beautiful human."

She purred against him and reached for his cock. He groaned. There would be no release for him tonight. His mouth moved along her neck, her delicate collarbone, and back up to her wet and open lips.

"I love your lips."

He grinned. "You love my fingers too."

"And your—" His lips swallowed her words as their tongues met and danced together in the now familiar way. Lifting her, Brayden laid her on the bed, her eyes questioning. He spread her legs; her eyes calmed. A lick, a satisfied gasp. He worked her clit in circles, flicking it with his tongue.

This could backfire on him, but he was out of options. An orgasm rolled out of her easily, and Brayden climbed up her body, wrapping her legs around his wide body.

There was risk in turning humans, he'd told her. Briefly. They hadn't dwelled; he'd made sure of it.

Inside he went. Deep. Slow. He held her sparkling eyes, and they smiled at each other in the way lovers do, her tongue running over her bottom lip.

Then her eyes began filling with tears.

He blinked. She knew.

"I love you," she said, a tear falling down her cheek.

"Willow..."

"Do it, Brayden. Do it, my love."

He hesitated a moment, then dropped his head into her neck. His fangs expanded.

And he bit.

CHAPTER FORTY-EIGHT

"Come in, Vince."

He could hear his brother's footsteps outside his front door. A moment later, those feet were walking up the stairs and into his bedroom. They glanced at each other then at the female lying on the bed. Still a dead person.

"How is she?"

Brayden shrugged.

"It's been seven days. I thought it would be quicker than this?"

After taking her blood, Willow had drunk from his vein, and he'd emptied her body of all her human blood. Over the next few hours, he'd fed her more and more blood as her body began the transition.

Then she had fallen into the deep sleep. Inside she was changing, developing stronger muscles, her heart and lungs doubling in size. Hormone production was supercharged, and unused parts of her brain were triggered.

Vampires used up to five percent more of their brains than humans, which didn't sound like a lot, but when you considered Homo sapiens currently only used ten percent, it was a big jump.

She'd sweat so much Brayden had put her in the bath and spoon-fed her electrolytes. She'd convulsed so aggressively that he'd called Kate, who had stood looking as hopeless as he'd felt.

"I just don't know, Bray. It's not usually this bad. I'm

sorry."

Finally it had stopped, and she'd slept. It had now been seven days with no change, her heartbeat at half the rate it should be. She was breathing awfully slow, shallow breaths.

Over the past one hundred and sixty-eight hours—more commonly known as seven days—he'd experienced a roller coaster of emotions. Regret, anger, sadness, utter anguish, shame, fear...and now he just really missed her.

"Our blood is strong, Bray; she'll wake when she is ready."

He wiped his face with a hand. "Or too strong."

Vincent sat on the side of the bed and picked up Willow's wrist, feeling her pulse. While he hated anyone touching his mate, his brother was the king. Willow was now one of his vampires.

"I do not pity you this, brother. May your vamp babies find their mates among our kind."

He smiled. "And yours."

Vincent shrugged. The words hung in the air, unspoken. Why Kate hadn't yet fallen pregnant, they didn't know. One hundred and thirty years.

"I need a shower. Can you sit with her for a few minutes?"

Vincent nodded. "Of course, go. I was going to say you stink."

Brayden grinned, his first smile in a few days. Then he felt guilty as his eyes dropped to his lifeless mate.

"Go," his brother said softly.

He stepped into the master bathroom and stripped off. Nikes, gray sweatpants, and his filthy white T-shirt all landed on the ground.

Brayden stood looking in the mirror at his long-drawn-out face. There were dark circles under his eyes, and he needed to shave. He rubbed at his jaw. He certainly didn't give a shit about that right now.

Stepping under the water, he ran his hands over his body, feeling his strong broad shoulder and muscles. Down his stomach, the ripples of his abs were defined and hard. He washed between his legs, soap covering his cock and balls. It felt good.

He poured shampoo over his dark curls and scrubbed. It felt robotic. Brayden knew his body was a powerful machine desired by millions of women. Yes, he'd taken advantage of it thousands of times, yet standing here with water pouring over him, he couldn't remember any of them.

Except his mate. Willow Moretti.

Brayden, get out here now!

His head jolted up. He turned the water off and ripped the door open. Nearly skidding on the floor, he flew into the bedroom.

"What? Fuck, what?"

Vincent covered his eyes, grimacing. Brayden shook his head. "For God's sake, you've seen my penis a million times."

"It doesn't mean I want to *keep* looking at the damn thing." He scowled, dropping his hand. "Willow. She blinked."

"Are you sure?"

The tilted head and raised eyebrow told him his brother was, in fact, sure.

"Fine. She blinked."

Twitch.

"Did...was that..."

Blink. Wriggle.

Vincent patted him on the shoulder and began to step away. His brother forgotten, Brayden knelt beside the bed and sat staring at her like she was an apparition.

A finger moved. Another eye. Her lips twitched, then opened slightly.

"Willow. Baby, I'm here. Come back to me." The words he'd repeated like a mantra for days spoken again. "Open your eyes, sweetheart. Breathe."

Suddenly she sucked in a deep breath and began coughing.

"Here." Brayden tipped her on her side in case fluids were caught in her throat. She wasn't the delicate human she once was anymore, but he found himself unable to stop taking care of her.

Willow sucked in breath after breath, then finally, her eyes opened.

Blink. Blink. Blink. Stare.

Blink.

"Hey." He wiped her hair away from her forehead.

Blink.

Er, she had her memories, right?

Blink.

CHAPTER FORTY-NINE

She felt her consciousness returning. She wasn't in a dream so much as outside of herself; not like in those movies where someone watched themselves during an operation or standing outside the pearly gates reflecting on their life.

No, this was more like floating in black space. Terrifying yet incredibly peaceful. Like a supercharged meditation session, except she wasn't sure she could get back to her body.

There was a reason she should, she just couldn't remember why. She barely had thoughts, so she just floated, enjoying the calm ease. Eventually, the desire to go back to her body grew, the reason for it still evading her.

Was she hungry? Barf, no.

She began to move parts of her body and felt different.

Voices. Male voices. It sounded like they were at the end of a tunnel. Echoey. A hand on hers. Warm, tingly.

Her reason.

She began to cough, then felt her body being tipped gently by strong hands. Forcing her eyes open, she began to blink. More blinking. She couldn't see. It began to clear. A body. The man, he was in front of her. Staring.

Her reason.

"Hey."

Blink, blink, blink.

"Hey, it's okay. Willow, you're back." He placed his hand on her cheek.

Her name was Willow. Yes.

Holy shit!

She sat up and grabbed him, her body hurting all over, and she groaned.

"Whoa, baby, take it easy."

"I'm alive," she croaked out before coughing.

"Yes," he confirmed, putting a straw to her mouth. She sipped on the yellow fluid and groaned at the delicious taste. "Do you know who I am?"

Her eyes flicked up to his. His forehead was creased, dread in his eyes. She smiled, her lips feeling tight as she did.

"The man I love." An eyebrow rose. "Brayden, why would you think I don't know who you are?"

He sat back on his heels, his head falling into his hands. "Thank fuck."

"Sorry I scared you."

He looked up, eyes full of relief. Then he launched at her, wrapping his arms around her and pulling her to him on the floor. Willow's body ached, but she didn't care. She let him envelope her in his cocoon of a body and gently rock. That he was completely naked wasn't lost on her.

"How long was I out?" she mumbled, her face squished into his chest.

"Approximately seven hundred and twenty million years."

She let out a laugh.

"A week, Willow." He let her go enough so she could look up at his gorgeous face. She laid a hand on his cheek. "How do you feel?"

"Achy. Happy. Strong."

He nodded, smiled, and sighed. "I believe the aching

will go away quickly once you start moving about. We heal fast."

Brayden carried her to the shower and washed every inch of her body, kissing her tenderly as he went. She reminded him he didn't need to be so gentle anymore. He shrugged. So, there'd be no changes in that department, then. Willow wasn't disappointed—she loved the way he protected and cared for her.

She brushed her teeth and looked around at the world which now seemed brighter and more vibrant. The desire to run for miles overcame her. She was now a vampire, and here she was, brushing her stupid teeth.

Oh. Teeth.

"How do I...?" She poked inside her mouth.

Brayden stepped up behind her. "It will happen naturally. You'll learn to control them."

"Where are they?"

He took her finger and pushed behind her incisors. Holy crap, they were sharp. A prick of blood appeared on her finger which Brayden sucked off slowly, holding her gaze. Heat pooled between her legs. Powerfully.

His eyes widened. "Wow, baby, I scent your desire."

A split second later, Brayden had her on the bed and was on top of her. He'd used vampire speed. This time, though, it hadn't been a blur.

Suddenly, he sat up. He stared at the wall behind them, frozen, then looked down at her.

"What's going on?"

"Brianna is here."

What?

"WHAT?"

CHAPTER FIFTY

Craig paced the driveway beside Brianna's car. Thank fuck it was evening.

Hurry the fuck up!

He'd telepathed Brayden as soon as he'd been advised of Brianna's arrival.

We're coming, but fuck, Willow has just woken up.

Jesus.

Five minutes. Keep her, um, occupied. Not with your dick.

He rolled his eyes.

"Craig! Where. Is. Willow?" Brianna shouted again. "I am not leaving until I see her."

Yeah, well, he guessed she hadn't flown across the country, hired a car, and driven here just to be waved off. What a complete fuck up.

"She's on her way."

"What, are you psychic or something?"

He narrowed his eyes in confusion. Oh. He'd used telepathy and hadn't, as far as Brianna was concerned, made any effort to call anyone.

"I texted Brayden on my way down."

Brianna reached into her car and pulled out her handbag. "Great. Let's go inside."

"No! No, ah, no," he said a little bit too fast. "Let's just wait out here."

She tugged her arms around her. "Fine. I'll stand out here and freeze to death."

"Don't you have a jacket?" he asked, receiving a raised eyebrow in return for his unhelpful effort.

"What is this place?" she asked, spinning around, taking in the enormous castle. No wonder she was cold, he thought, staring down at her short skirt. She had thin tights on which showed off all the curves and arches of her lovely legs.

Cough. Just legs.

"Brianna, how did you find us?"

When she looked back at him, her eyes burned with mistrust. "Why? What's going on? Where is Willow and why hasn't she returned my calls for over two weeks?"

He shrugged. "I don't know chick stuff."

"Don't lie to me, Craig. Something is going on. If you must know, I had her phone traced by a friend in the LAPD."

He frowned. "Isn't that illegal?"

She lifted a shoulder. "He's a friend, like I said."

He took a step forward. "Are you sleeping with this *friend*?"

Craig had to give her credit; she held her own, not stepping away.

"If I am, it's none of your business."

His jaw clenched.

"Bri!" Willow came flying out of the castle, looking fucking incredible. Vampire looked good on her.

"Where the hell have you been?!" Brianna yelled.

As the two girls neared each other, Craig stepped back, then saw Brayden's face and realized the mistake his mate was about to make. Craig stepped in front of Brianna and caught Willow before the new powerful vampire crushed her friend.

Realization lined her face and her mouth opened.

"Would you get the freaking heck out of the way, you big damn...ugh!" Brianna said, pushing and prodding at him.

Willow grinned and wound around him, hugging her friend. Gently.

"Fuck, thanks, man," Brayden said, rubbing his forehead.

Craig ran a hand over his short hair and walked over to stand beside the prince.

"What the fuck do we do now?"

Turn the page to read chapter one of The Vampire Protector – book three in the Moretti Blood Brothers series.

CHAPTER ONE

He knew this was all kinds of wrong, exposed in the castle's halls like this, but the redheaded seductress had flung her hair over her neck, and a juicy vein was pumping with excitement.

It wasn't her blood Craig wanted; it was her creamy skin.

For now.

He ran a finger over it and felt her shiver in his arms. The corner of his mouth twitched, and hey, look at that, so did his cock.

He glanced around, even though he knew no one was near, then leaned in.

Liiiick.

God, she was delicious.

She groaned softly, and it was all he could do not to scoop her up and take her back to his room. His mouth moved over her jaw and claimed her lips softly, then deeper, harder as she responded to him. Another moan against his lips…

Whomp.

Fuck.

That had been his own damn moan, he realized as his chin bounced off his chest.

Mother-fucking-fucker.

He'd fallen asleep at his desk, daydreaming about one sexy human redhead named Brianna Jones.

She was currently living at Castle Moretti because, apparently, they were taking in humans now. Well, not exactly, but over the past few weeks, there had been two different humans at the enormous royal structure.

The first had been Willow, who'd arrived as the mate and guest of Prince Brayden Moretti. And now she was a vampire.

Thank fuck.

Not that one walked in a human and came out a vampire. Generally.

The prince had given her the choice of turning immortal or remaining human, the later requiring him to wipe her memory and let her go back to her life—a near impossible feat for a mated male, especially one as dominant an alpha as Brayden. Craig wasn't sure if he respected the hell out of the guy for having the strength and courage to go through with it or if he considered him a fucking moron.

Probably both.

Most vampires turned their human mates then asked for forgiveness afterward. A dick move for sure, but one with far less stress.

The thing about bonded males was they lost their goddamn minds if they lost their mate. If Willow had chosen her humanity, he knew Brayden would have sunk into a very dark place. He would have been a dangerous flight risk to the race and a danger to humans, and very few vampires would've had the strength to bring him back besides Craig.

Thank fuck it didn't matter now. Craig was still wiping his brow. Capturing Brayden Moretti would not have been easy. Even for him.

But he would have. Not because he was the commander of the Royal Vampire Army, not because of their bromance, and not because he'd been close to the edge himself once. No. It had to do with the Moretti blood, something Craig shouldn't know about. The blue blood was uniquely powerful, and Craig had the juiced-up shit running through his veins. And he shouldn't. No one outside the Moretti family should.

Occasionally, the Morettis shared blood for all number of reasons; however, the small amount quickly flushed through a vampire's system.

Except for Craig's.

He'd always been one of the most lethal vampires in the race, and after Brayden had shared his blood one fateful eve, it hadn't left his system. He figured it was because he'd had a shitload of the stuff, but he couldn't be sure. In fact, everything was a calculated guess because he couldn't talk to anyone about it. Especially not the Morettis.

Over hundreds and hundreds of years, he'd witnessed the power of their blood, and had put two and two together. That he held some of their family power within him had remained his most closely warded secret, one he occasionally wondered if the prince was aware of.

And now there was a new Moretti.

The race was abuzz with the upcoming royal livestream via VampNet of Brayden and Willow's official bonding ceremony. The king had declared the royal ball and the prince's bonding ceremony would become one event, not wanting to delay their bonding nor hold two events given the rebel activity. Immediately afterward, Willow would be crowned a princess. And the sassy vampire princess-to-be wanted her human bestie attending the not-human, not-wedding ceremony.

Brianna.

He groaned, dropped his feet to the floor, and pushed his chair away from his desk. Standing and stretching his tall body, he reached down and gave his cock a rough squeeze. Damn thing wouldn't soften, not since the little witch had arrived.

Brianna had found her way across the damn country after some LAPD guy had traced Willow's phone. The same guy who was going to eat a bullet if the redhead was sleeping with him.

Shit, he should be grateful the cop hadn't gotten a task force together and shown up looking for Willow himself. They would have found a supposedly missing person with a new set of fangs; not that Brayden or Craig would have let any law enforcement or human retain their memories, but it would have been a big fucking cleanup job.

He groaned once more. This was why they strictly kept humans out of their world. It got messy. Fast.

Craig ran a hand over his short blond hair. He still couldn't believe the female he'd nearly fucked in the bathroom of a dirty LA bar was Willow's best friend. The same one who'd slammed her front door in his face and who stalked his damn dreams. Including, apparently, his waking ones.

He'd stopped short of lifting her skirt, and now the little witch wanted nothing to do with him. Craig didn't truly know why he hadn't just pushed insider her. She had been wet and ready after eye-fucking him all night. He'd gripped her neck and sucked on those full lips of hers, holding her up against the grimy white tiles while electric lights beamed down on them. Hardly the stuff of romance novels.

He remembered the sudden, overwhelming feeling that this female deserved so much better even as her body melted against his like a furnace. Something had stirred within him and made him stop. An odd nagging in the back of his mind he just couldn't grasp.

A conscience?

God, he was thinking like a human. Vampires fucked; they fucked a lot. Humans, vampires, males, females—it didn't matter. When you weren't mated, it was like a kind of sport, and he'd qualified for the Olympics a hundred times over. Craig wasn't lacking for options, and never had been. Females were drawn to his size, his raw masculinity, and his supposed bad boy vibe.

But he was no bad boy. He was the commander of the Royal Vampire Army and second in command to Prince Moretti, who also held the title of captain. Craig protected the Moretti family and upheld the vampire laws; he didn't break them.

But yeah, he was no saint. If you fucked with one of his, he'd snap your neck and rip your head off to hang on the washing line. Not that he had a washing line.

The old head rip was one of only three ways to kill a vampire; to step in the sun or a stab to the heart were the other options. Where the humans had gotten the idea it needed to be with silver was beyond him. A ruptured heart was a ruptured heart, whether done with plastic, silver, or steel.

He shook his head.

He really thought he'd done the right thing following his instinct and pulling her skirt down, especially after he'd all but dragged her in there. She'd been willing, sure, but shy. He had been taking advantage for sure. The reaction he had gotten in return had been anger, something which had confused the hell out of him while he was busy congratulating himself for being a gentleman.

He had walked an angry Brianna back out to her work friends, who were being charmed by one of his vampires, Lance, and come to a screeching halt. Brayden and Willow were staring at them. It turned out his angry redhead was Willow's bestie.

The saving grace at that moment was Willow not yet knowing the prince was a vampire, so she had grabbed Brianna and dragged her off for a dance while he'd been left to explain himself to Brayden.

He'd promised to leave her alone, and he had meant every word. At the time.

Except things hadn't quite gone like planned.

A few days later, he'd shown up at Brianna's house with a half-assed excuse so he could see her again. He had been confronted by a wild, stubborn female who turned his cock to stone.

She'd told him she had felt rejected.

He'd kissed her.

She'd slammed the door in his face.

So that had gone well.

He'd thought it would be the last he ever saw of her. Yet here she was, sleeping in the castle, and he was going out of his damn mind. No amount of jerking off was resolving the permanent ten-inch problem in his pants.

He needed her gone, and he needed to get laid.

Damn sexy little witch.

If only she'd let him explain.

He hadn't fucking rejected her. Not at all. He had planned to fill her with a few more drinks and then take her home. Actually, he hadn't been thinking quite that clearly; he just knew he wasn't fucking her in the damn bathroom. God, if only he could get her into his bed and take his time while he licked every inch of that creamy, soft body.

Instead, now when they were in the same room, she could barely look at him while he couldn't tear his eyes off her. Brayden would sneer at him, warning him off, but it didn't matter. Brianna Jones had no time for him. If she did speak to him, it was all sass. And that just made his body want hers even more.

But sass aside, Craig saw the shadows in her eyes. Her pain struck him. He didn't know what it was, but he had an overwhelming feeling of wanting to protect her. She would reject him, of course, but it didn't change how he felt. Even as he was trying to ignore it himself.

He needed to get her out of his head.

Later he was going to hit the bars, and if someone was looking for a blond, six foot four, tattooed bad boy built like a brick shithouse to ride like a cowboy, they were going to get lucky.

Male or female—he didn't give a shit.

He just needed Brianna out of his head.

… To continue reading grab your copy today from your favorite online bookstore.

MORETTI
BLOOD BROTHERS

You might also like my new series,
Realm of the Immortals.
Seven powerful archangel brothers. Eight books.

THE ARCHANGELS' BATTLE
Book one: Realm of the Immortals
Available late July 2021

Can Archangel Michael protect heaven and find the female who haunts his dreams?

The Olympians have just won the war against the Titans, leaving the skies in chaos. Archangel Michael has the enviable task of cleaning up the mess, until he discovers Zeus now has plans to invade heaven. Which he can't allow.

While they prepare for battle, the archangels enjoy the raw pleasures of the goddesses and angels. But Michael can no longer ignore the female in his dreams who stirs up feelings he shouldn't be capable of having. He turns to the new queen whose sexual demands provide the distraction he needs. But for how long?

Can Michael protect heaven from Zeus's powerful invasion and finally discover who his dream girl is?

Book two, THE ARCHANGEL'S HEART will be out in August/September 2021 - *date TBC.*